LONG VALLEY

LONG VALLEY

ROBERT E KREIG

WHITEKEEP BOOKS

For Suzanne.

FRIDAY

Thick clouds veiled the night sky and mist draped loosely around the towering, jagged mountains. Wisps of snow streamed across the ground like loose ribbons caught in the breeze. The trees swayed and creaked gently each time a gust of cold air blew down from the surrounding peaks. The wind swam through the pine leaves, sounding like a rapid stream. Occasionally a branch creaked loudly under the pressure of the building snow and dumped the load onto the ground with a sudden thump.

The only other sounds were of four trucks with large tanker trailers idling by the side of the state highway and the chattering teeth of a young private who was having trouble leaving his mark on a tree.

The highway loomed above the trucks like a great concrete monolith. They had just driven down the exit ramp and onto an intersecting road which passed under the highway to the right and snaked into the mountains on the left. The vehicles lined along the side of the road, ready to move in that direction.

"Come on, Private," the sergeant yelled from the lead truck. "We're on a tight schedule. You said you needed to go. Now go."

The private snorted back a ball of snot forming inside his nose and swallowed. It was disgusting. He should've spat. Instead, he now had something that reminded him of a cold oyster crawling down his throat.

"Sorry, Sarge," he called. "I don't get it. I was almost bursting before."

"Performance anxiety, sir," another private called from the second truck.

"Fuck you, Wilson," the private retorted from his tree.

"That's enough, both of you." The sergeant took a deep breath and shook his head. "It's the cold, son. You've been out there so long it's a wonder it ain't fallen off yet."

"Nothing there to fall off," Wilson laughed.

"Shuttup, Wilson," the sergeant bellowed. "Get in the truck, son. It's only another twenty minutes to the base. As soon as we get there you can piss until you're blue in the face."

The private zipped his pants and jogged back to the lead truck. He climbed into the driver's seat and slammed the door shut, closing the cold out and soaking up the heat in the cabin.

"Sorry, Sarge," he said bashfully as he knocked the truck into gear and pulled onto the road.

"It's okay. I understand. But you will cop some shit when we pull into the base. You got it?" The sergeant reached for the radio receiver sitting on the dashboard in front of him.

"Yeah," the private nodded, hoping he could hold it another twenty minutes before the internal dams burst.

"Okay boys," the sergeant said into the radio. "We're about to pass through 'the Eye' and then we need to be careful. The road turns tightly until we get to the valley floor. We'll have mountainside reaching up to our right and river down below us on the left.

"Be careful. The road should be plowed clear for us, but the fucker will be as slippery as ice. Copy?"

One by one, the other trucks' occupants replied as they followed the little road into a tight gap that wound its way into a wall of rock that rose from the pine forest like jagged teeth.

The road quickly swung to the right, following the mountain range to the north. A metal barrier covered in reflectors hugged the road on the left, giving fair warning of the long drop to the river beyond.

The private kept the vehicle in low gear and as close to the rock wall as he could. There was no way in hell he wanted to stray too far to the left and slip down that embankment.

Over the tops of the trees to his left, lights in the distance outlined the grid pattern of a town. Small islands of lights dotted the valley showing pockets of civilization in the form of tiny neighborhoods and farmhouses.

"Son," the sergeant started. The private, deep in concentration, suddenly jumped and felt he may have soiled himself. "Did you know these mountains are full of mines from the gold rush days?"

"Ah," the private appeared slightly confused. This was not the sort of thing the sergeant would usually converse about. "No sir. I did not."

"Yeah." The sergeant pointed past the private to the ridge beyond the river. "The first settlers here dug right over there. More came afterwards and soon there were tunnels going from one side of these mountains through to the other. It must be like a regular ants' nest, or bees' hive under there.

"Then the local natives decided they didn't like what was happening here. This place was special to them. Isolated and cut off from the outside world. I guess it was sacred."

The sergeant pulled out a pack of cigarettes. He plopped one into his mouth and offered the private one.

"No thanks, Sarge."

"You don't mind if I do?" The sergeant pulled the cigarette from his mouth.

"Not at all."

"Okay," the sergeant put the stick back in his mouth and lit it with a lighter he kept in his coat pocket. He took a couple of drags and breathed deeply. "What was I saying?"

"Sacred," replied the private.

"Oh yeah," the sergeant recalled. "So, some fighting happened between the settlers and the Indians. Eventually the army was called in to resolve any disputes."

"Resolve any disputes?"

"Yeah. They wiped out the local indigenous population. Men, women and children."

"Shit!" The private shook his head.

"Mm-hmm," the sergeant took a deep draw on his cigarette and slowly exhaled. "You know the worst of it? They didn't find enough gold in this valley to pay for one wagon wheel. The only thing this place was good for was the trees and setting up a fucking army base."

"Wait." The private's brow furrowed. "What do you mean 'the trees'?"

"Logging camps moved in after gold mining died off. They stopped years and years ago when they nearly destroyed every tree here."

"But there are plenty of trees."

"That was because the army moved base further into the valley back in seventy-six. As a goodwill gesture they planted trees and re-forested the whole valley so the hippies in town wouldn't protest about the new base."

"How do you know all this, Sarge?"

"This is my hometown, son." The sergeant raised the radio receiver to his mouth. "Get ready to lay it on, boys. We've reached the valley floor. Take care going through the town. Should be a straight run. It's around three-thirty. No one should be awake except the farmers. But take care. Civvies are unpredictable."

The trucks picked up pace as the ground beneath them leveled out. The land on either side of the road opened, exposing fields and farmhouses in the distance. The river continued to snake through the valley on their left. The mountain range encompassed them on both sides, moving further out on both sides and stretching into the distance ahead where they met some miles away.

The strong, high beam of the headlights connected with a green sign with white writing posted beside the road. It read:

CITY LIMIT

LONG VALLEY

POP 2495

The lights of the town grew larger as they kicked up speed and moved to the center of the road. The snow plow had done a good job. The road was clear, as if it had just been made so. Still, now and then, the wind sent small drifts of white across the path before the trucks. But there was no sign of any hindrance to their journey.

Slightly, the private slowed the vehicle as he passed through town. The sergeant grunted his approval as he lit another cigarette.

It looked like any other town in the middle of nowhere. They passed a gas station, Sheriff's Office, fire brigade and a string of stores with large awnings overhanging the sidewalk. There were signs pointing toward the hospital and school and houses lining the streets on either side.

Nothing special. Except that the road widened to an extremity amid the built-up area of the town.

"Welcome to Long Valley, Private," the sergeant said as they drove through. "My home sweet home."

"Why is the road so wide here, Sarge?"

"Logging trucks," the sergeant replied as he breathed out blue smoke from his nostrils. "They need the width to take the turn onto Old Mill Road there."

The private noticed a building with several signs displaying 'Town Hall', 'Library' and 'Post Office' as they moved swiftly through the intersection.

The trucks continued through the town and onward, moving deeper into the valley.

Trees began to fill the scenery on either side of the road as the mountain ranges crept closer and closer. Occasionally, he noticed a road or two leading off to the left and right and clusters of houses in the distance.

"Old army housing, Private," the sergeant explained. "A place for army personnel to raise their families. A strategy to promote a real community spirit and link the base with the town. It didn't take off too well, and they forced army families to move when the housing areas got sold off to civilians back in the eighties."

The private noticed a sign for traffic to slow down to five miles per hour. He followed the instruction and noticed a chain-link fence just beyond the trees running parallel on either side of the road.

Ahead was a checkpoint boom gate with guards on either side. Spotlights burst to life as the trucks approached. One guard signaled for the trucks to stop.

The private pulled up next to the guard and wound his window down. The sergeant handed the private some papers, which he gave to the guard.

"Says here you got four trucks," the guard stated.

"That's right," the sergeant replied. "You can count them if you like."

"I have," said the guard. "There's only three."

"Bull-fucking-shit." The sergeant opened his door and walked around the front of the vehicle. "You need to learn how to count. What's your name, you dumb ass..."

"Oh, shit!" the guard called. He was gazing back toward the road.

The private heard the screech of tires but could not see the source. He saw the glow from a fireball on the guard's shock-filled face and felt the truck slide forward with immense force. He felt the warm embrace of urine filling his pants as all self-control escaped him. *Finally.*

The sergeant disappeared from his view, but he knew the sergeant was somewhere underneath the vehicle and would not be leaving his home ever again. Then the truck lifted skywards as the other vehicles plunged into his. The sound of crunching metal against metal was sickening as he tumbled through the air and watched a wave of flame sweep past the cabin of his truck to engulf the guard station and its inhabitants.

The truck crashed to the ground and threw the private against the passenger window. Glass pierced his face, and he fell back to the driver's side as the truck came to rest on that side. The private hit his head one last time on the steering wheel with a loud crack.

Everything grew dark.

SATURDAY

I

Steam rose steadily from his coffee as he stared vacantly through the window to the quiet street outside. He was a regular here, always assured his place toward the front of the diner. His favorite booth, they assumed. Truthfully, it gave him the best vantage point to observe the occurrences outside on Main Street.

"More coffee, Sheriff Dawson?" the young waitress asked him, holding a pad and pencil at the ready. "Maybe somethin' else?"

"Hmm?" He glanced up from the window to meet her deep brown eyes. He knew deep inside where he saw a young, beautiful girl, she saw a worn-out old man. "No thanks, Betty Sue."

A smile formed as she turned and briskly moved behind the counter to a service window where another customer's order waited for delivery

Festive decorations of silver tinsel and bells adorned the service window. Above it was a tacky plastic sign, which read, 'MERRY CHRISTMAS.' In the back corner, next to an old jukebox from the fifties, sat a small tree fitted with red and green baubles.

Dawson could not remember a time when the jukebox had ever worked and only now wondered why the hell it was even there. They removed the records years ago and welded the coin slot shut. It was nothing more than an oversized ornament.

The lights flickered sporadically with no perceivable pattern, as if transmitting Morse code. Kill me. Kill me.

Dawson took a sip of his coffee as he returned his gaze to outside again. The wind had picked up and sent ribbons of snow along the road like streamers. Directly across the road was the County Sheriff's Office. A lone figure, a man, flung the door open and stepped into the cold morning.

The sheriff watched as the figure readjusted his coat around his ears and pulled his wide brimmed hat tightly down onto his head before jogging across the road. A little bell rung above the diner's door as both the man and a gust of freezing wind made their way in.

"Hey Deputy Vaughn." Betty Sue smiled. "Coffee?"

"Oh yeah." Vaughn smiled back. "How you doing, Betty Sue?" he asked as he sat across from Dawson.

"Fine," she said as she poured a cup. "You?"

"Cold," he replied as he rubbed his hands together before removing his hat.

"Might be cold out there, Deputy. But it's *hot* in here," Betty Sue stated as she brought his coffee to the table.

"Stop flirting with the customers, Betty Sue," a loud voice from the kitchen shouted.

"I wasn't, Daddy," she yelled back. "I just meant that Deputy Vaughn may want to remove his jacket before he gets too warm." She then turned to Vaughn and lowered her voice, "And so I can look at your big muscles."

Vaughn started to snicker, his face turning a bright red as Betty Sue strutted away to the counter.

"You done?" Dawson asked.

"Yes sir," Vaughn suddenly changed his composure to suit a more serious matter.

"So?"

"Jacob said he could get the plow up to Old Ridge Road after lunch. But the tree lying across it up near the Millar's lodge will have to be cleared by the fire brigade."

"Well, they can't get up there until this shit clears." Dawson pointed to the conditions outside.

"Satellite report says this weather front won't clear until Tuesday." Vaughn took a sip of his coffee. "It's just a good thing that no one is up there, so there's really no need to rush it."

The sheriff shifted his gaze from Vaughn to the still quiet street outside. Nothing living was moving out there. And why would it? It was too damn cold.

"Okay." Dawson nodded. "Get the signs and barricades over to Old Ridge Road and do your best to block it up. Then get a hold of Jacob and tell him not to worry about clearing it until there's a break in the weather and we can get the brigade up there to clear that tree. Tell him to make sure he keeps the road between here and the base clear. Those army guys will get pissed if their trucks can't get through. Even in this shit."

"No problem." Vaughn took out his phone and tapped some notes into it. "I'll get onto it right away, Sheriff."

"Have some breakfast first," Dawson ordered as he stood to his feet. He reached into his pocket and dropped ten dollars onto the table. "That won't pay for yours."

"Understood." Vaughn raised his cup to his lips as he shot a glance toward Betty Sue.

Dawson wrapped his coat around him and leaned in close to his deputy. "You bangin' her?"

"A gentleman never tells." Vaughn smiled.

"You ain't no gentleman." Dawson propped his hat onto his head.

"Only once."

"Bullshit." Dawson chuckled as he opened the door and stepped into the cold morning wind. Biting snow stung his cheek before he had the chance to tilt his coat collar up around his face. He quickly and carefully jogged across the road and headed toward the Sheriff's Office.

"Where the hell have you been?" called an elderly lady from behind a small reception desk as he entered. She was tapping away at a desktop computer, occasionally glancing across the desk to some hand-written notes. Behind her was a small space taken up with two workstations laden with papers, folders and junk food wrappers.

To the right of the workstations was an open door leading to a small corridor with a door to jail cells to the right and a tiny kitchen to the left. The smell of freshly brewed coffee filled the small office space. Dawson could only guess that Agnes had made a pot when she arrived at work.

"Having breakfast in the Bahamas," Dawson answered as he walked past the desk to heater next to a glass door with his name on it. "Where have you been, Agnes?"

"I've been right here answering your phone all damn morning," she snorted.

Dawson stopped dead in his tracks. His hand rested on the door handle. The door was slightly open and he was about to step in.

"What do you mean, 'all morning'?" he asked as he turned to face her.

"Since I got in here, around six," she replied. "They've been calling all morning about some noise they heard near the army base."

"Fill me in," he said as he moved around the reception desk and pulled up a chair to sit next to her.

"Well," Agnes started. "They've been saying that there was some explosion around three o'clock this morning. A couple of them even said they thought it was an earthquake. Martin Rigby said it knocked him right out of bed."

"Martin Rigby's an old idiot. A sudden fart would knock him out of his bed."

"Well, in any case, there were about nine calls saying pretty much the same thing. Something happened out there and the base hasn't called us at all about it."

"Did you try calling?" Dawson asked.

"No answer," she replied as she reached for a cup of steaming tea on the desk.

"Sons of bitches," Dawson stood to his feet. "They're gonna try to clean it up and cover it up. Whatever it is." He started for his office door again, then suddenly turned. "Did you check the messages from last night? They may have left one."

"Yes, I most certainly did." Agnes sounded offended. "Only people who called were those who heard or felt whatever happened out there. Oh, and one from Stan Butterworth about some dogs or wolves that broke into his chicken coop and had themselves a party."

"Nothing from the base?" he asked.

"I would tell you if there was," she spat.

"Okay." He shot his hands up in surrender. "I'm sorry. I know you would. Just let me know when Vaughn gets in. I'll be in my office trying to call the base."

"They won't answer. I've tried six times."

"Well, I'll keep on trying until Vaughn gets in. You call the Mayor." Dawson took another long look at the workstations behind Agnes. "And get those boys to clean that shit up when they get a chance."

"One more thing," Agnes stated.

"What's that?"

"Those boys in back are all sobered up," she pointed with her thumb toward the door behind her.

"Keys." He held his hand out toward her as he walked toward the door. She grabbed a set of keys sitting near her computer. Attached to the keys was a plastic souvenir key ring, a small plastic dolphin with the inscription *WELCOME TO MIAMI, BITCH!*

Dawson took the keys from her and strolled through the open door. He turned to his right and unlocked the deadbolt on the metal door. He gave the door a hefty push, which opened with a loud *SKREEK.* The door swung freely until it touched the cinder block wall that lined the inside of the room.

The room housed three small jail cells. Each cell had a cot and toilet against the far wall partitioned by metal bars. Cardboard boxes with numbers and dates stenciled on them filled the first cell. The other two cells held a person in each.

"Damn glad to see you, Sheriff," said the man in the second cell. He was a scrawny young man, sitting on his cot holding a mug of coffee and scratching the whiskers on his chin. The other man in the third cell was leaning with his shoulder against the bars trying to look out the small window on the adjacent wall.

"Glad to see you too, Frank." Dawson smiled. "How you holding up, Dwight?"

"I got me an incredible headache, Sheriff." He held up his empty coffee mug. "This stuff didn't help much."

"Don't s'pose it would with the bender you two went on last night."

"We didn't do nothing too bad, did we?" Frank asked as he stood up carefully. Dwight looked eagerly to the sheriff for an answer to his friend's question.

"Nah," Dawson answered with a smile. "Deputy Redhawke found you both crawling up the middle of Main Street about eleven thirty and brought you both here for your own safety."

"So," Dwight began. "We ain't being charged?"

"For what?" Dawson laughed.

He unlocked each cell and ushered the men out through the doors and into the front office. Agnes had already retrieved their belongings, taken from them the night before. Redhawke had placed each man's wallet and keys into plastic zip-lock bags and labeled the bags, labeled in permanent marker with their names.

"I'm guessing both you guys have duty coming up," Agnes snorted.

"How d'you know?" Frank quizzed.

"Because the last seven times you boys have been put in lock up was just before you got called in for guard duty at the base."

"Well," Dwight said as he stiffened himself, "it ain't gonna happen again."

"You said that the last seven times too." Agnes shook her head as she returned to the file on her computer.

"Stay out of trouble, boys," Dawson said as the men retreated through the front door with a wave.

II

It was another twenty minutes before Vaughn stepped into the office. A great gust of bitterly cold wind erupted into the room and blew a bunch of papers off Agnes' desk and across the floor.

"Look what you did, you clumsy oaf!" she hollered as she threw her hands in the air.

"What?" he said as he closed the door behind him and took off his coat. She stared at him and shook her head. "Am I meant to control the weather now? How was I to know the wind would blow in at just the right moment as I opened the door? Huh?"

He hung his coat on a rack near the door and walked around to behind her desk where he picked up the papers that had blown across the room. As he was doing this, Dawson opened his office door.

"Where've you been?"

"Uh," he grunted as he stood upright and placed the papers in front of Agnes. "I ate breakfast. Gave Betty Sue a big wet kiss. She gave me some tongue." He directed his response toward Agnes who shook her head. "Then I went to see Jacob about holding off with clearing Old Ridge Road until the weather cleared. He told me he was too busy watching Gator Boys or something, anyway. Then I went to see the boys at the firehouse and told them the same. Then I came here. Why?"

"Something happened," Dawson said as he moved toward a door behind Agnes' desk. "I'm gonna make some coffee. Where's the thermos?"

"Under the sink," Agnes called as he entered the kitchen. "Where it always is."

He opened a cupboard door under the sink in the office's small kitchen. He saw dishwashing liquid, dishcloths and bug spray.

"Where?"

"Oh, for crying out loud," she stood up and quickly strode into the kitchen, reached into the cupboard where the Sheriff stood and retrieved a large stainless-steel thermos. "There. Where it always is."

She returned to her post as Dawson grunted a *thank you* and unscrewed the lid.

"Why do you need a thermos?" Vaughn asked. "You going somewhere?"

"Yeah," Dawson replied as he ran hot water into the container, rinsing it out and heating it up at the same time. "You're coming with me, too."

"What? Why? Where are we going?"

"Mayor's on his way," interjected Agnes.

"At least someone is answering the phone," Dawson responded as he poured hot black coffee from the pot into his thermos. He screwed the lid back on and poured more into a cup that was sitting on the bench in front of him.

He strolled back into the office and placed the thermos and the cup on the desk next to Agnes. Vaughn watched as he strolled across the room to a large locked metal cabinet. The keys were on an extendable cord attached to his gun belt. He unlocked the cabinet and retrieved two rifles. One, he held out for Vaughn to take. The Deputy quickly took the rifle and reached into the cabinet for a loaded magazine.

"Better take a few," Dawson advised. "I got a bad feeling about this one."

"This one, what?" Vaughn asked as he grabbed a few more clips.

"I think I'll wait until the Mayor gets here," he replied. "Save having to say the same thing twice. And clean that shit up. You and Redhawke need lessons in organization."

"That is organized," the deputy replied. "Do you want me to grab a walkie?"

"No," Dawson answered. "But check that all the batteries are charged."

Vaughn crouched in front of the gun cabinet and ran his eyes along a power-board in the back. The power-board housed several cables that led to a long cradle dock that ten walkie-talkies sat neatly into. Below each of the walkie-talkies, on the cradle unit, was a stenciled number that ascended from left to right and a small, green LED light signaling full charge for each device. One cradle, however, spat an uninviting red glare. It was empty.

"Hey boss," Vaughn called. "Where's number seven?"

"Betcha Redhawke has it," Dawson stood at the window, peering into the street. "Or it's under all that shit on your desks."

"I told you," Vaughn stood and pointed to the deputies' stations. "That is a very complex and user-friendly filing system right there. You'll never be able to replicate that anywhere in the entire world."

"And who the fuck would want to?" Agnes put in.

A large black SUV pulled up outside with a screech, quickly followed by a bang as the driver slammed the door shut. The three of them watched as a tall figure moved briskly past the window and rushed in through the door.

"Damn, it's cold out there," breathed a large man wearing a long gray beard. He quickly threw his coat off and moved to the heater on the wall near Dawson's office door. "So, what's happened, Tom?"

"Well, Mister Mayor," Dawson started to answer as he took the cup of coffee from Agnes' desk and handed it to the man. "Something has happened at the base. We've had calls all morning about an explosion, an earthquake or something. The base isn't answering their phones but everyone around them who has called can get through to us."

The Mayor was taking a large gulp from the cup. "Good coffee," he said, nodding. "This means that the base is not holding up to their end of the bargain where they contact us in case of emergency. Or, they think they have it under control."

"If they have it under control," Dawson replied. "Then surely they would answer the phone when I tried to call them earlier."

"Then they're not holding up to their end of the bargain," the Mayor stated.

"My thoughts exactly," Dawson agreed. "And the coffee is shit."

"The coffee *is* shit," the Mayor agreed before taking another gulp.

"Or maybe they're all up shit creek at the base and can't get to the phone," put in Vaughn.

The Mayor's eyes quickly moved to Vaughn. The Deputy couldn't tell if it was a look of disapproval or wonder. He wished he kept his mouth shut when he moved his glance from the Mayor's face to his two work colleagues.

"You two old farts with all your experience didn't consider that," Agnes smiled. "Did you?"

The two older men looked at each other briefly and then back to the young Deputy who looked as if he just came out of grade school. Dawson thought maybe all old men looked at young men that way. Inexperienced, snot-nosed bastards who were opinionated because of their over-priced education and physical stamina enabling them to live oversexed lives. Then he thought maybe all old men were jealous of the young ones because they were too wrinkled, pruned and not getting any trap, like the gorgeous Betty Sue at the diner.

Lucky bastard.

"The kid could be right," Dawson muttered. "All the more reason to go out and have a look-see."

The Mayor shook his head and took in a few deep breaths. "I hope to God you're both wrong. That maybe it's just some training exercise out there."

"They would've let us know," said Dawson.

"I know," the Mayor replied. He took another gulp to finish his cup of coffee. "The coffee really is shit." He placed the empty cup on Agnes' desk and put his coat back on. "You guys let me know right away what you find out."

Before they could respond, the Mayor was out the door, back in his vehicle and gone.

Agnes picked up the empty cup and returned it to the kitchen as both men slid into their coats and retrieved their rifles.

"See you when we get back." Dawson smiled.

"Take care," she replied as she sat back down in her chair.

III

Vaughn practically tore his gloves off and placed his bare hands on the dashboard's air vents as they left town and started down the road toward the army base at the far end of the valley. The warm air drifted through his fingers like an unseen stream before it dispersed throughout the interior of the Cherokee.

Dawson wore his hat low, almost concealing his bushy eyebrows. He pulled his coat up around his ears and wrapped a scarf around his neck and covered his mouth. It was almost comical to Vaughn. All he could see was a cowboy hat and scarf with a nose and moustache sticking out between the two.

"Can you even see where you're going?"

"Don't be a smart ass," Dawson's muffled voice answered.

Vaughn snickered.

"Listen," Vaughn began as they entered a thick patch of forest on either side of the road. "Why do you call the Mayor by his title? Not his name?"

"Huh?"

"You know," Vaughn started to put his gloves back on. "You guys have known each other since the Stone Age. I just thought you would call him by name. That's all."

The forest opened up to reveal farmland with cows kicking at the snow to get to whatever plant life was underneath.

"A man in his position deserves to be called by his title," Dawson answered. "His job is harder than it looks. This may be a small town in the middle of nowhere. But, keeping everyone reasonably happy by making the tough decisions is draining on the mind and body. As far as I'm concerned, he has done a good job. Better than the last guy." Dawson stopped and shook his head as he quickly reminisced about a time passed. "Fuckin' Fraser. So, I give the Mayor my respect by calling him by his title. I advise you to do the same."

"Sure, boss." Vaughn turned his gaze out the window in time to watch more trees pass by.

They drove through two crossroads and passed a few small clusters of houses set a ways back from the road. These were old army housing estates now occupied by people on low incomes, unable to afford residences closer to town. Most were unemployed or seasonal workers such as loggers and farmhands. There wasn't much they could do during the winter months except spend their savings and try to make ends meet.

Dawson felt more akin to these folk than those who were in town. His own father worked as a farmhand and there were many Christmases that went without presents when he was a boy. He placed no blame on his father or the circumstances life dished out to his family. The fact was, he knew none better until he grew up and saw how other people lived. This made him respect and love his father even more. His father never brought alcohol home, never dished out his frustrations on him or his mother, and never said a negative word in front of him during his childhood. He had always made sure there was food on little Tommy Dawson's plate and a warm bed to sleep in on the coldest nights. Who needed presents?

Dawson slowed the Cherokee down to a crawl. The boundary fence of the army base was now on either side of them just beyond the tree line. It was still another half mile to the checkpoint.

"What the hell?" Vaughn whined as he glared through the windshield.

The army had set a small boom gate upon the middle of the road. A young soldier carrying an automatic rifle was flagging them down while another sat in an all-terrain vehicle to keep warm. Dawson stopped the Cherokee and turned off the engine.

"Grab the specs and put them in your pocket," Dawson ordered as he opened the door. Vaughn reached into the glove box and pulled out a small set of binoculars and shoved them into his coat pocket. He then donned his hat and joined Dawson in the cold.

"Sheriff," the soldier called. A warm, friendly smile etched onto his face. "Deputy. I wasn't informed of your visit. I'm afraid you will have to turn around and go back to where you came from."

"Go back?" Dawson sneered. He pointed at the chain fence stretching along either side of the road. "Son. That's your fence-line, is it not?"

"Yes sir," the soldier nodded. "It sure is. Goes all the way from the checkpoint out to just yonder and then right up to the mountains. Meets up on Maverick's Peak back there." The soldier pointed to a large jagged mountain peak some distance away, directly behind the checkpoint. Snow blanketed the mountain peak with occasional tears in the white fabric to reveal the harsh black rock beneath.

"From Maverick's Peak, you say?" Dawson smiled.

"Yes sir," the soldier replied.

"All the way 'round the ridge?"

"That's correct," the soldier chuckled, shooting Vaughn a quick look. *What is this old man up to?*

"Back to the checkpoint way down the road there?" Dawson stepped closer to the soldier. "Don't look at him. Answer the question, son."

"Ah, yes," the soldier replied. "That's right."

"Everything on the inside of that fence is yours, right? I mean the army's. Not *yours* as in *you*."

"Army property," the soldier pointed to the fence.

"And here?" Dawson pointed to the ground at his feet.

"Not army pro—"

"Not army property," Dawson interjected before the soldier could finish. "You're damn right. This is mine. So why the fuck have you set up a temporary checkpoint in my jurisdiction without informing me first, son?"

"I uh…" The soldier took a step back.

"What do you see?" Dawson asked.

The soldier didn't know how to respond to the question. That was until he realized the question wasn't directed toward him. It was for his Deputy who was holding a small pair of binoculars up to his eyes and was aiming them down the road toward the actual boom gate at the entrance to the base.

"Oh shit," the soldier said.

"Couple of burned-out tankers and a lot of tire marks on the road by the looks," Vaughn replied.

"You can't do that," the soldier interjected.

Vaughn moved the binoculars across the scene. Smoke was still rising from the wreckage and the ground was black from charring. It must have been a large explosion. The only recognizable object was part of the booth that once stood near the boom gate. It now laid on its side several yards to the right of its original position.

"Lot of people running around. Some heavy lifting and excavating equipment. Looks like a big ass clean-up job to me."

While this was occurring, the other soldier was speaking into a radio inside the all-terrain vehicle. Dawson couldn't hear the conversation, but he could guess it wasn't a pleasant one.

"We just follow orders and our orders were to set the checkpoint up here," the soldier stated. "You would have to talk to our superiors to find out why, sir."

"Well, that's good," Dawson said and smiled. "Because I think one of them is coming now."

The soldier turned to see another all-terrain vehicle heading their way. He gestured to the soldier in the vehicle by shrugging his shoulders. The other soldier exited the vehicle and approached the small gathering.

"Colonel Nelson is on his way, gentlemen," the second soldier informed them. "I'm sure he can answer all the questions we cannot."

"Well, you want to hope so, son," Dawson replied. "And he will want to do it quickly. I'm feeling cold."

The second all-terrain vehicle pulled up behind the first and a large uniformed man stepped out. He walked over to them, exercising his controlled, well-trained gait that informed Dawson that this was an officer with an agenda. They would not get any true answers today. The two soldiers jumped to attention as he moved closer.

"Gentlemen," the officer directed toward the Sheriff and his Deputy. "At ease, soldiers."

"Colonel Nelson," Dawson responded. "I'm Sheriff Tom Dawson and this is Deputy Sheriff Greg Vaughn. We would like to know why you set—"

"Why I've set up this checkpoint in your jurisdiction," Nelson said. "Well, as your Deputy with the lenses could tell you, our actual checkpoint has been destroyed. Now, we could set up something up there where the other one was. But as you can see, we've had a small incident, and some fuel was spilled."

"Now, hold on a second." Dawson threw his hands up. "Fuel spill? Why wasn't I, and the Mayor, informed of this? That little incident of yours looks as if it happened on my side of that fence."

"We have it under control," Nelson replied coolly. "If you take a look, all the fuel burned up. The vehicles were totally incinerated and sadly some lives were lost. I would appreciate it if we could deal with this ourselves so we can gather what remains there may be of the deceased to return them to their families. I hope you understand.

"We plan to be finished here in a few hours. We'll have the area cleaned up and with luck, a new checkpoint set up back in the fenceline by nightfall."

"I'm sorry about your men," Dawson stated. "I really am. But we need to be informed in the future. We can set up roadblocks from our end. We have worked with you guys in the past without a glitch. What you have done is a breach of the trust between the community and the army. We can't have that."

"You're right." Nelson smiled. "You're absolutely right. In the future, if anything happens, and may God forbid it, I will phone you myself."

"That's all I ask." Dawson put his hand out.

Nelson took it and both men shook on it then returned to their vehicles.

"Well?" Vaughn asked when they had turned around and headed back toward town.

"The Colonel is full of shit," Dawson muttered. "They're up to something but we got no proof of what it is. What did you *not* see?"

"What I saw was two tankers burned out," Vaughn said. "What I didn't see were the other tankers they must have removed sometime earlier. My guess is that only one tanker had fuel in its charge, judging by the expanse of the burn marks on the road.

"I have no idea what the other burned-out tanker was towing, but it wasn't fuel. The fuel burned up. The tank had torn open from the impact. Not an explosion. Something spilled, but it wasn't fuel."

IV

"What do you mean, *it wasn't fuel?*" the Mayor asked from behind his desk.

Dawson and Vaughn sat in leather armchairs across from the Mayor. Dawson had his legs crossed and his hat rested on his knee. Vaughn left his hat on the coat rack near the door of the front office where the Mayor's assistant now sat tapping away at her desk.

"I know it wasn't fuel," Vaughn answered, "because the other tank had no evidence of burn marks on the inside."

"You could tell that from where you were standing?" the Mayor asked.

"Yes sir." Vaughn nodded. "The other thing to consider was the remains from the other takers."

"What remains?"

"Exactly!" Vaughn thumped his forefinger on the edge of the Mayor's desk. "There were no remains. No burn marks. Lots of tire marks from heavy braking. More than what two loaded trucks would leave behind. I would say there were at least four vehicles involved in that accident."

"Small incident," Dawson corrected his deputy. "That's what Colonel Nelson called it."

The Mayor ran his hand over his bearded chin and looked at each of the men carefully. Eventually, he shook his head and turned his gaze to the window overlooking the main street of Long Valley.

He said, "I'm at a loss, gentlemen. If I call State Police, they will call the military and we will get stonewalled. If I call our federal representatives, the same thing will happen. I should do that, but it would be pointless."

He rose from his chair and strode to the window. Below him were the few civilians who braved the cold to fulfil their daily routines. There were people across the street buying groceries and supplies at a variety of little stores. Others were downstairs in the Post Office beneath him, paying their bills and posting letters, cards and parcels for Christmas.

The building served as a multi-purpose facility. It held the esteemed title of Long Valley Town Hall, but also contained the local Post Office and Municipal Library. It was such a big building for such a small town. Depending on whom you talked to in town, the building was one of the three, not all in one. One would call it the Town Hall, while another would call it the Library and another the Post Office. The Mayor had considered, at one time, moving the Sheriff's Office into a vacant section downstairs.

Dawson, however, turned the offer down before they had processed anything official. His reasoning was regarding safety. If they escorted a dangerous prisoner in or out and they got loose, there'd be hell to pay.

The Mayor glanced back over Dawson's shoulder to his closed office door. He read his reversed name on the glass. *Mayor Harold Waring.*

He was Mayor of a quaint town. Everybody knew everybody. Everyone was reasonably happy. No one was wealthy, but they all got by and helped those who had trouble. They raised money through school fundraisers. They pitched in when there was a need. He loved the people of this town and they trusted him.

The effort he had to put in for him to earn their trust was immense. The last mayor, Calvin Fraser, almost destroyed the town. His attempt to make the mountain ranges a nature reserve would have closed most of the seasonal operations and would have placed most of the valley's inhabitants out of work. His reasoning for this proposal was to bring tourists in. His strategy to bring tourists into the valley, however, didn't exist.

In all effect, Fraser was about to unintentionally close the town down.

This pissed off the loggers and farmers who formed some plans of their own. Most of it was just talk, but there were a few individuals who got the emotions of other influential people into a frenzy.

If it weren't for the intervention of Tom Dawson and Harold Waring, the town would have surely formed a lynch mob and had Fraser swinging from the lamppost outside the local library.

Instead, they offered Fraser to file an immediate resignation and get out of town before anyone came looking for him. Understanding the plight and offence he had committed, Fraser agreed. He wrote, signed, filed his resignation with his secretary and left the valley before sundown with his family.

That was two years ago.

Mayor Harold Waring wasn't about to make any decision like that. He would look out for the citizens of his town.

"What I am about to say to you…" His voice sounded shaky. "What I am about to ask you to do does not leave this room. Understood?"

"Yes sir," Dawson replied. Vaughn nodded.

"I want you to sneak back out there tonight. See if you can find anything suspicious. Find anything that could be a threat to the wellbeing of our people. Get the evidence. Tangible. Photographs. Whatever. Could you do that?" He was looking directly at Vaughn.

"I might need some help," Vaughn replied.

"What kind of help?" Mayor Waring asked as he plopped himself back in his chair.

"A pair of wire cutters, some bolt cutters and a couple of boys from the firehouse," he replied.

"Anyone in particular?" Dawson asked.

"Jeff and Shane will do nicely."

"Ex-Navy boys," Dawson said to Waring with a smile. "They hate those army guys. Don't know why."

"They keep trying to steal their girls," Vaughn stated. "They keep trying to steal my girl."

"Well," Mayor Waring chuckled. "We can't be having that, now."

V

Dawson jogged back into the foyer area of his office. A small barrage of discontented individuals filled the room. They looked slightly bored, sitting in a row of chairs that lined the wall, or red-faced as they tried to speak angrily over one another. Agnes held an emotionless expression as she repeated the same phrase over and over in a monotone as she continued to tap at keys on the computer.

"Please take a seat. The sheriff will see you in order of your arrival."

Suddenly, all faces turned their attention toward him. They thrust their concerns in his direction like a tidal wave of verbal terror. He peered past Agnes to see his other deputy, Colin Redhawke, interviewing another of the town folk at his desk.

The Sheriff ignored the upset individuals, of which he counted nine, and headed straight for his office.

"Send the next one into me," he ordered Agnes. "You take another at your desk," he said to Vaughn who was at his heels. With that, he entered his office and closed the door.

He sat down in his high-backed chair and grabbed a notepad just before Agnes reopened the door and ushered the first customer to a chair opposite the Sheriff's desk. An elderly man rugged up in a thick plaid jacket stared watery-eyed across the desk.

"There you go, Georgie," Agnes murmured. "Would you like a cup of something?"

"No thank you, Agnes."

"Sheriff?"

"No thank you, Agnes. But could you give each of them a number and split them between the three of us, please?"

"Already done," she replied as she closed the door.

"So, George," Dawson began, "what can I do for you?"

"Something ate my goat, Sheriff," George stated. His voice was shaking from emotion. Dawson couldn't tell if it was anger or fear.

The Sheriff lifted a pencil from out of a cup on his desk and wrote on the notepad.

"You sure it didn't run away?"

"Well, if it did..." George leaned forward. "It forgot to take its head and left shoulder."

Dawson stared at the old man for what seemed a long time.

"Okay," the Sheriff mumbled. "Start from the beginning. What happened? Did you hear something? See something?"

"I woke up around two or three. There was a loud bang. Sounded like it came from the army base."

"How far from the base is your house?"

"Oh..." he looked up to the ceiling as he quickly calculated the distance in his head. "Probably a quarter-mile."

"Okay." Dawson scribbled notes on his pad. "An explosion woke you up."

"Yeah. Well, I thought it might have scared Nanny. That's my goat's name," he stopped. His chin quivered. "*Was* my goat's name."

"Go on," Dawson said.

"I went to check on her in the shed and she was fine," he continued. "And I went back to bed. And when I woke up this morning, I had breakfast and went out to feed her. The shed door had been knocked down, and I found her..." He trailed off in a whimper as tears formed in the corners of his eyes.

"Okay, George," Dawson murmured. "I get the picture. I'll look into it when we get a chance. Is she still...?"

"No," George said as he got up. "I buried her in the garden before I came here."

George shuffled back out through the door and into the foyer. Sheriff Tom Dawson tidied his notes a little before Agnes brought the next person into the Sheriff.

"Hilary Zelski," Agnes announced as a young woman in her twenties parked herself where George had been sitting.

"How can I help you, Hilary?" Dawson asked, pencil at the ready.

"Something killed my cat and left it in pieces on my front yard."

VI

The three officers of the law gathered in the kitchen to compare notes. It seemed like a lot of the same. Besides George's goat and Hilary's cat, there were other forms of animal mutilations throughout the same area of the valley. All the complaints and concerns received were from an area within a half-mile radius of the accident scene.

"Something isn't right," Vaughn suggested. "First, we have this incident at the base and now all this."

"You think it's linked?" Dawson asked.

"I don't know," he replied. "We don't have proof. But you got to admit. Seems pretty weird that the two things happen on the same day."

Dawson nodded. He couldn't help wondering what the tanker trucks were hauling through his valley.

"Come on," Redhawke slurred. "Look at you two. Do you really think there's an army conspiracy happening here? In Long Valley? Where *fuck all* happens, and it makes the front page of the local newspaper? We just ain't that exciting.

"The most exciting thing to happen here was a couple of hundred years ago when my people flung arrows at your people. That's it. Since then, the most exciting thing to happen was Missus Gilroy winning first prize for the best pumpkin in oh-three."

"That was fixed," Agnes called from the other room. "That bitch was sleeping with the judges."

"That's just gross," Redhawke called back.

"Colin's right," Dawson stated. "That *is* gross and we need evidence if we're going to look into linking anything to the base. In saying that, it seems too much of a coincidence to ignore the possibility." He looked to Vaughn.

"I'll talk to the boys about a field trip," Vaughn responded.

VII

It was just after midnight when he turned the pickup truck right, onto the last crossroad before the fence-line began. The nearest group of houses was a few yards away. Vaughn drove into the small neighborhood and park the truck there, hoping not to draw any attention to the vehicle.

"You ready?" he asked the two men crammed in beside him on the bench seat. They were all dressed in dark clothing.

"Ready," one replied.

The other nodded before pulling the dark ski mask over his face.

They exited the vehicle and gathered their backpacks from the tray on the back of the truck. Vaughn started into the tree line first. The others followed suit, keeping low as they did so.

It was hard going as the snow had piled up to knee height. At the fence, they took time to catch their breath before one of the masked men pulled the bolt cutters from his pack and handed them to Vaughn.

"Thanks, Shane," Vaughn whispered before he snipped at the chain fence before them. After some time, he had made a large L-shaped cut that ran along the ground and up the side of a pole attached to the fence. He handed Shane the cutters and slid through the hole into the grounds of the army base.

Jeff, the other masked man, followed Vaughn as Shane threw the cutters into his pack before joining the other two. Vaughn pointed to the fence-line off to their left, toward the main road. He intended for them to follow the fence alongside the road until they reached a safe but observable distance from the crash scene. After they were in such a position, they could determine how to proceed.

Vaughn started off. Snow crunched gently under each footfall. He was careful to keep his balance and avoid obstacles such as fallen branches, pinecones and twigs, as these made loud sounds if trodden on that carried long distances in the night air.

A wolf howled in the distance. He hoped they didn't startle it as they moved northwards, keeping the fence to their left. If one wolf was nearby, then others wouldn't be too far away. Being attacked by wolves was one thing. Attracting the attention of army personnel to themselves was another.

They moved onwards. Vaughn could see the lights of the base in the distance. The Colonel was good to his word. The temporary checkpoint was gone. The army had set the new checkpoint up and manned it with guards.

This could prove a problem as the crash site was just beside the new checkpoint.

Vaughn signalled the boys to stop. He pointed at an angle slightly to their right. They needed to move deeper into the tree line and closer to the base. They needed to avoid the line of sight with the checkpoint.

Stealthily and carefully they moved, making sure their footfalls were as quiet as they could manage. The trees and shrubs acted as the perfect buffer between the checkpoint and themselves as they kept to the shadows.

Another howl from the wolf caused the three men to stop dead in their tracks. It was close by. The night air often played tricks on the mind concerning distances, but the men knew it wasn't far away.

A choir of howls to the east answered it. They too were not far away. Did the wolf want to join the pack? Or did the wolf want the pack to join it?

"Come on," Vaughn whispered as he dropped on his gut and crawled forward. After snaking their way to a point Vaughn considered being in line with the checkpoint, he stopped and sat up to take his bearings.

It was another few yards to go before the trees met a clearing that marked the beginnings of the base's main grounds. There were buildings beyond that looked like barracks and office blocks. Behind them was something that reminded Vaughn of an aeroplane hangar or TV studio. He saw it had a large door and no windows.

Thirsty, he took out a plastic bottle from his pack and drank.

"What's in that?" asked Jeff, barely audible.

"Water," Vaughn replied, offering the bottle to the men. Both declined. Shane picked up a handful of snow and shoved it into his mouth.

"Wolves could've pissed on that," Vaughn hissed.

"Flavor." Shane smiled.

Vaughn replaced the bottle and crawled on toward the checkpoint some fifty yards away. As he crawled, he noticed the ground dipping down to a hollow. If anything had spilled from the accident, it would have spread this way.

The vegetation grew thick here, giving him the impression that the hollow held water in the warmer seasons. It opened into a small clearing. Vaughn thought they must have ventured into a snow-covered water hole.

He stopped dead. His eyes locked onto something he did not expect to see.

The two men pulled up on either side of him. Jeff held his breath. The three of them wanted to get out of there so badly but knew that they would have to do so extremely carefully.

In the middle of the hollow was a stag with its stomach ripped open. It lay in a pool of dark liquid. The liquid wasn't water or fuel from the crash.

The viscosity reminded Vaughn of oil, but it glowed a dark florescent green whenever the chill breeze disturbed it, causing ripples across its surface. But that wasn't what almost caused his heart to stop.

A large wolf was ripping at the stag with its teeth, feeding on its prey. It buried its head deep in the stag's belly and was writhing back and forth making a sickening sound as it pulled flesh from sinew and bone. Slowly, it lifted its head from out of the stag's torso. Blood had spread along the sides of the wolf's face, giving it a grimacing smile that reached the base of its ears.

Jeff unloaded the camera from his pack, careful to not make a sound, and recorded the scene. He had the night vision set before they embarked on this adventure and just had to press record.

He tried to zoom in on the liquid so he could capture as much detail as possible. The problem with night vision technology was that it made everything look green, anyway.

"I think that's enough," Vaughn insisted. "Time to go."

The three men carefully slid back into the thick growth as splashing around the kill became more excited. They heard some growling and soft barking from the trees to the south as the pack arrived to join the one who called them earlier.

The men stopped and watched as four wolves trotted down an embankment to their left with heads bowed. The lone wolf placed its paws on the carcass and snarled. The others ventured in carefully to join the feast.

The first wolf suddenly leapt across its kill and grabbed the lead wolf by the neck. Blood spurted from the wound as the wolf ripped the throat of the other open. It then turned its attention on the other three.

Vaughn had never seen a wolf do this in his whole life. He didn't think they could conduct such a kill without the help of a pack. This wolf was strong and quick enough to kill a stag all by itself.

It grabbed a second wolf before the other two had the chance to turn and run a little distance away. They stopped and turned back, perplexed by the scene.

It was a silly mistake to make. The wolf had one in its jaws before it knew what was happening and was dragging it past the recently severed head of its packmate.

The last wolf took off at high speed, heading east from where it came. The first wolf looked toward the escapee and took a few steps in that direction.

Go back to eating, Vaughn desperately willed the wolf. His concern was that the wolf would pick up their scent and find them instead.

The wolf turned its back toward the men and returned to its first kill. It buried its head deep into the hole it made in the flesh and continued to eat. The sound of bones crunching was sickening.

Vaughn took this as an opportunity to leave.

The men quietly crawled back the way they came until they were at what they regarded to be a safe distance. Vaughn took a quick assessment of their situation. They had no weapons; no real protection. So, they made a unanimous decision to hightail it out of there as quick as they could.

Within ten minutes, they were back in the pickup truck, huffing and puffing, speeding back into town.

"Fuck me," Jeff muttered. "I've never seen anything like that before."

VIII

The men gathered around the pool table at the local bar next to the firehouse. It was dimly lit and quiet. A few people gathered at various places throughout the room. There was evidence that many others were in the bar earlier, enjoying themselves and leaving quite a mess of empty glasses behind. But now, the atmosphere was melancholy. Now and then someone got up from the bar or a table and left to go home. The group of men at the pool table was here, however, for a debriefing.

Dawson stood on one side of the table with his back to the wall. He knew it was a force of habit, positioning himself to see the whole room and everyone in it. Behind him, hung high on the wall, was a rack containing a variety of pool sticks. Like the old jukebox in the diner, the pool sticks and table were practically ornamental, not used in a game for about five years. During a few bar fights, the sticks acted as formidable weapons of choice when a few loggers had downed one too many whiskies.

Around the table were several other men who were more or less the unofficial town council. Mayor Waring stood swaying across the table from Dawson as he attempted to lift his beer mug to his lips. Carl Mason, the diner owner, was leaning on one end of the table with both hands. He was a largish man with thinning hair. His long goatee was wet with beer drool, and he was too drunk to care.

Another man stood next to him with a mug of coffee in his hand. He wore a bright orange parka and a New York Yankees baseball cap. This was Jacob Sorenson, the local snowplough driver.

On the other side of Waring stood Redhawke, Jeff, Shane and Vaughn respectively, still shaken by their experience and receiving odd looks after attempting to explain to the other men what had happened to them.

Waring started to shake his head, causing his swaying to increase to a violent rocking. He knocked Jeff with his left hand as he attempted to grab the table, continuing to shake his head in disbelief.

"Are you telling me that there's a fucking werewolf out there?"

"No one said anything about a werewolf," Vaughn corrected. "But it most definitely wasn't a normal wolf by any standard. I got the thing on camera."

"The thing was fast," Shane insisted. "It killed the others as if they were nothing."

"What do you think that liquid was?" Jacob asked.

"I don't know," Vaughn replied. "But if I were to guess, I would say it came from one of the trucks."

Jacob put his head down as he sipped at his mug. Dawson eyeballed him and saw the man was thinking. Jacob lowered his coffee and cleared his throat.

"If that stuff came out of the truck," he expressed, "where did it go?"

The Mayor seemed to sober suddenly. His eyes widened; his focus became clear as he stared down the table to Jacob who was scratching his chin. Mason stood up straight. He looked around the table at the other men who were all sharing the same confused face.

"What do you mean, 'where did it go'?" he asked. "Because what I heard was that there was a puddle of the goop lying up there with a deer carcass in the middle and a wolf who has magic powers."

Dawson started to nod. He understood what Jacob meant.

"What I mean is that a puddle the size that the boys showed us doesn't even come close to the amount a tanker would be hauling. So, where did the rest of it go?"

"Maybe they cleaned it up," Dawson suggested.

"And leave that much behind?" Jeff put in. "No way. I'm guessing they didn't clean up shit. They just covered it up."

"Oh, shit!" Mason shouted.

Some other patrons in the bar looked up to see if a fight was about to begin at the pool table. When they understood that no violence was about to occur, they all went back to their own little discussions around their own little tables or at the bar.

"What?" Vaughn asked.

"The stormwater drains," Mason explained. "About twenty years ago the town expanded the drains into the base grounds. Excess water would flow into our stormwater systems and be carried out into the river."

"I remember that," Waring agreed. "They requested it to clear melting snow so that the front of the base didn't turn into marshlands and stink up the housing estates."

"So that stuff," Redhawke slurred. "Whatever it is. It's on its way to the river. Can we stop it? Clean it up or something?"

The men fell silent and looked to each other for an answer. No one spoke. There was no way to clean up the army's mess. It was also clear that the army had no intention to clean it up.

"We need to talk to the Colonel tomorrow." Waring thumped his fist onto the table.

"Today," Vaughn said.

"What?"

"Today, Mayor. We passed midnight some time ago. And, no we can't."

"Why can't we?" Mayor Waring asked, starting to sway again.

Jeff put a hand on his shoulder to keep him steady.

"Because if we confront them, they will know we were trespassing on army land."

"Garn darn it," the Mayor whispered as he placed both hands on the pool table.

Dawson moved his eyes steadily from one man to another. He saw drunk, tired faces that needed rest.

"I need to get to work," Jacob announced as he stepped around the table and headed to the bar. He placed his mug near the waitress and walked out the door.

"I think we all need to go, too," Dawson suggested. "I'll walk you home, Harold."

"Thanks, Tom," the Mayor slurred. He stumbled as he turned toward the door.

"I better help you with him," Redhawke offered.

"Yeah." Dawson smiled. "I think you better."

"See you in a few hours, boss." Vaughn waved.

"No," Dawson corrected. Vaughn gave the Sheriff a quizzical look. "Take the morning off. Come in on the afternoon shift. I don't think any of us will make the morning shift today."

SUNDAY MORNING

I

It lapped at the miniature stream that snaked its way through the drainage system toward the river. Now and then, it stopped drinking to stand on its hind legs and listen. An occasional car moving past on the surface was enough to spook it into this position.

After it quenched its thirst, it moved on, scurrying against the flow of the trickling stream toward a small opening that led up to the street. It bumped into another of its kind and bit it. The other squealed and ran back the way it came as fast as it could.

Now it had tasted blood.

It wanted more.

Bounding up a slight embankment, it moved toward the opening. Once there, it paused. Carefully, it sniffed the air and made a quick assessment of the area outside the drain.

There was no movement. But there was the delicious odor of something alive.

It scampered across the road and onto a driveway blanketed with snow. Effortlessly and soundlessly, it ran across the white surface toward a gap between the snow and the base of the house.

The pitch-blackness and a dank smell would have been overbearing for a human. Not for this creature. It relished such conditions.

The scent of the living was powerful.

It climbed support beams and found the space where the scent was strongest. Slowly and carefully, it appeared from behind a refrigerator and into a small kitchen. Raising itself to its hind legs, it sniffed the air and determined its next action.

It bolted through the house and into the bedroom where it drowned in the intoxicating smell of living flesh.

A lump of breathing mass was moving underneath the blankets on a bed, but a large human foot with a blood-soaked Band-Aid wrapped around the big toe was sticking out from underneath the covers.

It locked onto the foot and ran open-mouthed toward the big toe.

The delicious, mouthwatering big toe.

He suddenly found himself awake and screaming. An immense pain shot up his foot and along his leg. Without thinking, he reached down to his foot with his hand only to receive a bite from something waiting for him down there.

"Shit," he yelled. Jumping to his feet, now standing on his bed, he kicked at the blankets. "What is it? What is it?"

Something scampered across the floor to his left and passed under the bed.

"Shit! Shit!"

He reached for the light switch on the wall and pressed. Intense brightness blinded him temporarily, but it was enough time for another attack.

The thing bounded onto the bed and went for the toe again.

Gnawing.

Gnawing.

Gnawing.

"Fuck!" He kicked. It, whatever it was, hit the wall near the door. His eyesight adjusted just in time to see a black figure, about the size of a football, dart under the bed.

"What are you?" he asked in vain. He knew it would not answer.

It bumped around under the bed; knocking small boxes he kept photographs in. Stamping his feet in the hope to scare the thing out, he left splotches of blood on his sheets. His toe was bleeding profusely.

"Oh shit," he expelled. The flesh was hanging in small strips. Whatever was under the bed had big teeth.

He needed medical attention. To get medical attention, he needed to get off the bed. That meant he would expose his feet to that thing down there, which would probably attack him again.

A quick glance around the room informed him that there was nothing in reach to use as a weapon. His best option would be to run out the door and close it behind him. Then he could either get his baseball bat to beat the thing to death, or get out to the car so he could get that medical attention he so badly needed.

He took a few deep breaths and leapt for the door. The sudden pain that shot up his leg after his toe smacked onto the floor almost caused him to collapse.

That was until he heard it scampering after him.

He corrected his balance and reached for the edge of the door.

It was fast. The distance between himself and the thing was closing faster than he could move.

He pulled the door toward him as he moved through the doorway and into the hall. The door slammed behind him.

The thing thumped into the door. Trapped.

"Yeah," he yelled through the door in triumph. "Suck on that."

THUMP! It bashed into the door again.

THUMP! Harder.

THUMP! Harder again.

He recoiled and backed hastily away from the door.

"Shit," he said, before limping down the hall and into the kitchen, leaving a trail of blood behind him.

He slipped on a pair of boots near the kitchen door and threw on a jacket hanging on the back of a chair before grabbing the keys from the table.

Before he knew it, he was driving into town. He didn't care that he forgot to lock his door. The throbbing in his foot was dominating every sensation he had.

Sweat was forming on his brow and he felt hot. A tingling sensation raced from his crotch, along his spine and into his arms. He thought he might have been having a heart attack.

Did heart attacks start in the balls?

He chuckled softly at his thought as he pulled into the emergency access of the Long Valley Memorial Hospital.

The car screeched to a halt, and he hopped out. Instead of making his way to the door, he fell to the ground. The tingling sensation had built to a rapid, pulsating flow of heat. Sweat drenched his head and the pain in his foot was overbearing.

He crawled toward the door but only made it a few feet before all strength left him. His eyes lost focus as his head lowered itself involuntarily to the ground.

"Help me," he cried. "Help me!"

An eternity passed before he heard the hospital's automatic doors open. Speedy footsteps and something that sounded remarkably like a shopping trolley's wheels was heading his way.

"It's okay," a man's voice announced. "We got you."

He felt himself being lifted onto a gurney and then moved from the cold night air and into the warm hospital.

"So hot," he said.

"You're feeling hot?" a woman's voice asked.

"Yeah," he muttered. "Thirsty."

"Get some fluids into him," another man's voice. "I see blood coming out of this boot. Remove it, please."

He felt some pulling and prodding at his legs.

"What did this, sir?" asked the second man.

"I don't know," he answered. "It was small. Like a raccoon."

"We need tetanus shots and blood samples."

"Yes, Doctor," the woman replied. He guessed she was a nurse.

"How long ago did this happen?" the doctor asked.

"Maybe ten minutes," he answered.

"What's your name?"

"Quentin O'Brien."

"Okay Quentin," the doctor rested a hand on O'Brien's shoulder. "I'm Doctor Vanderberg. I will put an I.V. in you to get your fluids stable. The nurse will take some blood and we will run some tests. As a precaution, I will give a tetanus shot and then see what I can do about this fever of yours."

O'Brien grunted a response and then passed out.

A nurse rolled a vitals monitor attached to a stand up to the side of the gurney. She attached a peg-like device to O'Brien's finger. A cable ran from the device to the monitor. The nurse pressed a button on the monitor which responded with a beep. The monitor's screen came to life with colored squiggly lines and numbers.

"Doctor." The nurse pointed to the screen.

"What is it?" he asked. He was young, slightly pudgy and his gaze was on the contents of a syringe he was administering to the patient. The nurse realized the doctor was engaged and read off numbers.

"Temperature one-oh-six and rising. Blood pressure one thirty over ninety. Pulse rate eighty-nine."

The doctor carefully pulled the needle from O'Brien's arm and placed it in a dispenser attached to the side of the gurney. He looked at the numbers on the screen and noticed they had changed again, for the worse.

Another nurse had finished applying an intravenous tube to the patient and was hanging the bag of saline on a hook next to the vitals monitor. She then clamped the monitor's stand to the side of the gurney.

"Is it a heart attack, Doctor?" asked one nurse.

"I don't think so. Orderly," he called. A tall thin man came darting out of a room halfway along the corridor. "Get some ice packs and meet us in…"

"Room twelve," a nurse responded.

"Isolation. Room twelve," the doctor repeated. The orderly had already gone for the ice packs before he had finished.

They quickly wheeled O'Brien down the corridor and into room twelve. As they did so, a nurse noticed a dark rash expanding around

O'Brien's eyes. His skin had turned a pasty white and his breathing had become rapid.

"Oh, my lord," she gasped.

"Donna?" The other nurse glanced over.

The rash had formed around the patient's already darkened lips. Doctor Vanderberg noted that the rapid expansion was following the blood vessels under the skin. Vein-like patterns were also expanding around the fingers, ears and throat.

"Vitals are normal, Doctor," Donna gasped. "How can that be? Listen to his breathing."

Doctor Vanderberg observed the four main vitals on the screen. The squiggly lines and the numbers had returned to within normal range. The breathing rate, however, was inexplicable. O'Brien inhaled and exhaled quickly like a panting dog.

Vanderberg pulled a small penlight from his pocket and pried O'Brien's right eye open. The eye was bloodshot around the edges and it had lost all pigmentation in the iris. The pupil was abnormally large and motionless.

The doctor turned the penlight on and pointed the light into the pupil. The pupil shrank to the size of a pinhole. This was a normal reaction for any eye when exposed to light, but not to such an extent. The eye's response reminded the doctor of some reactions with certain animals.

The eye moved and looked directly at Vanderberg. He jumped back with a shout. His action spooked the nurses, causing them to follow suit.

The orderly suddenly appeared at the door with an armful of ice packs.

"Doctor," he panted. "I got your ice pa—"

O'Brien leapt from the bed in one swift move and landed on top of the orderly. The peg-like sensor on the patient's finger slipped off, causing the monitor to flat-line and sound a loud uninterrupted beep.

The orderly fell backward onto the linoleum floor, dropping the icepacks. The packs slid along the corridor in both directions as O'Brien grabbed the orderly by the hair.

He dragged the fallen orderly back into the room and started violently banging his head against the floor as he moved toward the wall opposite the door. On the third hit, the orderly's skull fractured and blood streaks appeared on the white linoleum.

More hits— more blood appeared.

Vanderberg grabbed both nurses and fled from the room, pulling the door shut behind him. He saw O'Brien through a small window in the door. The patient was still beating the orderly's head into the floor.

"Nurse Stevens," the doctor whispered. "Can we lock this room?"

"Yes," she answered. "The keys are behind the—"

Screaming interrupted Nurse Steven's reply. Donna, the other nurse, had lost control of her composure and dropped to her knees. Doctor Vanderberg quickly looked through the window to see if O'Brien knew of their escape.

A pale, ashen face pressed up against the glass looking straight at him with pinhole pupils surrounded in a bloodshot sea.

Donna screamed and held her hands against the sides of her face.

The patient's eyes darted to the source of the screaming and back to Vanderberg. The doctor no longer saw the man who came in for help only five minutes earlier. What he saw was a predatory creature.

Donna screamed and screamed. The sight of the orderly's head smashing open was seared into her mind's eye.

O'Brien started to half-heartedly thump against the door. The doctor took some comfort in this as the door opened inward. Still, he gripped the handle and pulled the door toward him just in case O'Brien worked this out.

"Keys now," he barked at Stevens.

II

Redhawke was the only deputy on call during the night watch. He had been in a deep sleep when the cell phone on his bedside table rang. He jumped with a start, before collecting himself and answering.

"Hello."

"Sheriff?"

He recognized the voice as Doctor Vanderberg's. Shakiness in his voice gave the impression that something was wrong.

"No," he replied. "It's Deputy Redhawke."

"Deputy, we have a situation here at the hospital. How long until you can get here?"

"Give me ten minutes." Redhawke rose from his bed while holding the phone to his ear.

"Okay." The line went dead.

Redhawke tossed the phone onto the bed and lifted his uniform trousers from a chair against the wall.

He took ten minutes just to get into the SUV. After dressing, he made himself coffee and poured it into a travel mug. He was still wiping the sleep from his eyes as he pulled up outside the hospital.

O'Brien's car was still there. Its driver's door was open, and the headlights were still on. Snow fell gently, reminding Redhawke of coconut flakes as it drifted through the beams of the headlights and landing silently on the ground.

He took a small flashlight from his belt and directed it into the car. Splotches of blood lay on the seat and floor, but that wasn't anything out of the ordinary for the Emergency department of a hospital.

A nurse came to the door and waited for him just inside the foyer. He left the car as it was and strode through the automatic doors and into the welcoming warmth of air conditioning.

"Nurse Stevens," Redhawke greeted her.

"Hello, Colin. The doctor is this way," she said. She was middle-aged and stern in appearance. Turning and briskly walking away, she led Redhawke into the hospital and down a long corridor.

He saw Vanderberg peering into a small window positioned in the middle of a door. His eyes were wide and his face wore a confused expression. His breathing was stiff and came in small gasps.

"Doctor?" said the deputy.

The doctor pivoted. His head looked as if it would snap off from the speed. He looked at Redhawke for what seemed a very long time. It was as if he didn't recognize the deputy.

Eventually, the doctor's breathing eased. His countenance relaxed.

"Deputy," he replied. "Thank goodness you're here."

"What happened?" Redhawke asked.

"A patient came in with some strange symptoms. We treated him."

"Just you and Nurse Stevens?"

"No," Vanderberg replied. "Nurse Leggett was here also and Kyle Yancy, our orderly."

"Where are they now?"

"Donna is in the staff room," Stevens answered. "And Kyle is in that room with the patient." She pointed at the door the doctor had been looking through.

Redhawke saw speckles of blood on the glass.

"Who is the patient?" the deputy asked.

"His name is Quentin O'Brien," the nurse answered.

"What do we know about him?"

"Not much," the doctor replied. "He said something like a raccoon bit him. A weird rash appeared, and we took him into that room to isolate him. He suddenly went wild and attacked and killed Kyle."

It was eerily quiet behind the door.

"Did you sedate him?" Redhawke questioned, wondering why he wasn't hearing a 'wild' man now.

"No," the doctor answered. "We got the hell out of there when he attacked Kyle. There was no way I could have saved him."

"It's okay, Doctor." Redhawke placed a reassuring hand on the doctor's shoulder. "Mind if I take a look?"

"Brace yourself," Vanderberg stated.

Redhawke approached the small window cautiously. If there was an irrational person in there, he would make sure he didn't startle him into a frenzy.

Through the window, Redhawke saw blood spattered against the walls adjacent and parallel to the door. As he drew closer and closer, more and more of the room became visible.

The neatly made bed, positioned against the far wall, still had the gurney beside it. Blood had sprayed onto both in one long streak as if someone had tossed the contents of a cup in that direction.

He tilted his eyes down to the floor, smeared and puddled in red. He was finding it hard to believe that so much blood could come from one man.

But it wasn't the blood that made him turn from the window. He had seen blood many times before.

In the middle of the room were the remains of Kyle Yancy. His mashed head was an unrecognizable red pulp. His limbs were torn from his torso and his chest and stomach ripped open.

Hunkering over the mess was another individual who Redhawke could only guess was the patient, Quentin O'Brien.

He was kneeling with his arms spread wide with one hand on Yancy's crotch and the other in what used to be the victim's face. O'Brien was bent down low, his body writhing as he used effort to accomplish his immediate task. His face buried in Yancy's open torso.

O'Brien was feeding.

Redhawke turned away, aghast. He couldn't believe what he had just seen, nor could he bring himself to take another look.

Not right now.

"What the fuck?" Redhawke started to walk back toward the foyer of the Emergency department. The doctor and nurse followed him, unsure of where he was going. The deputy stopped near the reception desk and leaned against it with both hands.

"Are you all right, Deputy?" Nurse Stevens placed a hand on Redhawke's back.

"Yeah." He straightened himself and looked back toward the corridor from which he came.

"What do you intend to do?" Vanderberg asked.

"I'm going to attempt to arrest him," Redhawke stated matter-of-factly. He looked over to the doctor and the nurse. "Is there anyone else here?"

"A couple of overnight patients down the other corridor," the doctor answered. "We're the only person in the place."

"Okay." Redhawke thought a moment. "I want you to lock all the doors to the rooms with patients and then I want you to both go into your staffroom with the other nurse and lock the door behind you. Got it?"

"Yeah," Vanderberg replied as he handed the deputy a key. Redhawke took it and held it up. "For the door," Vanderberg said. "I locked it."

"You got keys for the other rooms?" the deputy asked. Stevens responded by holding up a set of her own on a key chain connected to her belt. "Okay, go."

The doctor and the nurse headed across the foyer and down an adjacent corridor. Redhawke watched them as they locked doors on either side of the long passageway before entering a room at the end. He heard the door close, followed by the rattle of keys as they locked the door from the inside.

His breathing had increased and his body was trembling. Something inside was telling him that this would end badly. He turned back toward the corridor which led to the room that housed the crazed patient and the half-eaten orderly.

He held the key in his left hand and pulled his revolver with his right as he slowly made his way toward the door with the blood-spattered window. Visions of blood and flesh flooded through his mind as he made each steady step closer.

Scenarios started to play out as he projected possibility after possibility of what could happen. It was a vain effort to try to drown out the horrific scene he was about to encounter.

He peered through the glass one last time.

There he was.

His head buried in the dismembered torso. Eating. Eating.

Redhawke suddenly tasted bile.

Slowly, carefully, quietly, the deputy slid the key into the lock and turned. He felt a slight vibration as the mechanism unlocked. He pulled the key out of the lock and placed it into his jacket pocket.

He made a quick assessment and went in fast, hoping to catch O'Brien off guard. The deputy placed his left hand on the door handle and turned. With his right thumb, he pulled back on the hammer of his revolver hearing it click all the way until it would move no more.

He took one more deep breath before rushing through the door with the gun raised.

"Mister O'Brien," he yelled. "You have the right to—"

O'Brien raised his head to see what the commotion was. His face was pasty white with dark patches around his ravenous, bloodshot eyes. Loose flesh hung from his teeth in strands and trailed into the torso like string. Blood smeared over his face from ear to ear like the smile of a macabre circus clown's grin.

The patient tore the flesh away from his mouth with his hands and stood to his full height. He fixed his eyes upon Redhawke as if he were new prey. Pieces of Kyle Yancy stuck all over O'Brien's clothing.

"Oh, my..." the deputy managed. He knew this would not end in any sense of a positive way. O'Brien lunged across the remains on the floor, expelling a terrifying, inhuman scream. His arms stretched out with blood-soaked fingers reaching for Redhawke.

Deputy Redhawke responded with a shot from his revolver.

Then another.
And another.

III

Dawson stood in the doorway of room twelve. He snapped photographs with an SLR camera he had slung around his neck. Carefully, he stepped over blood streaks to take shots from different angles.

"Tag" He pointed to a bullet casing lying on the floor near the door. Vaughn reached into a box he had next to him on the corridor floor and pulled out a tiny A-frame sign with the number 1 printed on it. He reached through the door and placed it near the bullet casing. Dawson snapped another shot with his SLR.

"I can't see the others," Vaughn croaked. He was having trouble keeping his breakfast in. The sight of the blood wasn't what triggered his urge to purge his bacon and eggs. It was the dismembered corpse on the floor next to the now dead man who had been feasting on it.

Feasting.

The sudden taste of bile stung the back of his throat. He winced and swallowed, feeling a slow, harsh burn as saliva moved down the inside of his neck.

"I think Mister O'Brien is lying on the other casings," Dawson replied. "I can't be sure."

The sheriff looked to his deputy as he lifted himself to his full height. He saw the unmistakable hint of green in Vaughn's face.

"You okay?"

"I'm just not used to this kind of thing," Vaughn answered.

"You wouldn't be human if you were," Dawson suggested. "Look. Let's take a break. Have some coffee." He moved back into the corridor, cautiously placing his feet so as not to contaminate the scene.

Vaughn picked up the box and carried it back to the foyer. He placed it on the reception desk and continued down the adjacent corridor to the staffroom. There, he found Redhawke nursing a steaming cup of coffee as he stared at the wall on the opposite side of the room.

Sunlight streaked through the window and landed on a large table in the center of the room. Sitting on one side were the two nurses and opposite them was the doctor. All shared Redhawke's expression. Disbelief, confusion and fear.

Vaughn was about to ask if anyone wanted coffee but noted that all had full cups before them. He moved to a little kitchenette near the window and grabbed a mug from the sink.

"He wasn't a man anymore," Redhawke offered.

Vaughn turned to look at the other deputy as he poured the black liquid into his mug. He put the pot down and sat near Redhawke.

"What do you mean?"

"He was an animal," he whispered. Tears started to well. "I could see it in his eyes. There was no way I could reason with him."

"It's okay, man. You did everything right."

"I shot him."

"He was attacking you," Vaughn reassured. He placed a hand on Redhawke's shoulder.

"He was unarmed, and I shot him," Redhawke sniffled.

Vaughn looked down at his coffee. Steam slowly rose from the mug like small streaming clouds wrapping themselves together, clinging on for survival until they disappeared from sight.

"He wasn't a man anymore," Vanderberg nodded, agreeing with Redhawke's statement. "He had changed. The man we found in the car outside was not the man you shot, Deputy."

The doctor lifted his mug and gulped its contents down. He placed the cup back on the table and turned his gaze upon the light streaming in through the window.

"Looks like it's going to be a nice day out there," he added.

"Doc," Vaughn began. "What do you mean, 'changed'?"

"Hmm?" Vanderberg appeared lost for a moment. "Oh. I mean, whatever happened to him changed him. I've seen cases of schizophrenia where people will change from one personality into another. But this was a total transformation. He changed from being Quentin O'Brien into something else entirely.

"I believe it was biological. Not psychological. One thing that needs to be done is a full autopsy on Mister O'Brien."

"State Police will be given full jurisdiction concerning any investigation," Vaughn explained. "They will order an autopsy on both the deceased individuals. It will be part of the procedure."

"What do you think caused it, Doctor?" asked Stevens, the older nurse.

"I don't know," he replied. "He mentioned something about a raccoon."

"A raccoon?" Vaughn stared wide-eyed at the doctor.

"Yes," Vanderberg remembered. "He said it happened ten minutes before he got here. It was only a few more minutes and then he turned."

Vaughn rose from the table and ran out of the room. He sprinted to the foyer and called to Dawson. The sheriff was attaching police tape in an X-shape across the now-closed door of room twelve.

"Yeah," he called back.

"We need to get to O'Brien's place and find a raccoon."

IV

Vaughn stood at the back door of Quentin O'Brien's house. It was a small two-bedroom brick shack made for withstanding cold weather. The steep roof had kept the snow from building up on top of the structure, but O'Brien had been reluctant to clean it up and clear his paths. The snow had piled up to waist height in different locations around the house. Vaughn saw the route that O'Brien had taken from the back door to his car as he waded through the snow.

The deputy pushed the door open with his gloved hand. Slowly, with a long squeak, the door swung open to reveal a dark passageway. Vaughn pulled a flashlight from his belt and pointed the beam into the room.

There were drops of blood on the floor, leading from the door into the blackness. He stepped inside and followed the blood trail with the light. Dawson crunched through the snow and stepped into the doorway after him. They were now in O'Brien's kitchen.

The blood trailed through the kitchen and into a corridor. Vaughn turned to his boss who gestured for the younger of the two to lead the way. The deputy, however, would have rather been sitting in the car with the heater on while his boss followed a fucking blood trail through a dark house.

Vaughn reached for the light switch on the wall. He flicked the switch up and down, up and down. Nothing.

"Power's out," Dawson stated.

"No shit," Vaughn replied. "This is how those scary movies always start."

"You've got a gun." The sheriff pointed to Vaughn's holster.

Drops of blood stained the carpet, leading toward a closed door at the end of the corridor. In between that door, and the two men, were two open doors, one on either side of the passageway.

Dawson pulled his flashlight out and directed it to the door on the right. Vaughn aimed his for the door on the left.

As both men reached the open doors, they turned their lights and gazed inside.

"Clear," Dawson announced.

"Clear," his deputy responded. "Bathroom."

"Bedroom," the sheriff noted. "No blood."

"Nothing here either."

The men returned their attention on the closed door less than three feet away. Vaughn reached for the handle and rested his paw on it. He turned his face to Dawson, who nodded *open the door.*

The deputy turned the handle with a slight rattle.

THUMP!

Both men recoiled.

THUMP!

"There's something in there," Vaughn said.

"There's supposed to be a raccoon in there," Dawson replied. "Remember?"

THUMP!

Dawson reached for the door.

"Wait," Vaughn muttered. "What do you think you're doing?"

"I'm gonna open the door," Dawson stated.

"Why?"

"We need to see what's in there."

"No, we don't," Vaughn insisted. "We can call the boys at the firehouse to come and deal with this. You know. *Hey, my cat's stuck up a tree inside some dead guy's bedroom.* Let them take the rabies shots."

"It's a fucking raccoon." Dawson flung the door open.

It stared up at them with mouth agape.

"Holy..." Dawson shouted.

Suddenly, it scurried toward them at great speed, its blackened claws ripping at the carpet as it emitted a high-pitched squeal.

BLAM!

Vaughn held his pistol steady, aimed directly at where the creature's eye once was. It lay still, seeping dark red liquid from the wound in its head.

"That's no fucking raccoon," Vaughn hollered.

V

"It's a rat," grunted an elderly man in a white laboratory coat. He held a lit cigarette between his lips as he pulled rubber surgical gloves onto his hands. Once the gloves were on, he pulled the smoke from his mouth and used it as an indicator as he explained. "You see here," he said as he jabbed the cigarette toward the rear of the creature.

It lay on its side with its mouth agape. Most of its head was missing thanks to the hollow point bullet Vaughn had given it. Its blackened claws curled, jutting from the end of stumpy limbs. Dirty-colored fur covered its long body. Not black or gray. Just dirty. The whole thing ended with a tail that reminded Vaughn of a fat earthworm.

"That's a rat's tail," the elderly man continued before taking a drag from the cigarette. "Also, here." He pointed to the mouth. Dawson and Vaughn followed his finger. "The front teeth are those of a rodent. It's either a rat or a fucked up hare. Except, hares don't got tails like that."

"It's too big to be a rat, Walter," Dawson pointed out. "Look at that body. It's the size of a dog."

"Not quite, Tom. Although, it is unheard of to get a rat this big and so deformed. Either, this is a new species and, I doubt it, or, that military base and its accident have done something to our ecosystem."

"Nothing can affect an ecosystem that quickly," Vaughn stated.

"You yourself spoke about a giant wolf attacking other wolves," the old man pointed out.

"Doctor Burkley," Vaughn said, "I don't know who it was that told you that, but it would be appreciated if you could keep it to yourself."

"Yeah, yeah." Burkley waved his hand. "It's a small town and every-one knows everything even if it's not true. The military isn't about to prosecute for trespassing when they could be responsible for introduc-ing a biological hazard into a community."

"Whoa." Dawson pointed at the elderly man. "What are you talking about and who has been talking to you?"

Burkley walked over to a desk near the only window in the room and sat down behind it. He lifted a notepad from his desk and handed it to the sheriff. Dawson took it and attempted to read the scribbled let-ters.

"Those are my notes I took when I visited MacCauley's farm early this morning," Burkley explained. "He called me about three this morn-ing about his cows. They were making a whole bunch of noise. When he went out to check on them, he found eight of them had jumped the fence from the field and into his yard. One of them near tore her udder off on the barbed wire.

"He put her down before I got there. But another one we found in the field had been ripped open right down the front from throat to ass. Most of the insides were missing. Not spilled out. Just gone.

"From what I saw, more than one predator had been enjoying them-selves over there. Reminded me of a lion kill where the whole pride would get in on the action. But, why leave the meat?"

Dawson looked at Burkley for a long time, waiting for him to finish. When the doctor didn't continue, he looked to Vaughn for the answer. The deputy shrugged.

"What do you mean?" Dawson asked.

"Hmmm?" Burkley lit another cigarette and turned his attention to the two men.

"Why leave the meat?" Dawson repeated.

"Oh…" The old man puffed a ball of smoke out. "Lions, or any preda-tor, will usually eat the rump or shoulders of their kill. It has the most meat. They will eat the guts too. But why leave the meaty parts alone? Not even a bite."

"Perhaps they were interrupted," Vaughn suggested as he leaned in to look at the dead creature's teeth.

"Maybe." Burkley dropped some ash in a tray on his desk and took another drag.

Dawson suddenly thought about the dismembered orderly in the hospital. His arms and legs were torn from the body, but not digested. The torso, however, had been the main attraction to the infected O'Brien.

Vaughn thought of the puddle of ooze he had discovered in the base grounds. His mind recalled the wolf with its head buried in the guts of a stag that laid in the pool of ooze.

"This thing didn't go for the guts," Vaughn said, pointing to the rat.

"Because you shot it." Burkley smiled.

"No." Dawson grimaced as he stroked his chin. "He means when it attacked someone else. It went for the feet."

"Probably because it's so small," the elderly man suggested. "What happened after it attacked this *someone else* you speak of?"

"Then *someone else* became sick and later attacked and killed another individual," Dawson informed him.

"Shit," Burkley stared at the sheriff. He glanced quickly to the dead creature on the table then to the deputy who nodded. *He's not kidding.* "We should backtrack that thing's journey. Where did it come from? How did it get infected? We need to find these things out."

"I have a theory," Vaughn put in. "Listen. O'Brien's place is in the housing estate. The old army housing area, right?"

"Who's O'Brien?" Burkley asked.

"The victim of that thing," Dawson answered as he pointed to the creature.

"The guy who killed the other guy?"

"Yeah," Vaughn continued. "Now, his house isn't that far from where we saw that wolf."

"And the puddle of goo." Dawson nodded.

"Puddle of goo? Has this all got something to do with that accident?"

The phone in the next room rang. Vaughn looked in that direction and saw movement through the door's frosted glass window.

"Seems like it, Wally." Dawson leaned against a bench and fiddled with his hat in his hands. "It looks like the army tried to quickly clean up its mess, but may have made it worse. MacCauley's farm? Isn't that out behind the estate?" He knew the answer to the question before he asked it.

"Yeah," replied Burkley. "You follow the last left turn right out to the end. The property backs onto the base's boundary."

There was a soft knock at the door before it opened with a tiny squeak. A young woman poked her head through the gap she made.

"Sorry Doctor Burkley," she said. "Agnes is on the phone. She wants to talk to the sheriff."

"Thanks, Shirley," Dawson walked out of the room and through the door. The woman shot a smile to Vaughn.

"Hi Greggy," she said before closing the door.

"I know about you and Betty Sue Mason," Burkley said. "Hell, half the town knows. Are you tapping my secretary too?"

"Not for a long time," Vaughn said bashfully. "What can I say? The ladies find me irresistible."

Burkley shook his head as he stubbed out his cigarette. "I need coffee."

Dawson re-entered the room and tapped Vaughn on the shoulder. "We gotta go, Wally."

Burkley grunted and pointed to the dead rat lying on the table. "What do you want me to do with this?"

"I don't know," Dawson answered. "I got no room at the office."

VI

Carl Mason was spending his Sunday morning cleaning his kitchen. The diner was closed for such an occasion once a week. His daughter, Betty Sue, religiously spent the morning cleaning the booths and front counter. Both would finish their section before noon and find they didn't have to do too much work at all.

This was because of the upbringing Carl had as a child. His parents were both sticklers for keeping things neat and tidy. His parents made him clean up after himself as a child and so he inadvertently gained an obsessive-compulsive disorder. At least, he believed he was OCD. He had frequently categorized items into particular groups and was two steps shy of labelling everything in his diner.

As it was, he cleaned the kitchen and front of the shop by wiping things down every night before closing up. He found that if he *kept on top*, it was a heck of a lot easier to take care of the bigger cleaning jobs on Sundays. The bigger jobs included cleaning the grease pits and discarding old stock.

Betty Sue entered the kitchen area with a rag draped over her shoulder, just as her father was placing a freshly cleaned hot plate over the grill. Just like clockwork. Both had finished at the same time.

"How did you go?" Carl asked. It was the same question every Sunday.

"Found fifty bucks in change," she answered.

"Bullshit." He stood upright and stared at her.

"For real," his daughter answered. "Three booths had change and a few of notes in between the cushions."

"Fifty bucks!" Carl shook his head. "Well, you can keep it in your purse I guess."

"Thanks, Daddy," she said with a wide smile.

Carl strode across the room to the sink where he washed his hands in a lather of soap. Betty Sue retrieved her little black handbag from the counter and placed the loose cash inside a little zip-up pocket on the inside. Her father followed her from the kitchen into the front of the shop soon after and gave the place a once over with his eyes.

It was tidy. He guessed his disorder had rubbed off on his daughter.

She made her way around the counter and to the front door. Once there, she took her parka from the hat stand and slid into it as her father flicked the lights off at a set of switches near the entrance to the kitchen.

Darkness filled the room. The only illumination was coming from the hazy daylight outside.

Carl grabbed his coat from the hat rack and shuffled into it as he opened the door for his daughter. He finished zipping up as he closed the door behind him. Betty Sue fished the keys from her bag and locked the door. Another Sunday ritual accomplished.

"Stop N' Save?" she asked. "Or something else?"

"Hmmm." He looked up and down the street. The snow had drifted into the street again. Wisps of wind lifted light frost into tiny spirals before letting them drop into the street. It was almost beautiful to watch except that the cold was stinging his face. That also meant it was probably stinging hers too. He had to get her out of this and into the car. "Stop N' Save," he answered.

He fished his car keys out of his coat pocket and pressed a button on a small remote dangling from the key ring. The car responded with a loud *BEEP, BEEP* and *click* as the doors unlocked.

Betty Sue was in the passenger seat with the door shut before Carl had even moved toward the vehicle. He moved around to the driver's side of the small sedan and opened the door.

A strange noise softly made its way across the air. It was hardly noticeable above the sound of the wind and static; everyday noise in the street. He turned his head to listen more carefully but couldn't determine its direction.

Looking up and down the street once more and not noticing any traffic in the streets, he ventured onto the road with his head tilted. The noise reminded him of the firehouse siren.

Given that the firehouse was across the street from his diner, he had to conclude that it wasn't coming from there or that he had suddenly grown severely deaf. He looked toward the Sheriff's Office up the street and couldn't see any movement there.

"Daddy," Betty Sue called from inside the car. Carl had left the door wide open, and she had hugged herself to beat the cold. "What are you doing?"

"Huh?" He turned back to her. She was shivering. Suddenly, he felt like the biggest pile of shit. He jumped into the car and shut the door. Before he finished his apology, he kicked the car over and turned the heater on.

"What were you doing?" she asked again.

"I thought I heard something," he answered. "Sounded like a siren or something."

He pulled the car into the street and turned left off the main street and into a side street, First Avenue. It was a short drive of a block and a half before he pulled into a small parking area outside the local supermarket.

It was a long building with large windows and an awning acting as a shelter from the weather stretching along the entire façade. On the top of the awning were large letters illuminated with fluorescent lights that read, "STOP N' SAVE."

Posters plastered the inside of the windows, large posters advertising specials and savings on particular items in store. In the center of the façade were two sets of automatic doors; one on the exterior and another set back inside, creating a foyer of sorts to act as a buffer from the harsh conditions outside. In summer, the area also acted as a buffer to keep the cool air-conditioned temperature at a constant.

Carl scored a parking space near the door to the Stop N' Save, which in his view, wasn't short of a miracle. It looked as if everyone in Long Valley had pulled in to do some shopping on his or her way home from church.

"Busy day," he said to his daughter.

"Must be all getting low on their beer and crisps," she snorted.

"Not everybody here is a hick, baby."

She mimicked playing the banjo, "Ning-a-ning-ning-ning. I'm my cousin's grandma."

"Shut it," he chortled as he climbed out of the car.

Father and daughter quickly made their way out of the cold wind and into the warmth of the Stop N' Save supermarket. Shopping trolleys were carefully stacked and positioned conveniently to the left of the doorway. Young adolescent girls manned eight registers, running products with bar codes over a scanner that sounded a loud electronic ring to acknowledge a clear reading. Zit-covered teenaged boys stood behind each register bagging the items as they tried to eye the girls inconspicuously.

Betty Sue grabbed a handbasket from a stack near small automatic gates to the side of the registers. Above the gate was a sign, "Way In." They moved through the gates and stopped in the fresh produce section.

"What do you want to get?" he asked.

"I don't know," she said as she watched a guy tapping his cell phone against a shelf with bright yellow bananas on it. He put it to his ear and yelled into it. *Weird.* "Those bananas can't be fresh."

"You don't want fresh produce, sweetheart," Carl stated. "Most of this stuff has been snap frozen during the warmer seasons and thawed out for winter. Those bananas could be a year old."

Betty Sue watched the guy shake his phone before returning it to his ear. "Are you there? Fuckin' phone," he hissed.

"Let's just get some lasagna or something and nuke it at home," she suggested.

"Now you're talking." Her father smiled as he wrapped an arm around her shoulders.

"Hey," a middle-aged woman called from the deli section. Both Carl and Betty Sue turned to respond. The woman wasn't calling to them. She had her cell phone up to her ear and was speaking into it. "Are you there? Hey!"

She lowered her phone and turned to another woman of similar age nearby. "My phone just cut off," she said.

Betty Sue scanned the area and noticed other people also having similar experiences with their cell phones. She quickly reached into her bag and retrieved her phone. The reception bar was absent.

"Check your phone," she instructed her father.

"Why?" he asked as he pulled a cell phone from his inside coat pocket.

"Check the reception."

He turned the phone on and looked at the screen. No bars. He turned it to show her as he looked around the room and saw many people with a phone in their hands but not able to get reception.

"Maybe a tower fell in a storm or something," he suggested.

Suddenly his mind ventured back to the noise he heard outside the diner; the siren faintly calling through the wind.

He thought of the conversation he had been privy to around the pool table at the bar. Army trucks leaking goo into the woods near the base.

Now the cell phones weren't working.

Was it all connected?

Was he just being paranoid?

What the hell was going on?

He looked to Betty Sue who looked back at him with wide eyes. The fear on her face wasn't something he had seen since she was much younger. Not since he took her to the county fair and rode the Ghost Train with her when she was thirteen.

She thought she was old enough to handle it.

Big thirteen now. Not twelve. A teenager.

He told her it would be scary. She insisted.

He sat beside her and she chuckled at first. Rubber skeletons and cotton spider webs. Then came the first turn and the recorded screaming began. Animatronic zombies fell through the walls. Reaching, reaching toward the carriage that father and daughter rode in.

A chill wind filled the tunnel as a werewolf howled to the left. More recorded screaming as a corpse fell from the ceiling with a noose around its neck.

She had buried her head into his chest by then and didn't dare look at anything else.

Big thirteen. But still a little girl.

He looked at her now, in the fresh produce section of the Stop N' Save, and saw that thirteen-year-old girl again. This, whatever it was, frightened her. He needed to get her home where it was safe.

"Let's get that lasagna and nuke it."

She smiled and nodded. He wrapped his arm around her again as they walked toward the frozen food aisle.

SUNDAY AFTERNOON

I

Jacob Sorenson sat inside the cab of his snow plow. The vehicle was nothing more than an old beat up tip-truck with a large grater blade attached to the front of the rig where the bumper bar would usually sit. The blade sat an inch above the road and angled slightly to allow built up snow to fall to the right of the vehicle as it moved along. A hydraulic system, controlled from a lever inside the cab, lifted and lowered the blade a few inches.

A large thermos of steaming coffee sat atop his dashboard console causing his windshield to fog up directly above it. He was sitting on the side of the Old Pass Road overlooking the town from high on a mountainside to the west of the valley.

He held a small cup that doubled as the thermos' lid in his woolen-gloved hands and sipped delicately at the black contents. The smell of coffee sifted its way through his senses and he savored the moment before lowering the cup to his lap.

A knock on his side window snapped him out of his coffee trance and he turned his head to see who it was. One of the firehouse boys, dressed in bright orange overalls and hoodie, was standing next to the vehicle. Jacob lowered the window to see what the problem was.

"Shouldn't be too long now, Jacob," he announced. "Sorry to keep you so long."

"It's okay, Shane," Jacob answered. He looked past Shane to the other six fire fighters who were hacking away at a tree that had fallen across the road with chainsaws and axes. "I can't clear anywhere else in the valley, anyway. Have a look at that." Jacob gestured to the valley be-low with his cup.

A thick haze of steady snowfall smothered the town. Jacob believed he would have a busy few hours ahead of him once the weather cleared.

"Geez," Shane breathed. "How long before you think it hits us?"

"Nah." Jacob shook his head. "We'll be okay. It's been heading a con-stant south since it started. It'll be out over the highway in an hour or two."

Shane watched the hazy blob above the town for a moment. "Still," he said. "We better get this done quick. We need to check the reservoir and logger cabins up here before we go back."

"The road between here and the water supply is your biggest prob-lem," Jacob advised. "It hasn't been cleared for few weeks. It might be slow going from here to there after you boys are done."

"That's okay." Shane smiled. "I'll get back to it. The sooner we clear this thing, the sooner we get finished up here."

Jacob raised his cup and closed the window as Shane returned to the fallen tree. He slurped the rest of his coffee down and poured another cup from the thermos.

It was going to be a long afternoon.

II

"I'm bored," whined a scrawny, zit-infested boy. His patchy stubble on his cheeks had iced over as he stamped his feet on the snow-covered football field the sat neatly behind the high school building.

Two other adolescent boys sat on the bleachers playing tonsil hockey with their girlfriends. He wished for what they had and was entirely envious of not having a girlfriend of his own. What was worse was the fact that he was their ride.

He paced back and forward along the sideline of the field. At least, he thought it was the sideline. The thick white blanket that covered everything made it hard to sense where anything thing was.

He wrapped his arms around his chest as he glanced back to the four teens on the bleachers embracing each other. Their body temperatures so high from excessive horniness it was a wonder they weren't setting themselves on fire.

"Fuck this," he yelled. His voice cracked from both the changing of his body and the frosty air. "I'm going back to Charlene."

One couple immediately broke their contact. "Come on, Andy," the boy hollered as he rubbed his girlfriend's back with his gloved hands. "Just a little longer."

"You can stay all you want." Andy waved his hands around him. "But I'm freezing my balls off out here. I'm going home." He started walking toward a small gate to the side of the bleachers. Beyond was a car park at the side of the school building where Charlene, a lone little red bubble-shaped Chevrolet Sonic, sat at an odd angle.

"He's our ride," said the girl to her boyfriend.

The boy looked to her and nodded before calling out to Andy.

"Andy." He stood up. "Hey, Andy. Let's take the girls home and hang out. Huh?"

"Aw, come on Brad," said the other boy. "Do you know how long I've been waiting to see Tiffany, man?"

"I know," Brad replied. He gestured to Andy who had almost reached the gate, "Andy doesn't have anyone since Trisha moved to Nebraska. Look at him. He needs us. We're his bro's."

"Dude." The boy shook his head.

"Bro's," Brad repeated. "He's always been there for us, bro."

"Fuck you, Brad." He stood to his feet. "Andy, wait up."

"Stan..." Brad smiled. "You're a real bro."

"Shuttup." Stan helped his girlfriend to her feet and held her hand as he followed Andy to the gate.

They squeezed into the Sonic like sardines into a tiny red can. The two girls sat in the back on either side with Stan between them. It wasn't long before he and Tiffany were back at checking each other's dental work with their tongues. Brad turned around from the front passenger seat to see his girlfriend staring awkwardly out the window at the passing scenery.

"You okay, Julia?" he asked.

"Mm-hmm," she nodded with a quick smile in his direction. Andy sensed the uneasiness and tilted his head slightly downward.

"I'm sorry, Brad," he sheepishly whispered, not wanting the passengers in the back seat to hear.

"It's okay." Brad laid a gentle hand on his friend's shoulder. "How about we take the boards out later and let off some steam, huh?"

Andy nodded. The corners of his mouth lifted slightly.

They drove past the Stop N' Save as they headed for Main Street. Julia saw people moving through the wide windows, which lined the storefront. They seemed to dart back and forth like frantic ants at a picnic. The supermarket moved from view as they passed the Library and slowed their approach to take a left onto Main Street.

Andy was about to go when he noticed two large headlights flash into view through the thick haze. He hit the brake and caused everyone in the Sonic to lunge forward. Stan and Tiffany clunked their heads together, causing an exchange of profanities between the pair.

"Sorry," Andy managed as a large green Humvee flew past them from left to right.

"Must be a late delivery for the army mail," Brad suggested as he watched the vehicle disappear out of view.

"Maybe," Andy replied. "But the base is the other way."

"Telegram for the President," Stan laughed.

Andy continued his turn into Main Street and drove north for two blocks before turning right.

"Can you take me to Tiffany's?" Julia asked. "I'll get my dad to pick me up from there."

"You sure?" Andy asked.

"Yeah. He'll kill me if he found out I was with you today," she said to Brad.

"Not before he kills me," he replied.

It wasn't a long drive. It never was in Long Valley. Andy stayed in the warmth of his car as the boys walked their girlfriends to Tiffany's door. They had another saliva exchange before stating their final *goodbyes* and the boys returned to the Sonic.

"Where to?" Andy asked.

"Your choice," answered Stan.

Andy had to think about it. Usually, he just agreed with whatever his friends wanted to do and went along.

"Snowboarding."

III

After a quick stop at each of the boys' homes to pick up their boards, they took the Sonic along Old Ridge Road which wound its way up the mountain range that enclosed the western side of the valley. It was a slow, steady drive as the road was becoming more and more slippery from the soft snow that fell.

"Should-a put the chains on," Stan chortled as he stretched out across the back seat. He was referring to a set of tire chains that Andy had left hanging in the garden shed behind his house.

Andy just didn't see the point in putting them on when Jacob Sorenson and his *Super Snow Plow* usually scraped the roads clear. Besides, the slipperiest sections of the road were only on the bends. If he took them slowly and stuck to the middle, he would be fine.

Eventually, Old Ridge Road flattened out as they approached an area often referred to as "The Lookout." It was here where most young couples would drive up to and park at night. You could practically see the whole valley from end to end.

Andy peered through his fogged windshield and beyond the wipers that scraped back and forth across the glass. He saw the *Super Snow Plow* with its yellow lights on top of the cabin flashing away. Jacob parked it at the lookout which was nothing more than a large flat section of gravel to the side of a bend in the road. The road then twisted sharply and disappeared into the trees before climbing steeply toward the reservoir that fed water from a spring to the town.

Sorenson climbed out of the plow and waved the Sonic over. He wanted them to park next to him. Andy waved to Sorenson and complied.

The boys climbed out of the car and heard chainsaws in the distance ripping through the timber. They stretched their necks in the sound's direction and saw some men in bright coveralls moving on the road ahead.

"Sorry boys," Jacob said. "Road's closed from here on up."

"Any idea when it will be clear?" Brad asked.

"Could be a couple of hours or more," he answered. "After that, we need to get the Sheriff over here to check the road with the firefighters for any safety concerns. Could be a few days before we give the full okay to go up there."

The boys looked at each other, sharing a common expression of bitter disappointment. Jacob looked from them to the Sonic. Strapped to the roof racks on top of the car were three snowboards.

"You know," Jacob offered, "you could just board down here."

Andy peered over the edge of the lookout and started shaking his head.

"The lookout is too steep," Stan interjected. "That's almost a sheer drop."

"Not there." Jacob's brow furrowed. "Over here to the side. Come on, I'll show you."

They followed Jacob along the road for about ten yards and stopped. The plowman pointed with his gloved hand to the section beside the road. The ground sloped gently downwards, covered with thick snow for as far as the trees would allow them to see.

"Just keep to the side closest to the road," Jacob instructed. "If you drift too far the other way, you will come to a steep drop. It might look smooth but it gets rocky underneath. Okay?"

The boys all responded with nods.

"Thanks, Mister Sorenson." Brad smiled.

"Just be careful and come get me if you need anything," Jacob called out as he returned to the warmth of his plow.

The boys unstrapped the boards from the roof racks and raced back to the spot beside the road that Jacob had shown them. It wasn't long before the three of them were winding their way between trees, ducking low limbs and laughing hysterically.

Weaving between trees or setting a path to follow was easy due to the logging company's planting of trees in rows and columns all over the mountain range. This allowed the boys to choose an open section between pines to call their own as they raced down the mountainside. Except, Stan liked to cut in front of the other two on occasions just to get a reaction from them.

"Fuck, Stan!" Brad called as he quickly steered to the left to overcome the intruding snowboarder's attempts to stir things up. Stan laughed as he turned sharply to direct his attention to Andy.

Andy saw Stan's approach and responded by turning his board sharply and bringing himself to a stop. Stan zipped past Andy with a look of defeat. He waved his fist in jest and stared back at Andy in mock anger. "I'll get you next time."

Stan turned to look in the direction he was travelling. His gaze fell on something to his right and he quickly pulled up to a stop.

"Get over here," he called.

The boys boarded down the slope toward Stan who leaned his board against a tree and started walking to the right, toward an open patch of ground.

Andy saw a clear patch of snow sullied with blood streaks. As he drew closer, he saw thicker pools of blood and chunks of flesh.

"Oh shit," Brad murmured as the scene came into view. Both boys leaned their boards against the tree next to Stan's and made their way over to him. The three of them looked down at the site for what seemed a very long time.

Something had flung blood and flesh in all directions from a central area where the torso of a large animal lay. It had its underside ripped open and its contents emptied.

"What is it?" Andy asked.

"I think it's a cow," Brad answered.

"Wrong question and answer, guys." Stan shook his head.

The other two looked to him, signalling, *what are you talking about?*

"You should have asked, what did this and why aren't we getting the fuck out of here?"

IV

Doctor Walter Burkley bent over the mutilated remains of the animal. His cigarette jutted from his pursed lips precariously as he squinted and tilted his head at an odd angle. Eventually, he moved around to the other side of the carcass and repeated his routine.

Dawson watched with avid interest. The veterinarian had been circling the body for twenty minutes only occasionally breaking the monotony with a scribble of some notes onto a notepad he kept in his inner jacket pocket.

Some heavy footsteps behind the sheriff announced Deputy Vaughn and Jacob who both carried two disposable coffee cups. Jacob handed one to Dawson, who took it with pleasure. Something warm inside was more than welcome in the bitter cold that surrounded him.

Vaughn approached Burkley, holding the cup out toward the doctor. Burkley waved it off with a grunt and scribbled more notes. The deputy retreated to the sheriff and sipped from his own cup in the other hand.

"Well?" Jacob asked.

"Nothing yet," Dawson replied. "I've been watching this since you left to get coffee."

"I reckon it was the wolf," Vaughn opined, referring to the creature he and the firehouse boys had seen near the army base.

"Weren't no wolf," Burkley responded.

"It speaks," Dawson joked.

"A man has to think before coming to a conclusion, Tom," he replied as he moved toward the waiting men. "Thank you, Deputy. I'll take that coffee now."

Vaughn handed the cup to the doctor who took it gratefully and sculled the whole contents in one go.

"That was well needed. Thank you," he said, handing the empty cup back to the deputy. "The wounds don't match that given by any wolf attack I've seen before."

"The wolf I saw wasn't like any wolf I've seen before," Vaughn responded.

"Touché." Burkley nodded. "I don't think the wolf you saw is a wolf anymore, Deputy."

The men looked at each other, curious and confused. Before any of them could ask for clarification, the veterinarian started speaking again.

"You remember the rat you brought to me?"

"How could we forget?" Dawson replied.

"After a closer look, I have to admit that it was no longer a rat as much as we would usually refer to what a rat is," he started. "In other words, that thing has mutated beyond being a rat."

"The next step in evolution," Jacob said.

"No. Not at all," Burkley replied. "I believe this was induced."

"Someone made that fucking rat?" asked Vaughn.

"In a way, yes."

"Why?" The deputy chuckled, not entirely believing what he was hearing.

"I don't think it was on purpose," the doctor explained. "You saw the wolf. You saw the goop that spilled from the trucks near the base. Put two and two together, Deputy, and you get this shit."

"The fucking army base again." Jacob shook his head.

"So, I guess we need to inform MacCauley we found another one of his cows," Dawson announced.

"Nope," Burkley interjected. "This is one of Gibb's cows. The brand on the rump is his."

"How did it get all the way up here?" Vaughn asked. "His farm's all the way down the south end of the valley."

"I have a feeling this one's been missing for a long time. It wandered up here and met its end," the doctor guessed.

"Doesn't matter," Dawson said. "My main concern is to tell Gibb about his cow, then visit Doctor Vanderberg to see if he's had time to do an autopsy on O'Brien. I might get you to tag along, Walter. Let's see if your mutation theory pans out."

"Yeah, okay," the doctor replied as he lit a new cigarette. "Right after I take care of my main concern."

"What's that?" Jacob asked.

"I'm seventy-one and I now have to climb all the way back up this fucking mountain."

V

The SUV slowly rolled along a gravel road that wound its way between fenced off fields up to a cluster of buildings at the top of a small hill. A large wooden barn sat to the left and a towering rectangular cinder block structure to the right of it. Farther to the right were two long cabins with several vehicles, mostly pickup trucks, parked in front. Beyond these buildings stood a modern two-story house.

It reminded Vaughn of something from the house and yard magazines that exemplified perfect suburban lifestyles. It seemed an odd choice of home structure to build and position in the middle of a farmyard. Its blocky architecture did not appear to complement the more traditional buildings it accompanied.

Dawson steered the SUV up to the giant cinder block building and pulled the vehicle to a stop. The building had a large roller door on the front, which was open. Inside the door was a loading dock for trucks. Beyond the loading dock was a large packing room.

An elderly man, accompanied by two younger men, leaned on a cane at the top of the loading dock. He gave a small wave with his hand to the men in the SUV. The younger men followed suit after seeing the elder's gesture.

"Afternoon, Anthony," Dawson said as he climbed out of the vehicle.

"Tom." The older man nodded. "Who's that with you?"

"I got Walter Burkley with me." Dawson waved his hand toward the doctor who made his way over to the sheriff. "And you know my deputy, Greg Vaughn."

"Afternoon, Mister Gibb," Vaughn said, with a tip of his hat.

"Good to see you, gentlemen." Gibb smiled before gesturing to the man immediately on his left. "You know my son, Donald. The other man here is Jerry. My leading hand."

"Hi," Jerry said with a quick smile. Donald responded with a short wave of his hand.

Gibb invited the men to join him on the dock by pointing to a small flight of stairs to the side of the platform he was standing on. "What can I do for you?" he asked as he turned to walk into the packing room.

"Well," Dawson started as he joined Gibb on the dock. "It seems we have some bad news."

"You found my cows." Gibb tilted his head to the sheriff as he headed for a large doorway at the back of the room. Large rubber curtains hung over the doorway. They allowed large objects through, like forklifts and people, but persuaded smaller objects, like insects, to keep out. Above the door were large vents that blew a strong stream of air straight down the front of the door as a further deterrent to persistent pests.

"Ugh..." Dawson gave the other man a quizzical look. "Cows?"

Donald opened one half of the rubber curtains to the right while Jerry opened the other half to the left to allow the men through. The room was cool. Frost had built up on conduit lines around the walls. Essentially, the room was a large fridge.

Extending from the ceiling was a rail that wound its way through the room from the rear to a packing station near the curtained door. Attached to the rail were many large hooks, some of which hung carcasses of freshly skinned cows.

There were several stainless-steel tables positioned around the room where men were butchering the carcasses into manageable portions. As Dawson watched, men placed the portions into Styrofoam containers which were taken by other personnel to the small packing station. There were six such containers neatly stacked at the station waiting for the next step of the process.

"I've lost seven cows in the last week," Gibb replied. "Five of them in the last forty-eight hours."

"We found one up near the reservoir," Dawson said.

"That's near all the way across the other side of the valley," Jerry interjected.

"Probably one of the two that went missing last week," Donald stated.

"A tree fell onto the fence," Gibb explained. "Jerry and the boys fixed it then did a count of the stock. We came up two short."

"We checked the rest of the fences," said Jacob. "They were all fine. Five more have gone missing since and no fences down. I can't explain it."

Dawson looked to Vaughn and Burkley. Both men shared his concerned expression. Gibb picked up on this and looked to each of the men.

"What is it?"

"We found your cow mutilated," Burkley informed. "Attacked by something big and strong."

"What?" Gibb asked. "A mountain lion? A bear?"

"We're not sure," Burkley answered. "We know it happened recently and that it's not the only attack that's occurred in the valley."

"You said your other cows went missing within the last forty-eight hours?" Vaughn asked Donald.

"Yeah," he replied. "I don't understand. Is someone taking our cows?"

"This isn't a vendetta, son," Dawson reassured. "The other attacks have not been specific to cows."

"I think we need to take this conversation up to the house, gentlemen," Gibb said. "I don't think we need any eavesdropping in here. I can inform my men later if I need to."

VI

An older, well-dressed woman poured the steaming black liquid into a mug and handed it to Burkley.

"Thank you, Sallie," he replied as he took the cup and sipped. It was bitter, strong and contained tiny black floating particles. Not to Doctor Walter Burkley's liking at all. "Very nice."

"I use real coffee beans and grind them myself," she announced with a sense of pride.

No shit, the doctor thought to himself as she left the room beaming with a smile. Gibb waited until she was out of earshot before he addressed the men who were all seated around the room on deep-cushioned couches.

"The coffee is crap," he announced. "I stopped drinking it years ago. Ever since she got that grinder, she insisted on making it. I prefer the canned stuff. Anyway, down to business. You were telling us about some attacks. Are other farms having this problem?"

"We're not sure," Dawson answered as he placed his mug on a coffee table in the center of the room. "What we know is there have been a few attacks involving small animals. What we think is doing this varies depending upon the story and what we know so far."

"Okay," Gibb shook his head. "I'm more confused now than I was five minutes ago."

"I guess you best start from the beginning, Tom," said Burkley.

"Okay." Dawson thought for a moment. "Two nights ago, there was an accident up at the army base. A couple of tanker trucks collided and resulted in an explosion."

"Yeah," Donald interrupted. "I heard about it from someone at the Stop N' Save. They said it woke them up and shook the house."

"It was big," Dawson continued. "But that, we think, was just the beginning. The stuff in the tankers spilled out either before or after the explosion."

"Fuel?" Gibb asked.

"No," Dawson replied. "I don't think so. See, if it were fuel, it would have burned up. This stuff pooled downhill. Deputy Vaughn got a pretty good look at the stuff the other night."

All eyes turned to Vaughn who was not expecting the need to tell his part of the story. When a moment passed, and no one removed their gaze, he knew he had no choice. *Thanks, boss.*

"All right. A couple of guys and me did some reconnaissance of the crash site. The only thing was, we didn't get to the site because we found a huge wolf blocking our way. I mean this fucker was huge.

"He was buried head deep in a deer's guts when we found him. Right in the middle of a puddle of some goo that I believe came from those tankers. Then some other wolves came up, and he started killing them. He tore their heads off and ripped them apart. We got the fuck out of there as quickly and quietly as we could."

"Shit," Jerry whispered.

Dawson nodded. "Now I reckon that goo made its way into the drainage system under the town. We got reports from people in that area about mutilated and missing pets. That was just the start.

"Early this morning, my other deputy plugged a guy who killed an orderly at the hospital. From their report, the guy came in feeling ill. Something in his house bit him so he went straight to the hospital. Within minutes, he attacked like an animal and killed the orderly. Then he started eating the orderly."

"Fuck me." Jerry shook his head.

"Deputy Redhawke shot and killed the guy," Dawson continued. "Deputy Vaughn and I went to the guy's house and found the creature."

"I shot it," Vaughn stated.

"We took it to Walter who told us it was a rat," Dawson finished.

"It *was* a rat," Burkley stated. "It had mutated, but it once was a rat. I think the same thing happened with the wolf that Deputy Vaughn saw and with Mister... What was his name?"

"O'Brien," Vaughn replied.

"Mister O'Brien who attacked and ate Mister Yancy, the orderly," the doctor continued. "I'm not sure what creature attacked your cow near the reservoir, but I think it is all linked to that accident that happened the other night. I wouldn't be surprised if other animals have been infected and possibly have contaminated other creatures."

"We need to tell the army," Gibb said.

"They cleaned that accident site up pretty goddamn quick," Vaughn said. "I don't think they're willing to admit or acknowledge such shit."

"What do we do?" Donald asked.

"Keep your eyes open and tell us if you see something out of the ordinary," Dawson instructed. "I'll try to get through to the State Police and see if they can offer help."

VII

Dawson swung the SUV back onto the road kicking up gravel and muddy slush as he hit the gas. He held his cell phone in his right hand. His thumb firmly pressed down on the zero to speed dial his office when he did this. He then turned on the speaker so he could place the phone on the console and speak hands-free.

The phone remained silent.

He looked from the straight road before him to the phone which was lit up like a Christmas tree and back to the road. At least he knew he had turned the thing on.

Frustrated, he snatched it back up and dialed the individual digits of the office's number before holding it to his ear.

Nothing.

"What the fuck?" he said as he pulled the phone away from his head to scrutinize the display screen.

It looked fine.

Correct time and date at the top.

Dialed telephone number in the center.

Reception bars were...

"Shit," he snorted as he slammed the phone against the dashboard. "Greg, can you..?"

"Already checked, Boss," Vaughn announced from the back seat. "No reception."

"Mine's getting nothing," Burkley stated as he waved his phone in the air next to Dawson.

"What do you think?" Dawson asked as he lifted the radio out of the cradle near the center consol. "Tower down?"

"A lot of trees fell last week in that blizzard," the doctor said as he pocketed his phone.

"Nah," Vaughn replied. "Phones were working this morning, and no storm has hit since that one last week."

"Agnes," Dawson called into the radio. "Agnes, you there?"

"…uck me. Tom?" replied a static voice. "You scared the shit out of me. I almost forgot how to use this thing; it's been so long."

"Agnes, what's up with the phones?"

"All cell phones are down," she answered. "The land line is fine for calls inside the valley but damned if you try to call anyone outside."

"Is it a storm or something?" Dawson asked.

"There is a storm coming. But it doesn't explain what's happening with the phones. I talked to the boys at the firehouse. They said the tower reception is strong. Weather reports are still coming in. Television reception is good. General communication is shot. It's a mystery."

"Okay." Dawson paused to think. He couldn't call the State Police. The only way to communicate was radio and landline. Perhaps the radio could reach the outside world. "Agnes, can you try reaching the State Police by radio? My CB just isn't powerful enough."

"I'll try," she said.

"Try the…" Vaughn leaned forward. He stopped short so he could grab the radio from Dawson. "Agnes?"

"Yes," responded the crackly voice.

"Try the internet," he suggested. "Email them."

"Nice try, sonny. No Internet reception. Don't you think I've been trying to update my Facebook?"

Vaughn swore as he handed the radio back to the sheriff.

"Agnes, we're going back to the hospital and then we'll come back in. We'll see you in around an hour."

"Okay," she replied. "Over and out."

The three men sat in silence for a short while. Dawson saw dark clouds behind the mountains at the far end of the valley drifting toward them. There was the storm that was heading their way. He estimated it would be on them by nightfall, which would make sleep for him a near impossibility.

Ever since he returned from Vietnam, night noise made him restless. He knew there was nothing in the noise that could hurt him. Mostly, it was just the house creaking, or a tree in the wind. Once, he jumped out of bed and grabbed his shotgun in response to a noise he had heard at his back door. He raced out in his underwear and exploded onto his back porch ready to blow someone away only to come face to face with a raccoon that had discovered how to open the garbage can.

Storms were the worst.

Strong wind raking against the side of the house accompanied by the rattling of windows would be enough to set his nerves on edge. Thunder claps and lightning would bring on involuntary shivering and tightening of his stomach.

He knew it was a physical memory that acted like an instinct. A fear brought on from a mortar barrage he survived and wished he could forget. A fear that returned every time those dark clouds moved in from the north and settled over the town.

God, how he hated storms.

Eventually, Burkley broke the silence.

"Army's blocking communications."

"Yeah," Dawson agreed. "But why?"

VIII

"This way, gentlemen." Vanderberg led the men along the corridor, past the taped off room where O'Brien had killed Kyle Yancy only a few hours ago, and into a small operating room.

In the center of the room was an operating table with the naked body of Quentin O'Brien laying face up. A large light hung from a crane-like arm, protruding from high upon the wall to illuminate the table. Next to the table was a tray which sat at waist height upon a small stand. Bloodstained surgical tools rested neatly on the tray. Vaughn moved his gaze across each of the shiny metal implements and couldn't help noticing how the blood glistened in the bright light.

The body of Quentin O'Brien stared into the light with glazed white eyes. His pupils remained the size of pin-pricked holes. Burkley noticed this and relayed his amazement by pointing at the body.

"What's up with the eyes?" he asked the young doctor.

"You noticed that too?" Vanderberg replied as he moved around to the opposite side of the table.

"Noticed what?" Vaughn asked as he moved in closer to have a look.

"The pupils dilate, or shrink, when they're exposed to light," Vanderberg explained. "When someone dies, the light doesn't have this effect as brain activity and nerve systems have shut down. So usually, the pupil will expand as yours would if it were dark."

"And?"

"Mister O'Brien is dead," the young doctor continued. "But his eyes have remained in a dilated condition. I have a theory but have not had time to investigate."

Vanderberg moved around to O'Brien's head and removed scalp and top of the skull as if it were a hat. He placed it on the tray near the table. It reminded Dawson of a coconut cut in half. He suddenly imagined someone clapping two skull tops together to make horse-galloping noises.

"Doctor Burkley," the younger doctor called. Burkley squeezed past Dawson and moved around the table to stand next to Vanderberg. "Do you notice anything strange?"

Burkley looked at the gray twisted tissue inside O'Brien's head that was his brain. At first he noticed nothing out of the ordinary, until he switched from animal doctor to human practitioner. Suddenly it all became clear.

"You say this man attacked like an animal?" Burkley asked Dawson.

"That's what the good doctor told us," the sheriff replied.

"I was there," Vanderberg reported. "There's no other justification. This explains it all."

Burkley adjusted the glasses on his nose and leaned in for a closer observation.

"What?" Vaughn burst out. "What explains it all?"

"The brain," Vanderberg replied. "The frontal lobe has decreased significantly. The cerebral cortex is practically gone. There are other sections that have increased in size while sections that control language and rational thinking have decreased."

"In other words, Deputy," Burkley interjected. "This man became an animal acting upon instinct. It's clear that the changes took their toll on the body. Dark patches around the eyes and vascular scarring through the skin. I dare say that this man wouldn't have lived for too long, regardless."

"I agree," said Vanderberg. "I would estimate a few days at most. But if this metamorphosis occurred from the simple bite from a..."

"Rat," Burkley responded. "A mutated rat."

"From a rat," the young doctor continued. "And within minutes of that bite. The consequences of what could have followed if Mister

O'Brien wasn't killed may be immensely damaging in proportion. We could have been talking total infection of the valley within days."

Dawson rubbed his forehead, "I have got a real bad feeling about this."

Vaughn nodded his agreement.

"We got one rat, one human and who the fuck knows what running around out there mutilating cattle," the deputy informed. "Not to mention a big fucking wolf."

"That's what I'm afraid of," Dawson explained. "There may be other people and animals infected already. We've only scratched the surface here."

"But maybe we stopped it cold here as far as human contamination is concerned," Burkley reckoned.

"I don't think so," Dawson replied. "Phones are down and other communications have been cut. What does that tell you?"

"The army knows," Vaughn answered matter-of-factly.

"We need to take a drive," Dawson said to his deputy. "We need to get to the State Police ourselves. I'll take you back to your surgery on the way, Wally."

"Yeah." Burkley nodded. "I think I'll send Shirley home and incinerate that rat."

"Thanks for your time, Doctor Vanderberg." Dawson shook the young doctor's hand. The other men followed suit and filed out of the room. Vanderberg followed them out into the corridor.

"Uh, Sheriff," he called. "What should I do with Mister O'Brien?"

"Burn him, son," Burkley replied.

IX

Dawson pulled the SUV to a halt outside the Sheriff's Office. He had dropped the veterinarian Doctor Walter Burkley off at the animal surgery on his way back to home base.

Vaughn jumped out of the passenger seat and onto the icy road making a loud crunch as his boots made contact. He briskly walked to the office door and waited for his boss to catch up.

The deputy opened the door for the sheriff and followed him inside. The warmth hit them like a sledgehammer. Both men hastily unzipped their coats and ripped off their gloves.

"What's going on out there?" Agnes asked as she tapped away on the keys of her computer.

"Don't ask," Vaughn managed as he passed by her on his way to the kitchen.

"A major cover-up," Dawson answered. "That's what. How did you do with the State Police?"

"No response," she replied. Her tapping stopped, and she picked up a steaming mug of coffee that had been resting beside her computer.

"Anyone out there talking?"

"If they are, I can't hear them," she took a sip and put her mug down. "No truck chatter. No warbled static. Nothing. Just dead air." She pointed over her shoulder with her thumb at a gray box with an orange light emanating from a small panel on it.

The panel displayed the radio's current channel, volume level and signal strength. Dawson saw the volume sitting on 8. It maxed out at 10.

"I ran through all the channels twice trying to get someone," explained Agnes. "I couldn't even get white noise. Smells fishy to me if you're asking."

Dawson grunted his agreement and followed Vaughn into the kitchen. "We're gonna top up our coffee and take a run to the pike."

"Why do you want to go out there?" Agnes swivelled in her chair to face the kitchen door.

"We can't get hold of anyone from inside the valley," Dawson replied. "So we thought we might try from out there. Should only be gone an hour or so."

"It's going to get dark soon," Agnes interjected. "You better not be too long out there."

"Meet you in the truck, boss." Vaughn zipped his coat up as he crossed the room. He carried a flask of fresh coffee in one hand and his gloves in the other.

"Get Redhawke back in," Dawson instructed. "I got a feeling we might need him tonight."

"Right away," she answered as he passed by and headed out the door.

Dawson pulled his hat down hard as the bitter cold smacked him in his exposed face.

"Listen," he heard someone say from beside the SUV. It wasn't Vaughn. The deputy was standing beside the sheriff facing the newcomer. "Can you hear it?"

Carl Mason, the diner owner, was standing in front of both men pointing with his gloved hand toward the northern end of the valley. Dawson saw Vaughn craning his neck, trying to listen. The sheriff attempted to do the same but could hear only the wind whistling through the buildings up and down the street.

"I don't hear a damn thi..."

"Shhh!" Vaughn hissed at his boss. A small amount of silence followed before he spoke again. "I hear it."

"It's a siren, right?" Mason asked.

"Yeah," Vaughn replied. "Like an air raid alarm. Like in the old movies."

Dawson cocked his good ear in the army base's direction. He still couldn't hear anything except the wind.

"I heard it earlier today too," stated Mason. "Around midday."

"There's something else," Vaughn put in.

Both older men looked to the younger for answers.

"Like a thumping," he muttered.

Mason and Dawson watched the deputy carefully.

"It's getting louder."

Dawson could hear it. Faintly in the distance, carried on the wind, a rhythmic thumping carried down the valley and along Main Street.

"Fucking chopper. I don't like this at all," Dawson said as he headed for the SUV.

"Where are you going?" Mason yelled.

"I'm going to the pike before it gets dark," Dawson replied.

"You should go home, Mister Mason," Vaughn suggested as he climbed into the vehicle. "Get inside where it's warm."

The tires spun on the icy road as the SUV launched away and headed south on Main Street at top speed.

Dawson planted his foot on the gas once they were on the open road. The vehicle lurched forward as he knocked it up a gear.

"I can see it," Vaughn announced. His head lowered to look past the sheriff and out of the side window. "Moving along the eastern ridge."

"Where?" Dawson turned his head to glance quickly to his left. He saw darkening clouds sweeping the tips of the mountains that enclosed the valley on his side of the vehicle.

"Almost level with us." Vaughn pointed. He twisted his body so he could view the chopper more comfortably. "They're moving fast. Just below the peaks."

Dawson had returned his gaze to the road ahead. They were passing the entry road to Gibb's farm when he risked another look to the east.

He barely noticed a dark object moving quickly in front of snow-capped mountains. It was barely a blurry dot to his eyes, but there was no mistaking the fact that it was heading the same way as they were.

"What are they doing?" he asked.

The road started to incline. It wouldn't be long before they began the winding journey to the pass in the ridge that would allow them to access the outside world.

"I lost them," Vaughn said. Trees had built up around them as they continued to rise out of the valley.

The road started to turn to the right. Whitened trees and a snow-kissed road filled the view. Dawson placed all of his attention on the twisting path before them. Vaughn continued to turn his head, looking through each of the windows for any sign of the chopper.

"What do you think they're up to?" queried Dawson. "You're an ex-navy man. What would they be doing?"

"You're an ex-army man," Vaughn replied.

"I'm not in the same league as these assholes," the sheriff snorted. "I fought in 'Nam. These guys send robots in to do their shit."

"Could just be a supply run," Vaughn suggested. "They might be transporting someone. Who knows?"

"Purely innocent." Dawson nodded.

"Innocent," Vaughn agreed. "Totally coincidental."

"Maybe you're right." Dawson swung the SUV to the right. The road was steep and his speed was slow. The thought of the chopper flying out of the valley on a very ordinary, mundane job eased his train of thought for the time being.

Vaughn looked to his right and could see over the valley. Lights were coming on in houses as the sky grew darker. The thick, black clouds to the north had crept over the range and were sealing the valley in like a blanket being pulled over a sunken bed.

Flashes emitted from inside the swirling dark clouds. Vaughn believed they would be in for one hell of a night. The sound of thunder caused his nerves to set on edge.

"What the fuck was that?" Dawson breathed.

"Thunder?" Vaughn half suggested before realizing how stupid that was. The clouds were too far away for the sound of thunder to reach them so quickly.

Suddenly there was another flash from above them with an immediate explosive sound. Dawson pulled the vehicle to a complete stop and glanced through the windshield.

A large object burst from above the tree line before them and flew directly over their heads. Both men turned in their seats to look out the rear window to see the tail of an Apache helicopter laden with guns and rocket launchers flying off toward the valley.

"Shit!" Dawson edged the SUV forward. The road bent to the left then back to the right before straightening out to pass through the small gap in the mountain range.

The sheriff hit the brakes hard and slid to a stop. The headlights of the SUV illuminated a tall dust cloud and a wall of rocks. Both the sheriff and deputy suddenly understood what the chopper was doing. It had blown holes in the sidewalls of the pass to block any access with fallen debris.

"Fucking assholes," Vaughn hollered.

"Too steep to climb," Dawson stated, maintaining his cool. "Looks like we're trapped in here."

"Why?" Vaughn shouted. "Why the fuck would they want to do that?"

"I don't know." Dawson performed a careful three-point turn and started back down the winding road toward the valley.

"If there is any danger, isn't it their job to get civilians out?" Vaughn asked. "Fucking bastards."

Dawson remained silent and kept his composure on the outside. Inside, he was *fucking* furious.

SUNDAY EVENING

I

Dawson screeched to a halt outside the Town Hall. Vaughn was already bolting for the door with a shotgun in his hand. The Sheriff stood beside the SUV. He held the door open in his hand as he gazed along the empty street toward Maverick's Peak.

Dark storm clouds had veiled the snow-covered caps of the mountain range to the north. Violent flashes of light emitted from deep inside occasionally revealing the ebbing turmoil that carried through the air toward the township.

Dawson turned his head to see Jacob's snowplough approaching from Old Ridge Road. A bright red pickup truck followed him. It was easily recognizable as one of the Firehouse vehicles. Both pulled up nearby.

"What's happening?" Jacob called as he jumped out of the plow.

"Just about to see the Mayor," Dawson replied.

"Mind if I join you?"

"Not at all."

Soon after, eight men had crowded into the small office upstairs from the Post Office. Waring leaned with his elbows on his desk and his face in his hands. Dawson had just informed him of what had happened at the pass.

"That's bad," Jacob stated.

"Bad?" Waring looked at him in disbelief. "That's all you got to say about it? Those fuckers just blew up our only way in and out of the valley."

113

"Now hold on," Vaughn said, trying to calm the situation. He turned his attention to the fire crew. "You boys just spent a few hours clearing the Old Ridge Road up near the reservoir. Right? Surely there's a track or something that can get us over the ridge somewhere."

"We cleared it to the reservoir," Shane replied. "There was too much damage beyond for us to get to today. Just not enough manpower."

"As melodramatic as Harold can be," Jacob started.

"Hey!" Waring retorted as he made his way to the window.

"He's right," Jacob continued. "We're trapped. There are a few goat tracks around the valley. But in this weather? One slip and you're gone."

Dawson shook his head. The pieces of the puzzle just didn't fit together.

"I don't understand why," the sheriff confessed. They all turned their attention to him. "Why would they want to close us in?"

"It's simple, boss," Vaughn replied. To him it always was simple. "They want to cover up a mess they made and the easiest way is to bury it."

"For a fucking accident on the road?"

"No," Vaughn replied. "For the shit that was being carried by the convoy that had the accident on the road."

"It got away from them," Shane commented.

"Exactly." Vaughn nodded.

"What the fuck?" Waring exhaled.

All men crowded around the window that overlooked Main Street. Their heads turned in every direction to spot whatever grabbed the Mayor's attention.

"What are you looking at, Harold?" asked Jacob.

"That." Waring pointed to the north.

A large vehicle with its lights blaring was speeding toward them. As it drew closer, the distinct color of a bland khaki chassis became clear. It was an army troop carrier.

"They coming to finish the job?" asked one of the firehouse boys.

"I don't think so," Shane answered.

Dawson and Vaughn were already out the door and bolting down the stairs to intercept the vehicle.

Vaughn was the first to reach the lobby. To his right was a door that led to the Library. Directly opposite was another door leading to the Post Office. An elderly woman was slowly shuffling her way from there toward the lobby's large entry.

"Stay there, ma'am." Vaughn waved to her. She suddenly looked alarmed.

"I didn't do anything, officer," she whimpered as she clutched her bag to her chest.

"For your safety," he replied. "Could you please go back into the Post Office?"

She didn't hesitate. In the time it took Vaughn to direct the elderly woman, Dawson had overtaken him and exited through the large oak doors of the Town Hall lobby and pulled his handgun from its holster.

"Stop right there," he barked as he levelled his firearm at the driver's side of the vehicle.

It screeched and slid to a standstill a few inches from the sheriff's SUV. A jumble of hands poked out from the side windows of the vehicle's cab.

"Don't shoot, Sheriff," a familiar voice shouted from inside.

"Who's that?" Dawson asked as Vaughn pulled up alongside him with weapon drawn.

"Dwight," came the response. "Dwight Krane."

"Who's in there with you?" Dawson eased a little.

"Dennis Edry, two other privates and some lab guy," Krane replied. "I don't know his name."

"Any of you armed?"

"No," Krane stated. "But we got a shitload of weapons and ammo in the back."

"All right," Dawson said. "Step out of the vehicle. All of you." He holstered his gun and stepped toward the truck. Vaughn kept his gun aimed at Krane as he opened the door and slid out of the driver's seat.

Krane held his hands above his head and moved toward the sheriff as the others exited the vehicle from the passenger side. Deputy Vaughn swung his aim to his left and levelled his weapon on a young woman in khaki. She in turn raised her hands and stepped to the side to allow the others out of the truck.

"I don't understand," Krane said as he shifted his gaze from Dawson to Vaughn's gun.

"We haven't been having a great day concerning the army," Dawson replied.

"Fuckers used missiles to blow the Eye shut," Vaughn sneered, referring to the nickname that locals had given to the passageway in and out of the valley. "What did they send you to do?"

"They left us," the young woman announced.

"What do you mean - they left you - and who are you?" Vaughn asked.

"My names Sandra Upton," she replied. "This is Dwight Krane, and that's Frank Sharpe."

Dawson and Vaughn watched as Sharpe stepped forward.

"We know Dwight and Frank," Vaughn said. "You, I don't know, sweetheart. And I definitely don't know him." The deputy nodded to a scrawny man in civilian clothing and thick, black-rimmed glasses who stepped out of the vehicle and moved toward the others.

"My name's Neville Edry," he said as he held out his hand and took a step toward Dawson. The sheriff quickly drew his gun and aimed it at Edry's chest.

"Step the fuck back," Vaughn called out as he swung his gun around on the newcomer. Edry jumped back and quickly lowered his hand to his side. Upton's eyes went wide with fear. "You too," Vaughn returned his aim upon her when he realized his boss had Edry covered. "You go stand next to him."

She complied and choked back tears as she moved alongside the other. The deputy pointed to the side of the truck where they both repositioned themselves.

"Hands-on the vehicle, legs spread," Vaughn instructed.

"You got them?" Dawson asked his deputy.

"Yep," replied Vaughn as he started patting down Edry with his left hand, keeping his gun on Upton with his right.

"Now boys," Dawson said calmly to Krane and Sharpe as he holstered his weapon again. "Show me what you've got."

The three men circled to the back of the truck. Krane lowered the tailgate and climbed onto the deck, lifting a flap of the dull green canvas that covered the rear of the vehicle, so Dawson could see inside.

There were boxes and crates of various sizes stacked and packed from end to end, bottom to top. Dawson took a quick mental note of the numbers and letters stamped on the sides of the containers as his eyes scanned the contents of the truck.

"We grabbed what we could," Sharpe said. "We just got a bad vibe when they started fueling up all the choppers. Something didn't seem right."

"It was before that," Krane corrected. "It was when the first alarm went off."

"Alarm?" Dawson suddenly remembered his conversation with Carl Mason. Mason heard an alarm earlier in the day, then again just before the Apache helicopter blew the entrance to the valley shut.

"Yeah," Sharpe affirmed. "Something happened before they started fueling the choppers. We started grabbing this shit just after that. Then another alarm went off, and the choppers bugged out. All of them. Took off straight over Maverick's Peak."

"Who went in the choppers?" asked Dawson.

"Most of the brass from what I could see," Krane answered.

"They loaded the regular army personnel into three Chinooks," added Sharpe. "All the reserves and I think all the civilian staff are still there."

"Well, what the heck made you load all of this up if there are still people there?"

"There's something up there, Sheriff," Sharpe replied. "I don't know what exactly. But you don't have so many lab coats and brass in one area for no reason. They have these big buildings up there. Kind-a like airport hangers with giant doors. They're always under lock and key and guarded only by the 'regs'. I mean, regular army personnel."

"I used to be military, son," informed Dawson. "You can use the terminology."

"Sure." Sharpe nodded. "Anyhow. They have a few guards facing out toward the main yard. But they got the big guns pointed toward the building. That's always had me wondering what the fuck they have got in there."

Dawson peered back into the truck and looked to both men before him. "All right," he said as he lifted his hat a little to scratch his head. "Do you trust these people you brought with you?"

"I'm not sure about the civvy," Krane shook his head. "He's a lab rat."

"Get yourselves inside the bar and have some coffee," ordered Dawson. "Tell Max to charge it to me."

The men didn't hesitate. It was freezing. They closed the back of the truck and walked inside the bar as briskly as they could.

Dawson rounded the vehicle again to meet up with Vaughn who was shaking from the cold. He still stood with his weapon pointed at the two newcomers. They still stood with their hands pressed against the side of the truck and teeth chattering.

"Let's get them inside," Dawson instructed. "This one's fine." He pointed to Upton. He then aimed his finger at Edry. "This one we're not sure about."

Vaughn nodded and kept his gun pointed at Edry as they headed for the bar.

"Everything all right?" Waring was standing at the main entrance to the Town Hall.

"We're heading inside." Dawson waved toward the bar. "I think we need everyone."

"I'll get on the phone and see you in a few," the Mayor replied before returning inside.

II

Charlene slid to the right as Andy pushed her hard around the bend. Her wheels spun on the ice as she fought hard to find traction. Suddenly, the Sonic lurched forward and headed in the direction her driver intended to go.

"Just a fucking taxi service," Andy yelled as he planted the gas pedal to the floor and flicked the headlights on.

He had just dropped both the well-built, muscular jock friends of his at Tiffany's house. Both Tiffany and Julia were there waiting. They invited all three boys in, but once the making out began, Andy felt out of place and quietly made his way outside and back to Charlene.

Wheels slid sideways again as Andy pulled to the right into a side street. He was winding his way through the back streets of Long Valley, making his way toward Main Street.

His intention was to head home and sulk. A pillow to scream into and some heavy metal music to increase the feeling of depression was what he wanted originally. But now, with Charlene, he just wanted to drive as fast as he could.

Andy hit the gas as she found the road again and sped to the next intersection. He pulled the wheel to the left. Charlene spun out of control momentarily making his heart leap to his throat.

"FUCK!" he shouted out of anger more than fear.

She straightened out, and he hit the gas again.

The next intersection was Main Street. In what little time he had before reaching it, he had to decide whether he would turn left toward town or right toward the army base.

It wasn't a hard decision to make.

In his current condition, he wanted to be alone. He knew turning left would take him toward people, and he just didn't want to talk to anyone right now.

He yanked the steering wheel to the right.

Charlene swung her ass across Main Street so far that she was almost facing the way she came from before Andy could correct the turn.

He slammed his foot onto the gas.

The car's wheels whirred loudly as they spun on the icy surface.

Andy steered to the left and Charlene lunged in the direction of Maverick's Peak.

Andy noticed thick dark clouds covering the tips of the mountains ahead of him as he sped toward them. The occasional flash of lightning inside the blanket of darkness made the vision appear deadly.

It looked the way he felt.

Why do they always get the girls?

The surrounding scenery seemed to blur as he focused on the yellow line in the middle of the road.

Why can't I ever meet someone that wants me the way Tiffany and Julia want Brad and Stan?

Wisps of snow-streaked across the windshield at the intervals of each stroke that the wipers made.

What's wrong with me?

Tears in his eyes made his focus fuzzy.

I hate them all!

He slammed his foot on the brake and seemed to slide forever before coming to a complete stop.

He dropped his head onto the steering wheel and sobbed.

"I hate them all!"

After spending some time feeling sorry for himself, he lifted his gaze to the road ahead of him. Everything was blurry from the tears in his eyes. A bright light was just in front of him but he couldn't make out what it was.

He wiped his face on his coat sleeves and looked through the windshield to get his bearings.

The beam from his headlights bounced off a sign that was only a few yards from where he sat.

It was large and attached to a small brick building that was roughly the size of a cargo container.

LONG VALLEY ARMY BASE
CHECKPOINT
PLEASE PRESENT IDENTIFICATION

Andy breathed deeply.

If he had hit the brakes a second later, he would be part of the building right now.

He shook his head as he took another deep breath and gently put Charlene in reverse.

Slowly, and carefully, he manipulated the car back into the middle of the road so she was facing toward town. He shifted the stick to first and checked his mirrors to see if the guards at the checkpoint would approach him.

It was then that he noticed the boom gate was up.

The door to the checkpoint building was wide open, and no one was sitting inside.

He then noticed in the distance, far beyond the checkpoint, some figures moving around.

They sauntered back and forth aimlessly, seemingly unorganized and confused. Nothing like what Andy would expect from army personnel.

A few were looking in his direction.

Their appearance frightened Andy to the core.

Their skin was sickly white and there was no hair on their heads.

Some were wearing army fatigues. Others were in civilian clothing. There was also a number wearing barely anything at all. Male and female. They were standing in the freezing cold and appeared unaffected by the low temperature.

Andy could see dark lines on their limbs and piercing white eyes. A knot formed in his stomach.

One of the few that were looking in his direction opened his mouth and bellowed.

A guttural sound loudly reverberated toward him. The pitch changed from a deep roar into a high scream, which made Andy want to cover his ears.

Suddenly, the sound stopped.

The other figures that were moving about paused. They all looked at the creature that had been screaming. One by one, they shifted their gazes toward Charlene.

Now all eyes were on Andy.

The knot in his stomach tightened. His heart leapt to his throat. "Shit!"

They ran toward him, faster than Andy thought was humanly possible.

He planted his foot down and Charlene spun her wheels.

"Come on," Andy screamed.

They gathered ground quickly and would be upon him in a few seconds if Charlene didn't move soon.

Suddenly, she lunged and took off like a rocket toward town. Andy laughed and shot a glance at the rear vision mirror.

His pursuers were still running for him. Slowly, ever so slowly they seemed to get smaller in his mirror.

He shot a glance to the road, then to his speedometer.

It said 65 MPH.

Andy looked to the mirror again and could still see some figures running for him in the distance.

"Shit!"

Before, he drove because he was angry, depressed and lonely. Now he drove for his life.

He didn't want to die.

"Come on, baby," he shouted to Charlene who was now hitting a steady 70 MHP.

Andy looked to the mirror again.

They were still there.

Small and blurry, but still distinguishable against the white back-drop

Running.

Running.

Running.

III

"I got a real bad feeling," Burkley announced from the bar.

"You're not the only one, Walter," replied Max Dooley as he poured whiskey into the veterinarian's glass. The doctor swallowed the contents in one gulp and placed the glass on the table before lifting himself from the barstool and returning to the table with the rest of the men.

Frank Sharpe and Dwight Krane had both finished retelling their story to the men surrounding them. Mayor Waring shook his head in disgust more than disbelief. Carl Mason nursed a coffee as he listened to the conversation and was now eyeballing Private Upton and Neville Edry who had been sitting in a booth at the far corner of the bar, as far away from the conversation as Vaughn could take them.

Redhawke sat at the bar as he had been for some time. His fingers were gently touching a tall glass of beer, which had almost gone flat. He fixed his eyes, staring at the top of the bar. His mind was in the Long Valley Memorial Hospital ward where Quentin O'Brien had been eating Kyle Yancy.

Dawson thought it best to leave his deputy alone to his thoughts and his untouched beer.

"We need to find a place to hide," Jeff Burrows, one firefighter, put in.

"The question is, where?" Sorenson questioned.

"No." Dawson shook his head. "The question is, what the fuck do they have up there?" The sheriff pointed to Edry. "And that asshole knows the answer."

Vaughn took the cue. He grabbed Edry by the collar and lifted him to his feet.

"Come on," the deputy ordered. "You get to talk now."

He pushed Edry toward the other men. Edry complied and crossed the floor as quickly as he could.

Dawson grabbed an empty chair and placed it at the end of the table. Vaughn forced the small man onto the chair and held him there with a heavy hand.

"Now Mister Edry," Dawson said as he sat next to the man.

"Doctor," Edry corrected as he pushed his thick glasses back upon his nose.

"What?" Dawson quizzed.

"My name is Doctor Neville Edry," he said as he peered around the table to each of the men surrounding him.

"I don't give a shit if you're the Ayatollah Imrani, motherfucker," Vaughn stated as he pressed down hard on Edry's neck with his hand. "You will speak when this man allows you to speak. Until then, shut the fuck up."

Dawson leaned in closer to Edry, "Now, Doctor Neville Edry. What have you got hidden behind those big doors up there at the army base?"

"I'm only a lab assistant," Edry began. "So I didn't see too much."

"Tell us what you know," Dawson insisted.

"Okay," said Edry. "We mainly looked at blood work from specimen samples. They took the samples before exposure and then after exposure."

"Exposure to what?" Burkley asked.

"I don't know exactly," Edry answered. "The paperwork just stated 'pre-exposure and 'post-exposure. I have no idea what we exposed them to."

"What were they using for their samples?" Sorenson asked. "I mean, what kind of animals or plants were the specimens?"

"Soldiers."

The men stared blankly at Doctor Neville Edry. They weren't sure they heard the answer correctly.

"Sorry." Waring blinked. "Can you repeat that?"

"They were using soldiers as test subjects," Edry informed them. "All were single males with no family. The blood samples at pre-exposure indicated that all were in good health with no infirmities. The samples at post-exposure showed cellular reconstruction had occurred. They were no longer the same men they once were, if we could call them men at all."

"Super soldiers," Redhawke slurred.

"Welcome back to planet Earth, buddy." Max smiled.

Redhawke let go of his beer and turned to face the gathering of people. "They were creating super soldiers."

"Now hang on a minute." Edry lifted both hands up in surrender. "I just looked into a microscope at samples. Your army guys who took off in the choppers were the brains behind whatever was happening out there. And from what I could guess, they weren't creating super soldiers.

"The idea of super-soldiers gives the impression of someone who follows orders. If these things followed orders, why did they have the big guns facing toward the lab buildings?"

"My guess," Vaughn began, "is that one of the fuckers got out and started making trouble."

Dawson scratched his chin.

"How many?" he asked.

"Excuse me?" Edry looked perplexed.

"How many of these soldiers were tested?"

"I've got no idea."

"Sure, you do," Burkley stated. "You saw all the blood work results."

"How many, Doctor?" Dawson asked again.

"Forty," Edry said. "I saw results from forty specimens."

Dawson stood up from the table and looked at the surrounding men. The thought crossing his mind wasn't the best he had, but he felt it was the only one that made sense.

"We have a truckload of weapons," he began. "We could load up and try to take these 'specimens' out."

"I'm with you, Tom," said Mayor Waring. "But you forget that we also have an outbreak occurring in the valley. My guess is that it's all connected. You could stop what's happening at the base. But how are you going to stop rats that bite people that turns people into ravenous freaks?"

"And big fucking wolves," Vaughn added.

"And big fucking wolves," the Mayor repeated.

Dawson sat back down to think this through again.

As he did so, he heard the screeching of tires coming from outside the bar on Main Street. A loud slamming of a car door followed.

Redhawke was the first to his feet and out the door. Through the haze of falling snow, he saw a Chevrolet Sonic sitting in the middle of Main Street facing south and a hooded figure running toward the Sheriff's Office across the road.

"Hey," Redhawke called. The figure stopped and turned his head toward the north. "Over here."

The figure turned to face Redhawke.

"Are you looking for the Sheriff?"

"Yeah," came a reply.

"He's in here." Redhawke opened the door. The figure ran quickly past the Sonic and straight into the warmth of the bar.

Redhawke closed the door behind him as he entered the bar behind the hooded figure.

"Who's this?" asked Mayor Waring.

"Andy Parson, sir," replied Andy as he lowered his hood. "Look, we need to get everyone out of the valley, now."

"Sit down, son." Dawson gestured to an empty chair. "We'll get something hot into you and you can tell us what's going on."

"There's no time," Andy replied nervously. "They're coming."

"Who's coming?" Redhawke asked.

"The zombies."

"What the fuck are you talking about?" Max queried.

"At the base." Andy looked to each man in desperation. "You gotta believe me. They started to chase me. I was going to head straight for the pass and get out of here. But then I saw the Sheriff sign and thought I had better tell you."

"It's okay, Andy." Dawson put a hand on the boy's shoulder. "We know about them."

"Then why are you still here?" Andy yelled. "They're coming!"

"We got weapons," Krane informed the newcomer. "We can take on forty, no problems."

"Forty?"

"That's right," Sharpe smiled.

"I saw hundreds," Andy objected. "And they are all heading this way. We need to leave the valley."

"Shit," Dawson muttered. "Valley's blocked in. Nobody can leave."

"What?"

"Army blew it shut," Vaughn replied.

"We need to find somewhere fast, Harold," Dawson said to the Mayor.

"I don't know of anywhere fortified enough in the valley to protect us except the army base," the Mayor responded.

"The high school," Andy suggested.

"What's that?" Sorenson asked.

"The high school would be perfect. We can lock the upper level off by big metal gates at the bottom and top of the stairs. There are bathrooms with showers and classrooms. Bars on all the windows. We could get people in there and hold out until help comes."

"Help ain't coming, boy," Krane stated. "Army shut us in. Who do you think's coming to help us?"

"Still," Sorenson put in. "Andy has a point. The school would be a good place to defend from. They built the whole thing out of steel and cinder blocks. There are bars on the windows. Electric heaters in each room will keep us warm. It's perfect."

"I got no other ideas," said Dawson. "We should get the weapons up there and get as many people as we can in there with us."

"Okay," Mayor Waring agreed. "Go home, back to work or wherever. Grab what you can and who you can and meet at the school in ten minutes. Got it?"

All men headed for the door. Vaughn gestured for Upton to join him. She had been sitting in the corner the entire time, listening to their conversation.

"What about him?" she asked as she tilted her head toward Max who was wiping down the bar with a towel.

"Max," Vaughn called. The bartender lifted his gaze to the deputy. "Weren't you listening? That means you too. We gotta get out of here."

"I can't leave the bar," he replied.

"If the kid is right," Vaughn strolled over to the bar with Upton in tow, "your bar is in the path of a large mob of flesh-eating fuckers. Now, get moving."

Max nodded.

He put the glass down and grabbed a full bottle of whiskey from the bench behind the bar.

"I'm taking this with me," he said as he headed for the door.

IV

George stared silently at the kettle as he waited for it to boil. It was sitting on the stovetop and just starting to make a strange whirring noise as the water heated inside.

His hand gripped at the mug that rested on the kitchen bench beside the stove. Inside was one teaspoon scoop of instant coffee and two scoops of sugar.

The wind howled outside his little cottage and rattled the tiny kitchen window loudly. His senses, however, focused internally as his memory kept returning to the carnage that was once his pet goat, Nanny.

Slowly, his eyes welled again as the kettle continued to whir.

His tattered blue dressing gown covered a dirty gray tracksuit that he had been wearing on and off for a week. His feet bore bright red socks inside his scuffed brown snow boots. They were the warmest things he had besides his old parka.

The window and the door rattled loudly as the wind shook the side of the house, almost bringing him out of his trance.

The kettle's whirring turned into a rumble as the water inside began to bubble. Steam rose from the water's surface and collected inside the kettle's cap. Pressure built inside and streamed through a little hole in the cap's side emitting a high-pitched whistle as a jet of steam escaped.

George turned the stovetop off and the kettle's whistling died.

But he could still hear it.

A high-pitched whistle.

No.

Not a whistle.

A scream.

Coming from outside.

The door rattled again. It wasn't the wind this time. Perhaps it wasn't before either.

It was someone trying to come in.

Or something.

George looked around for a weapon to defend himself with.

In his hand was a mug. All but useless.

He let it go and looked around. Next to the stove was a wooden block with knives slotted into it. He lifted the biggest one out and held it at the ready as the intruder outside violently thudded at the door.

The door cracked and splintered with each blow. The old man's heart nearly leapt from his chest as he tried to maintain steady breaths. Eventually, the top hinge snapped, and the door fell inwards and onto the kitchen floor.

A naked, white figure stood motionless in the doorframe. It stared blankly at George with piercing white eyes as it breathed rapidly. The old man's eyes went directly to the creature's breasts, and he felt repulsed. Not by his own actions, but by its appearance.

Dark veins twisted up the intruder's legs and across its abdomen. They eventually crossed the chest and blackened nipples and regrouped at the neck.

George felt pity for the young woman that once was. He knew, somehow, that she no longer existed, and this thing had replaced her.

Her head was bald and her skin appeared almost transparent. She spread her dark lips and bore her yellowish teeth in a grimace that revealed her blackened gums.

The old man waved the knife nervously in the air toward the intruder.

"G, go on," he stammered. "Get."

She opened her mouth and hissed as she lunged toward the old man.

She was quick.

George felt her teeth break the skin on his arm causing him to wince in pain. He dropped the knife and fell to the floor.

The intruder lurched above him momentarily.

The old man grabbed the knife from the ground and stabbed upwards just as the creature bent down to attack again.

The knife slid into her cheek. She recoiled instantly and lifted her pasty white hand to the wound under her eye. Dark blood oozed between her fingers like black syrup.

Before George could understand what had happened, the creature retreated through the back door and out of the house.

He lay there for what seemed an eternity, staring at the broken doorway. Waiting for that thing to come back and finish him.

His arm was throbbing, and he dropped the knife to the floor again. It landed with a clang as the thought of dying crossed his mind. He had just survived an attack just to crap out from a heart attack.

But the pain didn't feel like a heart attack. He'd had one of those before.

This was different.

Sweat built upon his brow as his limbs started to spasm. He felt bile rise in his throat with a taste of blood among it. He let it escape, throwing up a mess of white and red across the floor.

It was then that he understood.

The bite from that thing had done this to him.

He lifted himself to a seated position and placed his back against the fridge. His fingernails had turned black as blood vessels under his skin darkened, expanding like spider webs across his paling flesh.

The room started to spin.

He fought with every ounce of strength that he had, but he knew he would pass out.

He closed his eyes and slipped into darkness.

His body continued to spasm and transform as he rested against the fridge on the kitchen floor.

After a few seconds, he was still. He was silent.

His eyes opened.

His memories and sense of logic were now replaced with instinct.

He needed to move.

There was nothing here that served his desire.

Hunger took control.

V

Redhawke crossed the road and entered the Sheriff's Office.

"Close the damn door," Agnes called from behind the reception desk.

"Grab what you need, Agnes. We're leaving," Redhawke announced as he unlocked the gun rack.

"Shit." She immediately rose from her chair and disappeared into the kitchen.

"What are you getting from in there?" Redhawke asked as he retrieved a large tote bag from a drawer at the base of the rack.

"Bathroom supplies," she answered matter-of-factly.

"What?" he murmured. "Like toilet paper?"

"No. Not like toilet paper. We keep spare toothbrushes, toothpaste and shit like that. Not to mention the urn and coffee. That kind of stuff always comes in handy for situations like this."

Redhawke placed four shotguns into the tote bag. Suddenly, he paused.

"What do you mean, 'situations like this?'" he queried. "How do you know what's going on?"

"Come on, Deputy," she said as she reappeared at the door. "We lost communication. Army blew the only way in and out of the valley shut. The big accident and the coverup. The man at the hospital that you encountered. It doesn't take a genius to work out that some big heavy shit is hitting a fan somewhere."

Redhawke reached into the drawer at the base of the gun rack and pulled out boxes of shotgun shells and placed them into the tote bags with the guns. He admired Agnes for her bluntness.

"It's good to see you back and focused again," she said as she patted him on the head. "Now, where are we going?"

VI

Sorenson pulled the snowplow to a stop next to the gas pump. He jumped out of the cab and jogged around the front of the vehicle, making a beeline for the front door of the gas station store. The automatic doors slid open with a chime as he entered the small shop.

Three tiny aisles had been set up with shelves of snack food, leading to the rear of the store where glass-fronted wall fridges housed soda of various kinds and some milk; everything for the passing traveller or midnight stoner.

Behind the small counter at the front of the store sat an incredibly overweight woman with long, dark hair. Sorenson had never seen her in any other position in his whole time in Long Valley, except for behind that counter.

He imagined that they had wheeled her in as a kid and allowed her to grow in that spot, feeding upon the contents of the shelves in the store. Another train of thought took him to a dark place where they had built the store around her and that she slept, ate, drank, pissed and shit right there because she sat on a pipe that opened directly to the sewers below.

The flaw in his theories was that she was always wearing something different each day and he couldn't come up with anything plausible to explain that except that she had to get up to change.

On the left breast of her circus tent sized shirt hung a name badge with "MAUDE" stencilled onto it. She had her face buried in a magazine as Sorenson entered. She lifted her head to smile and squeak, "Good afternoon, Jacob." Her face then changed to a quizzical expression. "Didn't you just fuel up this morning?"

"Yeah," Sorenson answered. "Afternoon to you, Maude. I need to top up again. Everyone's making their way to the high school. Town emergency. You should get everyone and follow me over there."

"What are you talking about?" she asked with a cheesy grin.

"Uh..." Sorenson suddenly felt as if he was talking to the wrong person about impending doom. Maude was the type of person who read and believed in such literature that professed the existence of extra-terrestrial beings who conducted anal probe experiments on innocent inbred hicks in unheard-of backwater counties. He peered around. "Where's Dewey and the boys?"

"They're all in the garage working on that fire truck."

"You mind if I go in there?"

"Help yerself." She smiled as she went back to the magazine in her hands.

Sorenson made his way through an open door between the counter and a glass-fronted refrigerator filled with a variety of soft drinks in cans and plastic bottles. Cinder blocks hemmed the short passage between the store and the garage. A door halfway along the hallway opened into a small lunchroom with a kitchenette.

An old, small, metal frame dining table with a red laminated top sat in the center of the room. Its edges were lifting from age, exposing the fraying particleboard underneath the coated surface. A bench with a sink and faucet in the middle ran the length of the back wall, allowing just enough space for an old Kelvinator fridge from the fifties to stand to the far left.

Four matching chairs sat around the table. They were all part of a set that probably looked good once. Now they appeared cheap, tattered, tacky and trashy. A thin young man with a scruffy beard dangling over his gut sat on the left-most chair forcing an oversized BLT into his fur-covered mouth with little success. He needed to use both hands to hold the thing together as he angled it against his lips, tongue and chin to get the best leverage for his teeth to bite through the monstrosity.

He glanced sideways to the door and mumbled something through the hair, lettuce, tomato, bread and who knew what else. A quick wave with his hand told Sorenson that the man probably said, "Hey, Jacob."

"Hey, Farris," Sorenson responded. "Dewey around?"

Farris let go of his sandwich with his right hand to throw a thumb in the garage's direction. "Ihm..airh." *In there.* He returned his hand quickly to his sandwich, but it was too late.

The lower half of the edible package gave way and fell to the table's surface with a loud *SHLOP!*

"Haw-phsit!" he grunted disappointedly.

"Thanks, Farris." Sorenson smiled, holding back a chuckle.

He entered the open area of the garage and was struck by the sight of a large fire engine lifted into the air on a hydraulic hoist. Gigantic and bright yellow. Not red like most fire engines. Sorenson had never given the color of the local firefighter vehicles much thought until now, seeing one balancing on metal tracks so high off the ground.

Two men in blue overalls stood beneath the monstrosity. One was young and reaching up with a spanner, turning something near the front left wheel. Sorenson recognized him as Saul Albright.

The other was older, a cigarette jutting from his lips as he pointed to something near where the other man was working.

"That one there," he mumbled as a plume of smoke wafted from his face.

"Dewey," Sorenson called.

The older man turned around and smiled. He wiped his greasy hand on a rag that was sticking out from his back pocket and strolled over to Jacob. The two men shook hands.

"What can I do fer ya, Jacob?" Dewey asked. "That old plow givin' you a hard time?"

"Plow's fine," Sorenson replied. "Everyone's headed for the high school. Something's happened at the base that's got the council pretty riled up. I need you guys to come with me."

"How bad is it?" Dewey questioned as he shoved his hands into the pockets of his overalls.

"It's bad, Dewey," Sorenson said. "People will probably get hurt or worse."

Dewey took the cigarette from his lips and wedged it between his fore and middle fingers. He then scratched his head as he gave the concept some thought.

"Will guns be needed?" he asked.

Sorenson didn't hesitate with the answer. Dewey had always been up-front and honest with him. It was the least he could do to be the same back.

"Yes."

Dewey nodded. He took a long drag on his cigarette, held it a short while and exhaled through his nose.

"We'll stay here, thank you, Jacob."

The plow driver couldn't believe his ears.

"The high school will be safer, Dewey," Sorenson informed the other.

"I know," Dewey agreed. "But getting Maude out of here..."

Sorenson pictured the obese woman behind the counter reading tabloid magazines and eating chocolate bars. He then tried picturing her running and couldn't. His mind then moved to a crane lifting the lady out through the roof of the garage and placing her in a tip-truck.

Jacob understood Dewey's predicament.

"You got guns?"

"We'll be fine, Jacob," the older man stated. "You just get yerself over there and help those people. We'll be just fine here."

Sorenson stood and stared at the man for a short while that seemed like an eternity. He knew he wasn't going to see Dewey again.

Eventually, he nodded and moved his eyes over the large yellow fire engine.

"You do good work here Dewey," he said before turning and walking away.

VII

Vaughn drove the SUV to the church hoping to find some people still inside. Sometimes they held lunch after service. And sometimes lunch turned into an early dinner as Long Valley church folk liked each other's company so much that they didn't leave until late in the day.

"Why are we stopping here, Deputy?" Edry asked from the back seat.

"People come here, Doctor. My job is to look after them. Your job is to ride in the back seat and do what I tell you when I tell you." The deputy turned his attention to Upton who was sitting in the passenger seat next to him. "Wait here. I won't be long."

She nodded as he lifted himself out of the vehicle and shut the door behind him.

The snow crunched under his boots as he crossed the empty yard in front of the church building. The devoted Sunday attendees usually parked cars all over this area, but it looked untouched.

Vaughn guessed that everyone had gone home, or to the Stop N' Save to get out of the cold. He knew people had been here today, congregating together as they sang hymns and felt the warm embrace of the Lord.

He imagined the rows of seats inside filled with townsfolk in their Sunday best, nodding with audible *Amens* as the minister chided on and on about how sin is bad and how blessed the church is. In his mind, he saw people like old Mrs Gilroy, secretly judging the immoral lifestyle that others openly lived and gossiping about it to others as if it was the daily news.

Bitch!

Vaughn banged on the door with his gloved hand, palm flat against the wood. He tilted his head, touching the brim of his ten-gallon hat against the building, as he listened for anyone inside.

It was hard to hear anything as the wind had picked up and was whistling through the leafless trees lining the churchyard. They reminded him of skeletal hands bursting from the ground and reaching for the sky with twisted, blackened fingers.

He banged on the door again and waited.

The cold was working its way through his parka and into the three layers of clothing he wore underneath. The snow started to bite at his face and his discomfort grew as he listened intently.

Nothing.

Enough was enough.

He glanced back to the SUV and watched as the wipers pushed building snow off the windshield. Inside were two people keeping themselves much warmer than he was just by being inside the damn vehicle.

"Fuck this," he snorted as he started back across the yard.

The door creaked open.

Vaughn turned to see an elderly man with a long beard rugged up in a thick overcoat. "Can I help you, young man?"

"Uh..." Vaughn approached the door again. "I'm Deputy Sheriff Greg Vaughn, sir."

"Why don't you come on in?" the man gestured as he opened the door wider. "I'm Paul Harris."

"No, thank you, Mister Harris," the deputy answered. "I'm here to inform you we need to move everyone to the high school for emergency reasons. Is there anyone else inside?"

"No," Harris answered. "Everyone has gone home. I was just finishing cleaning up. I'm about to leave myself."

"Well, don't go home," Vaughn instructed. "Head straight for the high school. Okay?"

"Sure thing, Deputy," the elderly man agreed. Vaughn turned back toward the SUV. Harris had started to close the door when it suddenly dawned on the deputy that the only vehicle in the yard was his.

"Mister Harris," Vaughn called.

"Yes, Deputy."

"Do you have a mode of transport?"

"No sir," Harris replied. "I find walking everywhere always clears my head. Even in the worst of times. Gives me a good chance to talk to God."

"Well, you are not walking in this," Vaughn informed the elderly man. "We have got a heavy storm coming and we need to get to the high school in a few minutes. I'm afraid you'll have to come with me now. I'm not leaving you here."

VIII

Dawson jumped out of the Cherokee and ran to the automatic glass doors of the Stop N' Save. He desperately wanted out of the freezing cold. The doors seemed to take their time opening, making him wonder if they had frozen shut.

With a slight rattle, they parted and allowed warm air to sweep over him. He quickly moved inside the store and approached the service desk in the middle of ten register lanes.

He quickly looked up and down the length of the store and counted about thirty people that he could see. Others, hidden from his view, strolled along the aisles and near the cool racks at the back of the store.

Three girls were currently manning the registers with two bag boys. A few people lined up to purchase goods and one middle-aged woman was heading for the door. She nursed two bags of groceries in her arms and was attempting to fish her car keys out of her jacket pocket.

"I'm afraid you can't leave," Dawson instructed her.

"I— I..." She looked shocked. "I paid for these. I've never stolen a thing in my life."

"It's not that," he informed her. "I'm about to make an announcement and you should hear it."

"Hey Sheriff," called a young man from behind the service desk. "What can I do for you today?"

"Hi, Evan. I need to use the speakers," Dawson replied.

"Sure thing." Evan reached for a silver microphone attached to a stand. He toggled a switch on the base of the stand and handed it to the sheriff. "All yours."

143

Dawson held the microphone near his mouth. He wasn't sure what to say. How was he going to inform these people what was coming? How could he tell them without inciting panic?

It doesn't matter. They need to know.

He took a deep breath and spoke.

"This is Sheriff Tom Dawson," he began. His voice boomed through the store, immediately grabbing the attention of everyone in earshot of the speakers. "I need to evacuate this store and instruct everyone to head to the high school immediately. There is a storm bearing upon us, so I don't have much time to explain.

"All I can say is that you need to grab what supplies you can. Think of the bigger picture. Grab what *we* need. Not what *you* want.

"We have five minutes and then you need to get in your vehicles and head for the high school. If you choose to go home, you will place yourself and your family at risk. Thank you."

Evan looked at the sheriff with utter disbelief as he took the microphone back.

"Just who will pay for this?"

"I don't think that will matter much after tonight, Evan," Dawson replied as he grabbed a shopping trolley and entered an aisle.

IX

Carl Mason grabbed crates of water and soda from the cool room in the back of his diner. He had been carting the crates through the eating area and out the open door to his pickup truck where he stacked them in the tray. The truck was purring away to prevent her freezing up and to keep the cab warm by powering the heater inside.

Betty Sue had been gathering as much of the dried goods as she could. She carried bread, cookies, chips and cake to the pickup and placed them toward the tailgate.

"I think I got it all, Dad," she called as Carl entered the cool room again.

"Just one more crate of water," he hollered back. "Get in the truck and wait for me."

She opened the passenger door and slid into the seat before closing the door behind her. Betty Sue instinctively shuddered as she felt the last of the outside chill leave and allowed the warmth of the heater in the cab to engulf her.

Her eyes scanned Main Street ahead of her. Maverick's Peak had disappeared in the darkness of the looming cloud. The valley had grown a dull gray as the sun hid behind the mountains to the west.

Streetlights began to flicker to life as the automated system kicked into gear. The falling snow seemed to create luminous balls of energy around the brightening globes that dangled from tall metal poles that lined the empty street.

It was almost hypnotic.

A ball of fire rising in the distance caught her attention. She watched as it transformed into a cloud of smoke. Slowly, it vanished into the growing darkness and into oblivion.

She tried to estimate the distance, guessing that it was less than a mile away. Just inside the town limits. Fear gripped her, and she suddenly felt that she needed to be with her father.

A heavy thud behind her made her turn.

Carl Mason had just placed the last crate of water in the tray. He hurriedly made his way to the driver's side of the car and jumped in.

"I just saw…" Betty Sue began.

"I know," he answered as he knocked the vehicle into first gear. "I saw it too. It's only a few blocks away."

He started to drive. Betty Sue glanced back to the store and saw the door swung wide open.

"You forgot to lock the door," she stated.

"I didn't forget," he replied as he swung the vehicle onto Old Ridge Road. "We need to get out of here. The diner can look after itself."

Her heart raced so fast that she thought it would leap out through her throat and into her mouth. She had never felt such fear and excitement.

It wasn't long before they reached the Stop N' Save where traffic forced them to a crawl. Other vehicles were leaving the car park and heading in the same direction as they were.

A figure ran from the parking area toward them. It was waving its arms as it approached and something was hanging from its neck, swinging back and forth.

"Who's that?" Betty Sue asked, her voice shaky with fright.

"It's the sheriff," Mason answered as he wound his window down. Dawson moved around the truck to speak to its driver. He had a set of binoculars dangling around his neck by a strap.

"Carl," Dawson puffed. "Good to see you. Did you guys see that explosion?"

"Yeah," Mason answered. "Any ideas what it was?"

"Not a clue," he answered. "Listen. The drive will get a little slow for some of these guys. The road has iced over and Jacob has gone ahead in the plow to try to clear as much as he can. I don't think we have enough time to wait for him to do his usual job. Can your truck go off-road?"

"Well, yeah," Mason replied. "But I don't see how that's gonna help us."

"Drive up the nature strip in front of the properties." Dawson pointed to the left side of the road. There was a patch of open ground between the fences of the properties and the road just wide enough for a vehicle. "The fire truck can make it easy enough. You'd think this thing could do it too?"

"Ain't no fire truck, but I'll give it my best."

"Okay," Dawson nodded. "I'll see you at the school."

With that, Dawson retraced his steps back around the vehicle and disappeared into the car park area.

Mason swung the truck to the left and humped the gutter. Once he had all four wheels off the road, he carefully applied the gas pedal. He noticed Betty Sue breathing heavily.

"Don't worry, baby. We'll be fine."

She smiled, but her wide eyes told him she was scared shitless.

He was too.

X

Dawson directed the last of the vehicles out of the Stop N' Save car park. He returned to his Cherokee where three checkout girls waited for him.

"Okay girls," he said. "Everything will be fine once we get to the school."

"Sheriff?" one of the two girls in the back seat piped up.

"Yes, Nancy."

"Do you think my mom will be all right? We live right near the base, you know. I mean, these things you told us about are coming from there. Do you think they might have missed our house and that she will be okay?" The girl had become a blubbering mess, and it broke Dawson's heart.

"Nancy," he replied. "Girls. I don't have all the answers. Your guess is as good as mine. I'm sorry that I can't be more specific than that. I hope everyone is okay. But the truth is, I don't like our chances."

Dawson maneuvered the Cherokee through the car park, which still housed quite a few empty vehicles. He had instructed people in the store to carpool to the high school. Most had listened to him.

He pulled up at the exit that opened out onto Old Ridge Road and looked to his right. He could see the red glow of taillights from some vehicles making their way to their destination.

The sheriff turned his head to the left and peered out of the driver's side window. The glass had fogged a little, and he needed to wipe it with his glove to get a better view. In the distance, he could see the streetlights on the corner of Main Street and Old Ridge Road.

His foot planted itself on the brake a little more heavily as something grabbed his attention.

"Sorry girls," he said. "Rug up. I'm about to lower the window."

"Aw. Come on!" the girl next to him grumbled.

He wound the window down and freezing cold air blew into the cab of the Cherokee. He squinted his eyes against the chill and snow and saw some movement.

Dawson lifted the binoculars to his eyes. It took a moment, but he framed the light-filled intersection pretty well.

He saw the awning sign for the Town Hall and the Library clear enough to read them both. He moved the glasses to the right to put the street square in his view, and then he saw them.

Three men stood in the intersection staring in his direction.

Do they see me?

He dismissed the thought as he watched intently. A few more figures ran past the three from left to right and continued out of view.

Dawson noticed one man dressed in army fatigues. The others wore nothing but black undergarments.

Their skin was white like the snow surrounding them. Blue veins seemed to pop out all over their bodies from their hairless heads to their feet.

But the most haunting part of the image that Dawson now observed was their eyes.

White, lifeless eyes.

Darkened skin immediately surrounded their eyes. Almost blackened.

The same pigmentation surrounded the mouth, giving the impression that the men had black lips.

They continued to stare toward him.

How could they see me from that distance?

He found it mesmerizing that they would stand in the cold, unaffected by the low temperature.

Staring.

Standing.

Watching.

Scrutinizing.

Thunder clapped overhead. The dark cloud above roared to life.

"Holy shit," Nancy screamed.

"Can we go?" asked the other girl in the back.

Dawson watched as one man opened his mouth and screamed.

The sound was faint at this distance. But even over the roar of thunder and the constant howl of the wind, they could hear the scream.

All three men started running toward them.

"Shit!" Dawson exclaimed.

Others, too many to count, suddenly appeared from around the corner and followed the three men into Old Ridge Road and ran toward the Stop N' Save.

"They saw me." The sheriff hit the gas as hard as he could as he swung the Cherokee to the right with his right hand and wound the window up with his left. "Hold on, girls."

XI

"Take these straight up the stairs and around to the left," instructed Doctor Vanderberg.

A young man took a hulking pile of blankets from the doctor and ran inside the high school building. Vanderberg grabbed a large plastic tub filled to the brim with first aid supplies from the back seat of his car with both hands. He kicked the door shut as he turned toward what was to become his home until otherwise informed.

His feet slipped a little in the slush that had formed on the ground from all the pedestrian traffic in the area. He looked around him and saw a variety of vehicles parked precariously across the front yard of the high school, creating a labyrinth for any newcomers to navigate before they reached the safety and warmth of the building.

A few people lingered as they calmly grabbed equipment from their cars and waited for their kids to catch up. Their casual demeanor was almost enough to infuriate him.

Had they seen what happened to poor Quentin O'Brien, they wouldn't be acting so oblivious to the danger. If they had witnessed what O'Brien had done to Kyle Yancy, they would run their legs off and leave their luggage in their cars.

"Move it," Vanderberg cried. "Get inside, now."

"Come on, Doc," called one man carrying groceries as his two little boys ran circles around him in the snow. "Don't tell me you're buying into this exercise in futility."

"Listen, dipshit," Vanderberg replied.

"Hey!" the man grew defensive. "Come on now, Doc. There are kids here."

Vanderberg looked to the two laughing boys. They could be no more than ten years old and were enjoying every moment they were having in the snow this late at night. Their mother standing nearby, wearing a look of shock at how the men were behaving.

"There won't be if you don't get moving."

"Are you threatening my kids?"

"Let's just get inside," the woman said. "It's cold out here."

A loud screech made the men turn their heads toward the street.

A Cherokee was sliding sideways along the road at breakneck speed. It suddenly slammed into a parked car and came to a complete stop.

Vanderberg dropped the crate and ran toward the accident.

The Cherokee's left side was pinned against the car it crashed into. Three young ladies in Stop N' Save uniforms climbed out of the passenger side doors.

"You okay?" the doctor called as he ran toward them, weaving between parked vehicles.

They didn't respond.

The wind was loud and the storm above had grown fierce.

The Stop N' Save girls saw him and started in his direction. Vanderberg slowed his pace as another figure appeared from the front passenger door.

It was Dawson.

He lifted the binoculars to his eyes and peered back toward the direction he had come from.

"Shit," he bellowed as he dropped the glasses from his eyes, allowing them to swing from his neck. He turned and headed toward the school. "Get inside, girls," he called as he ran.

"Sheriff?" Vanderberg said confusedly.

"Not now," Dawson replied as he drew nearer to the doctor. "Get inside."

The men ran quickly, keeping the girls in front of them. The sheriff occasionally shot a glance over his shoulder as he instructed everyone to pick up the pace.

He saw the troop carrier nearby and noticed that someone had emptied it of its contents. He presumed everything had been unloaded and taken inside. If so, it would be the best thing that had happened today.

"Hurry up," Vanderberg called to the man and the little boys.

"Hey, fuck you," the man called back. "I'm taking my kids home. I don't need this shit."

"Get inside," Dawson barked.

"Get in the car," the man ordered his children. The boys looked to their father, disappointed. He had extinguished their fun.

"If you don't get inside now," Dawson called, "then I'll need to lock you out."

The man shot Dawson and Vanderberg a disapproving look.

"Warren," the woman pleaded.

"In the car now, Dorothy," the man ordered as he dropped the groceries and grabbed the boys by their sleeves.

"Dad," they protested together as he shoved them into the car. He stood and looked back to his wife.

"Dorothy," he bellowed.

She turned and strolled back to the car reluctantly.

Dawson watched solemnly as the car started up and the headlights flickered to life. He turned and headed for the high school door as Vanderberg lifted his plastic crate from the ground.

Both men entered the building where a large middle-aged man dressed in bright orange firefighters' overalls waited near the door.

"You're the last," he announced. "Unless those guys come back."

"They won't be back," Dawson informed the man. "Lock it up."

XII

"We should have just gone in, Warren," Dorothy said to her husband.

"It's all bullshit," he replied as he reversed the car onto the road. "It's just some safety drill. We'll be better off at home."

"How do you know?"

"Okay," he straightened the car up and shifted the stick to drive. "How do I know? Okay. Where are the Gibbs? On their damn farm. That's where."

"What's that got to do with anything?" she asked.

"If this was a real emergency, don't you think everyone in the valley would be present?"

"Not if they're dead," she yelled.

"Who's dead?" one boy asked from the back seat.

"No one's dead," Warren answered. "See what you did. You scared the boys."

"Are we going home now, Daddy?" the other boy asked.

"Yes, we're going home." Warren started rolling forward a little.

His headlights fell onto a line of white, hairless figures standing in the middle of the road.

"Holy shit," Dorothy breathed.

The figures stared blankly at them. Their chests were heaving, and their darkened lips hung open. Long puffs of steam emitted from their mouths as they breathed.

They scanned the car with their milky white eyes, seemingly confused by what they saw.

"What is this?" Warren asked. "Some kind of town prank?"

He hit the horn, hard.

The sound made the figures jump back slightly.

"Screw this," Warren said as he flicked the high beams on.

Suddenly the line of figures became a crowd that filled his view.

"Oh shit," he said as he quickly knocked the car into reverse.

A few of the creatures started screaming at the car. Others soon joined in and moved toward the vehicle.

Warren planted his foot on the gas and the car lurched backward.

The crowd ran toward him.

One of the lead figures leaped into the air and landed on the hood of the car. It started beating on the windshield with its fist.

BANG!

"Fuck," Warren bellowed.

BANG!

His wife and children started screaming and crying.

BANG! SMASH!

The windshield shattered into a million pieces.

The cold wind filled the car and drowned out their cries for help.

The car veered off the road and smashed into the sheriff's Cherokee.

The crowd of white figures encompassed the car. A few crawled in through the smashed windshield and attacked.

Warren watched wide-eyed and speechless as one figure bit into his wife's face. Blood sprayed across the interior of the vehicle in all directions as she went into spasms. Her arms and legs flailed as the creature sank its teeth deeper into her flesh.

Another white figure bit into his throat as others crawled past him and attacked his children in the back seat.

He tried to fight.

He wanted to protect his boys.

They were too young to defend themselves.

They called for him as the creatures started to feed.

It pained him that he couldn't see what they were doing to his kids.

But the sound.

Oh, the sound was horrific.

He heard screams of agony.

He heard the sickening crunch of bone and flesh as the creatures chewed into their bodies.

He heard their cries turn from shrill screams into gurgles as they drowned in their own blood.

It wasn't too long before he couldn't hear them at all.

SUNDAY NIGHT

I

The man in firefighter overalls locked deadbolts on the main entrance doors. He quickly slid the upper and lower bolts on each door, which penetrated both the concrete floor and stone door jamb. A quick rattle of the doors informed him they were secure.

"Come on," Dawson pleaded as Vanderberg climbed the main stairs behind him.

The sheriff stood on the bottom step of a wide stairwell. Brick walls hemmed it on both sides and a long banister split the passage into two halves. There were bright yellow adhesive arrows positioned on the front of each step, directing the right half for upward traffic, and the left half for those coming down.

On the floor, sunk into the concrete just in front of the first step, was an iron rail. It ran the width of the stairwell and the same length again to the left as it hugged the brick wall that lined the corridor to rooms in the lower level. An identical rail ran along the ceiling directly above the other.

Attached to the rail was a large iron gate with long vertical bars. It stretched from floor to ceiling and was slightly wider than the stairwell. The firefighter grabbed the gate and pulled it toward him as he got onto the first step with Dawson.

Both men heaved the gate along the rail. It was heavier than Dawson thought it would be. The rollers on the top and bottom of the gate that held it onto the rails desperately needed a greasing. The soft screeching it made as both men pulled it into position was enough to set Dawson's teeth on edge.

Eventually, the gate made it across the passageway with a thud.

The firefighter shifted the pins at the bottom and top of the gate into position and secured them with large padlocks. He gave the gate a shove and a tug to see if the locks would hold. It didn't move.

Both men turned and started climbing the stairs.

"I've already locked the two lower gates at the back of the building," the firefighter informed the sheriff. "I asked a few of the guys to throw furniture down into the stairs before we close the upper level gates. Should act as a deterrent, or at least an obstacle if anything gets through. Hope that was okay?"

"Okay?" Dawson laughed as they reached the top of the stairs. "That's good thinking. Tom Dawson," the sheriff held his hand out to shake.

"Miles Freeburg," the fireman replied as he took Dawson's hand. "Now, if you don't mind stepping aside for a moment, Tom."

Dawson looked around, perplexed. Then he understood.

A few of the other firefighters had carted some classroom furniture to the top of the stairwell. The sheriff stepped to the side as he watched a teacher's desk get thrown down the stairs. A cupboard immediately followed with student desks in tow.

"We have coffee around to the right in the teachers' lounge. We've made it into a makeshift cafeteria," Freeburg announced to the newcomers. "It's about halfway down that corridor. If you follow the passage all the way to the end and turn left, you'll come to the bathrooms. There are more bathrooms at the end of this corridor behind you."

All heads suddenly turned to see signs in the distance posted above two doors that stated *MALE* and *FEMALE*.

"We have one major rule tonight. Anything you brought with you benefits everyone. Don't be greedy. Take nothing, unless you absolutely need it."

Everyone that had just entered the building headed toward the teachers' lounge. The sudden need for coffee was overbearing.

Vanderberg, still carrying his large plastic crate of supplies, started to follow the crowd.

"Not you, Doc." Freeburg placed his large hand on the doctor's shoulder. "We have a room down that way for you." Freeburg pointed to the bathrooms in the distance behind Vanderberg. "If you follow this corridor and turn to the right, you'll find a room where your nurses are setting up. We also have a private stash of coffee and some food for you and your staff set up already."

"Thank you, Mister Freeburg." Vanderberg smiled before turning to head off.

"You guys got organized in a very short amount of time," Dawson observed.

"That's our job," Freeburg replied. "We run drills out here frequently. We test the emergency equipment every couple of months. So we know the place pretty well."

More furniture crashed down the stairwell as Dawson listened to the firefighter.

"I've been doing this for some time, Tom," Freeburg continued. "My kid came here before he went off to college. If what I've been told is true, then I thank the Lord above he's studying law in DC tonight and not here with us."

Dawson nodded. He didn't have words to say. All he could manage were three words.

"Thank you, Miles."

II

Tiffany slept on her parents' bed, curled up and snuggled deep in Stan's arms. He held her gently, occasionally stroking her hair as she softly breathed puffs of air onto his neck.

Stan had just woken up. He felt as if someone had disturbed his sleep, but he didn't see anyone in the room. A part of him wanted to look for Julia and Brad, just to find out if they had done something that had forced him from his slumber. He decided against getting to his feet when he noticed how cozy and tranquil Tiffany appeared. There was not a reason in the entire world to wake her. So, he held her.

Tiffany and Stan had both disappeared into her parents' room to talk. She was worried about her parents. They were meant to be home hours ago and hadn't called to tell her when they would be back.

"I wish I went with them to Wentworth," she had told Stan.

"It's okay," he reassured her. "They only went this morning. Maybe they got stuck in traffic or the storm shut the roads down."

"But they haven't called." She started to tear up.

"Phone lines could be down," he said as he wrapped his arms around her. "They'll be fine."

She had snuggled into him then. They somehow ended up lying down together and fell asleep.

Now Stan was awake.

A faint rustle at the window above the head of the bed forced his eyes in that direction. The blind was half open, and it was dark outside. Occasional flashes of light in the clouds above exposed snow streaking across the glass and building up in the corners of the window.

The window rattled gently as the wind howled.

Just the storm.

He looked back down to Tiffany. She hadn't moved except to wrap her leg around his.

Stan breathed deeply, fighting the urge to get aroused. He closed his eyes, intending to go back to sleep.

Rustle!

His eyes flicked open.

Rustle!

It wasn't at the window.

Rustle!

The sound was coming from lower down.

Rustle!

It was as if it was coming from just behind his head.

Rustle!

There were no bushes or trees below the bedroom window that could brush up against the wall. Something must have moved there. Something like a plastic shopping bag or another piece of light trash.

Rustle!

Perhaps the wind blew it there, and now it stuck in place and couldn't get free.

Rustle!

Thump!

"What was that?" Tiffany asked as she jumped awake.

"I don't know," Stan answered. "There's a nasty storm out. Maybe the wind blew something up against the house."

Rustle!

Rustle!

Thump!

"Sounds like it's stuck," she said, tensing up.

"I'll check it out." He lifted himself from the bed. As he did so, the door opened. Brad stood in the doorway holding a finger to his lips.

"What?" Stan asked with a cocky smile.

"They're out there," Brad whispered almost inaudibly as he pointed to the window behind Tiffany.

"Who?"

"I don't know." He shook his head. "But they look scary."

Rustle!

Rustle!

"That's them," Brad stated.

"Cut it out, Brad." Tiffany got off the bed. "Stop trying to scare me."

THUMP!

THUMP!

THUMP!

"Oh shit," whispered Brad. "They heard you."

THUMP!

THUMP!

THUMP!

THUMP!

"They're trying to break through the wall!" Tiffany ran to Stan and gripped his arm with both hands.

"Like to see them try. Brick walls." Stan put his arm around her.

"Glass window," Brad informed them.

"What do we do?" Julia asked, standing near the bedroom door.

"Find somewhere to hide," suggested Tiffany.

III

Gripping his shotgun, Dewey peered through the window as a lone figure ran away from the town, right down the middle of Main Street. He was screaming for someone to help him.

"You gonna help him?" Maude whispered from behind the desk.

Dewey could only see her silhouette as her frame moved against the light coming in through the window. Farris had moved through the rooms within the garage and turned off all the lights. He had left the heater in the lunchroom on, allowing a red glow to emit through the door into the short corridor between the store and the workshop.

The elderly man moved to the store's door, which he had locked a short time earlier. He placed his left hand on the door handle.

"Wait, boss," Saul Albright, holding a three-oh-three and peering through the window near Maude grunted. "Look."

"Shit!" Farris hissed as he clutched his stainless steel.357 Magnum against his chest. "Shit!"

Dewey followed the screaming man with his eyes. He looked tired and was surely about to collapse. Movement to the right caught his attention. He moved his gaze back along the road toward town.

At least twenty figures were running pell-mell toward the lone man.

"Help me," he cried in desperation.

White skinned, some in army fatigues, others in regular clothing, the pursuers squealed like gutted pigs at the sight of their prey.

"Please," the man cried into the otherwise emptied street.

"Maude," Dewey whispered. "I want you to move into the lunchroom now."

She didn't hesitate. Something bad was about to happen and she definitely did not want to see any of it.

"Help," the man called into the night as he desperately ran past the garage to flee his predators. "Anyone?"

Squeezing herself from behind the counter, Maude shuffled out of the shop front and down the corridor.

The creatures made the distance between the man and themselves in mere seconds.

He screamed as one of them leaped upon him, forcing him to the ground. It sank its teeth into his neck and ripped a large chunk of flesh from the man.

"Help me," he called one last time as dark blood poured from the wound and spilled onto the road. The other creatures engulfed him and buried their heads into the man.

The sight reminded Dewey of documentaries where lions had taken down a zebra and covered the prey as they squabbled over their share. He could no longer see the man.

His stomach turned at the vision, but he could not look away. If he could, he would have noticed that Maude was closing the lunchroom door behind her.

THUD!

A number of white eyes suddenly glared back toward the garage.

They had heard the door close.

"Oh, shit!" Farris breathed. "Oh, shit! Oh, shit! Oh, shit!"

"Shuttup," Saul ordered.

The white figures lifted themselves to their feet and glared directly toward the windows. Blood covered their mouths and cheeks like freakish circus clown makeup.

One of them crept on all fours, closer and closer to the garage, sniffing the air as it moved.

"What do we do, boss?" Saul asked.

Dewey watched as the creature drew nearer and nearer. His heart pounded so hard in his chest and head that he thought he would explode.

"I don't know."

IV

Dawson moved to the northern section of the building and now sat in a chair drinking hot coffee. He sipped carefully and ran his fingers over the thickening stubble on his cheeks.

The classroom he sat in was roughly halfway along the northern corridor and overlooked the courtyard in the center of the complex. He rested the back of the chair, usually occupied by the teacher, against the windows and peered toward the open door. The number 34 was etched just above the handle.

They had emptied the room of all furniture except for the teacher's desk, the chair he now sat on and a few students' seats. All the other classrooms had suffered the same fate, having most of the furniture removed to be used as barricades in the high school's stairwells.

"You should get some rest, Tom," Agnes told him as she sat in one of the student's chairs nursing her own mug. "You haven't stopped all day."

"I don't think I'll get a chance to stop until this is over," he replied.

"What do you think they are?" she asked, referring to the things he claimed to have seen before arriving at the school.

"I don't know." He shook his head. "Some infected people like what we saw at the hospital. You know the guy that Redhawke shot. Fuck, what was his name?"

"O'Mally or something," she said.

"O'Brien," he suddenly remembered. "Maybe something like what he became. Maybe something the army always had, but it got loose. Maybe they let it loose. I don't really know."

Privates Sandra Upton and Frank Sharpe entered, pushing two large khaki crates into the room.

"M-16 assault rifles and ammo," Sandra informed the sheriff. "We're placing two crates in each quadrant."

"Quadrant?" Dawson asked, getting to his feet to inspect the new items. Agnes noticed the look on his face. She saw an adult version of a kid on Christmas morning about to unwrap his presents.

"Vaughn's idea," Sharpe informed them. "Southern at the front. Western for the surgery."

"The western side is also the farthest point from town," Upton interjected, "so we're speculating that it will be the least likely to be attacked in a first-wave assault."

"So that's why you put the doctors and medical gear over there?" Dawson queried.

"No," Sharpe replied. "That was just a coincidence."

"Okay." Dawson nodded. "So, let me guess, eastern quadrant around to the side where the staffroom is, and this is the northern quadrant."

"Yes sir," said Upton as she opened a crate to reveal twelve M-16 assault rifles neatly racked side by side. "There's another twelve beneath and boxes of ammunition in clips beneath. We're storing these in rooms in each quadrant. All the rooms are interior rooms about hallway along each corridor."

"Interior rooms?" Agnes asked.

"Rooms that overlook the courtyard," Upton informed her. "Away from external walls that might be penetrated."

"Oh." Agnes nodded nervously as she held onto her mug tighter. "Okay."

"What rooms are being used?" Dawson asked.

"Eight and fourteen in the southern quadrant," Sharpe began. "The staffroom in the eastern. Lab five in the western and this room for the northern quadrant."

"Why two rooms for the southern quadrant?" Dawson questioned as he lifted a rifle out of the crate to inspect it. It was heavier than he thought it would be.

"Just in case they breach the stairs," Sharpe replied.

"Fair enough." Dawson placed the rifle against the wall near his chair. "That one's mine."

V

They huddled together in the basement, pressed up against a wall beneath the staircase that led back up to the house. Each held a golf club, taken from Tiffany's father's supply, and draped themselves in sleeping bags.

There was clutter everywhere, yet somehow neatly organized so that access to any item was within grasp. Camping gear was against the far wall. Laundry supplies were near the washing machine. An adjustable incline bench with a barbell resting in a cradle sat near the middle of the room. Around it was various sports equipment including a golf bag with an assortment of clubs.

Julia shivered under her sleeping bag. It was cold down here and the smell of damp was strong. Brad drew her in close to him. He was cold too.

The thumping from outside had stopped some time ago and now they sat in silence listening to the howling wind and roaring thunder. The storm was directly over them and snow covered the slither of glass that acted as a window high upon the wall above the washing machine. Now and then, a flash of light seeped through as lightning burst through the darkness, illuminating the room and quickly casting odd shaped shadows on the surrounding walls.

The teenagers' hearts skipped a beat every time light momentarily entered the room. Their minds raced with fear as they saw someone, something, peering back at them from the dark in that moment.

But there was no one.

Nothing.

"We should probably try to get some sleep," Stan suggested.

"Should we take shifts?" Julia asked. "Someone needs to be awake in case one of those things gets in."

"What's the time?" Brad asked.

"A little after nine," Stan replied as he glanced at his watch.

"I'll take first shift and wake you at midnight," Brad stated. "You stay up until three and the girls can watch until daybreak."

Stan nodded. "How's that sound to you, girls?"

Tiffany and Julia agreed with the plan.

VI

"This is the M-16 A2," Private Sandra Upton informed a small crowd that had gathered before her. Dawson and his deputies had assembled along with Mayor Harold Waring, Groundskeeper Barry Webster, Carl Mason and his daughter Betty Sue, Jacob Sorenson the snowplow driver, Miles Freeburg the eldest firefighter and several others from the community. She was standing in the *Teachers' Lounge.* In her hands was a black assault rifle, which appeared impressively large against her small, athletic frame. "It kicks like a bitch if you don't handle it properly.

"To hit what you want to hit, you line the site here..." she pointed to a section mounted atop of the rifle to the rear before moving her fingers to the tip of the barrel, "...with the site post here.

"It has a case deflector behind the ejection port so you southpaws can pretend to shoot as good as us normal people without hot shells bouncing off yer faces.

"There are three settings." Her fingers moved to a toggle on the left of the rifle. "*Burst* gives you three rounds with each pull of the trigger. *Semi* allows you a single shot with each pull of the trigger, and *Safe,* which will prevent you from firing a round off if you pull the trigger. Keep yer rifle on *Safe* unless you intend to shoot something."

"This girl is giving me a boner," Redhawke whispered into Sorenson's ear.

"The magazine," Upton continued, holding a metallic, rectangular box in her hand. "This baby holds thirty rounds. They are preloaded.

Your job is to shoot until it is empty, discard it and replace it with a new one. Simple.

"To load. Make sure the safety is on. Pull the charging handle all the way back and lock the bolt." The private demonstrated by extending a long lever at the back of the rifle. "Return the handle back to its original position and push the magazine up into the magazine catch. Do not force it in. If you find you need to force it in, it's probably because you haven't pulled the charging handle all the way back first.

"Once you have the magazine in place, press the top portion of the bolt catch button to release the bolt." She inserted the magazine into her rifle and pressed a small button above the magazine well on the rifle's left. A small click sounded for all to hear.

"You may or may not hear that noise depending on what's happening around you," she explained. "So, to make sure, tap the bottom of the magazine to check that it's securely in place.

"To unload. Safety on. Press the magazine release button on the right side of the mag well. The magazine should slide right out. Put another magazine in if you want to keep firing. Otherwise, lock the bolt open by pulling the charger handle back. Press the bottom of the bolt catch button and return the charger handle forward. Remove any ammo from the chamber and press the top of the bolt catch button to allow the bolt to move forward. Then pull the trigger to release the pressure on the firing pin spring."

She moved her eyes across the room, taking in the varied expressions on the faces in front of her. Some appeared knowledgeable; others examined the rifles they held in their hands to make sense of what they were just told, and a few looked at each other perplexed. It was a lot to take in.

"You'll pick it up quickly," she told the room. "Trust me. Magazines will be distributed in each sector. Grenades and heavy artillery will be left for those with training to operate. Please do not attempt to use any other item besides the assault rifle. Just because you saw someone in a movie do it doesn't mean that that's the correct way to do it."

The teachers' lounge started to clear. Dawson thanked the private for a well-informed presentation. She thanked him with a smile and a nod before leaving the room.

"Boss," Redhawke called from the far end of the teachers' lounge. A small group had gathered around a large table near a kitchenette that sat snugly in the room's corner.

Dawson strode over to the gathering, comprising his deputies, Mayor Waring and Miles Freeburg.

"I grabbed these from the office before coming here." Redhawke placed a duffle bag on the table for all to see. "I put them down somewhere so I could help get the supplies out of the army truck earlier. They totally slipped my mind until some kid out there found them and brought them to Miles."

Redhawke unzipped the bag and started placing walkie-talkies onto the table.

"My man!" Vaughn gasped in appreciation.

"They all charged?" asked Dawson.

"All of these ones are," the deputy replied. "We're missing one."

"Yeah," Vaughn interjected. "The boss shit a brick over that the other day."

"We thought you had it," Dawson directed to Redhawke.

"You took it," Redhawke replied.

"What?"

"When you went out to talk to Missus Friel about some teens screwing about in her front yard."

"Oh yeah." Vaughn smiled. "That's right. You took it out there because… Well, it's no secret what you get up to with Missus Friel. My guess, the walkie is still on her bedside table as we speak."

"Shit," Dawson spat.

"Losing your memory in your old age, Tom?" Waring chuckled. "And Missus Friel? She's more than half your age. You old dog."

"All right," the sheriff grumbled. "That's enough. Back to this. How many have we got?"

"Nine," Redhawke answered.

"Okay." Dawson ran his hand over the stubble that was forming on his cheeks as he thought things through. "The three of us take a walkie. I'll be in the northern sector. Redhawke, you're probably the best shooter out of all of us. You take the southern sector. Vaughn, you'll stay here in the eastern sector."

"That's three," Waring said. "What about the other six?"

"Give them to the army guys," Miles Freeburg suggested. "You've got two of them over in the western sector with the doctors."

"Good idea," Dawson agreed. "The last three go to Carl Mason who will be in this sector with his daughter." The sheriff quickly eyeballed Vaughn as he spoke. Deputy Greg Vaughn understood. His boss was placing Betty Sue, the only person Vaughn truly cared about in the whole valley, under his care.

"Miles, I want you to take one and coordinate the southern sector. Most of your boys are ex-military and I intend to use them. From what my deputies tell me, there is already a large gathering on the road out there and we will need people who know what they're doing. You up for that?"

"I can do that," Freeburg assured himself more so than the sheriff.

"The last one should go to Barry Webster," Dawson instructed.

"The groundskeeper?" Waring asked.

"He knows this school and all of its little secrets," the sheriff explained. "We need that kind of knowledge."

"Agreed," Freeburg grunted. "Barry has been a tremendous help when we've conducted emergency drills and assessments out here. He knows this school. Also, Sheriff?"

"Hmm?"

"I think we should move all the kids under fifteen into the rooms in your sector," suggested Freeburg. "It's the farthest place at the moment from where these things are gathering."

"Okay." Dawson nodded. "Let's get these walkies to those people," he said to Redhawke as he grabbed a radio from the table for himself, "and let's get those kids into the northern sector," he directed to Freeburg as he headed for the teachers' lounge door. "We've got about one hundred people in here with us, guys. Including kids. It's our job to protect them."

VII

SMASH!

Tiffany opened her eyes.

It took a moment for her to realize and remember where she was.

The basement was very dark and the howling of the wind had died off somewhat. She could hear Stan's heart racing as her head pressed against his chest.

Something was wrong.

"Stan," she whispered.

"Shhh," he replied.

The silence was unbearable. Both listened intently. Something loud had woken them both but now there was nothing.

"Brad," Stan whispered after some time had passed. "Brad. You awake?"

"Hmph," came a muffled reply. "What do you want?"

"Brad, you fuck nut," Stan snorted. "You were meant to keep watch."

"I was," he answered. "I must have dozed off. Why? What's wrong?"

"I don't kn—"

CRASH!

"Shit," Julia muttered. "It's in the house."

Something padded its way across the floor above them as it moved through the living quarters of the house. Now and then it would pause momentarily before moving to another location.

"What do we do?" Brad whimpered a little too loudly.

It stopped.

Their eyes all flickered to the ceiling of the basement.

They waited for it to move again.

They hoped it hadn't detected them, heard them, smelled them.

Waiting.

Hoping.

They silently prayed and wished for the thing above to go away.

Julia started to tear up and breathe shallowly, uncontrollably. Brad pulled her in closer to him to comfort her and help calm her nerves.

Her condition only worsened.

Wheezing gasps of air moved in and out of her lungs. The sound bounced off the walls around them.

The thing moved, shuffling quickly across the floor above in their direction.

It had heard her.

Julia's breathing quickened.

"Shh," Tiffany hissed as she placed a hand on Julia's arm.

It stopped moving again.

Directly above them.

Julia stopped breathing.

They all stopped breathing as they waited.

Their heads cocked toward the ceiling as they listened and willed the creature to move.

THUMP!

THUMP!

Soft screams escaped from the girls as the boys jumped to their feet, golf clubs at the ready.

THUMP!

THUMP!

THUMP!

It had discovered them.

VIII

They had been staring out through the windows of the garage's storefront for what seemed an eternity. Dewey couldn't take his eyes off the mess that lay in the middle of the street.

The lone man was not much more than a pile of meat. Three of the creatures continued to strip flesh from the bones with their yellowish teeth and lap at the blood on the ground with their blackened tongues.

The other beasts had moved closer to the garage, positioned near the gas pumps in front of the shop. They were glaring at the windows, seeming to know someone was inside but appearing confused by their own images being reflected at them in the glass.

Dewey counted his blessings as he recalled a time some years before when he had the windows tinted. The glare from the sun bouncing off the road during the height of the snow season was near unbearable. The thin film that now covered the glass not only proved a benefit for his eyes but also acted as a protective barrier against impending death.

One creature moved toward the shop. Crawling on all fours with its head tilted and body twisted at a side angle, it reminded Dewey of an ape on a TV documentary.

It reached up to the glass with its hand and quickly recoiled.

Dewey was mesmerized. The pale skin of the creature almost appeared translucent as blackish veins twisted from beneath a collar of the shirt it wore, up the neck and along the jaw. Its eyes had lost all pigmentation, leaving only tiny pin-prick pupils in a sea of tumultuous bloodshot white.

Black fingernails reached for the glass a second time and touched the window before recoiling again.

It was getting more game as it appeased its curiosity.

Saul lowered the three-oh-three, aiming it directly at the creature's head.

Don't you fucking dare, Dewey screamed in his head to Saul. One-shot would bring all the others tearing into the store. The old man knew they wouldn't have time to reload for the next shot before those things out there would have them. He shook his head.

Saul Albright must have seen the old man through the darkness. He lowered his gun and moved farther into the store positioning himself in the aisle between the crisps and soda.

The creature touched the glass with an open hand and held it there. It emitted a tiny whistle as it hissed. The others reacted by creeping closer and gradually placed their hands onto the windows one by one.

Several started scratching their nails down the glass or wiping the palms of their hands across the surface, creating scraping and squeaking sounds. One started padding the window softly as it pressed its face against the glass. Its eye darted this way and that as it attempted to see into the store.

Dewey moved toward the corridor. He signalled for Farris, who was still near the counter, to do the same. The old man had to pass the aisle that Saul hid in before he reached the passageway, so he hoped that the other would pick up on the signal and would move with them.

The padding on the window started getting more intense, turning into an open-handed strike.

Harder and harder.

"Lunchroom," Dewey whispered to Farris. Saul crept carefully along the aisle of fridges at the rear of the store, behind the aisles and toward the entry of the corridor.

Others had joined in hitting the glass.

It started to bow and make a sound resembling a bounce.

The men knew it wouldn't hold.

Farris opened the lunchroom door.

Light exploded into the corridor and into the store.

The noise suddenly stopped.

The creatures glared toward the source of the sudden illumination.

"What's going on?" Maude asked loudly as she sat at the table drinking coffee.

The creatures made a high-pitched scream that pierced into the eardrums.

"FUCK!" Saul called.

BANG! The monsters returned to hitting the window with intensity. Some threw themselves against the glass in desperation to get in.

"Get inside," Dewey ordered the other two men.

BANG!

CRACK! Dewey snapped his head around to see that the window had a great split from ceiling to floor. The only thing holding it in place for the moment was the thin film of tint.

Farris and Saul quickly moved into the lunchroom.

SMASH!

Five figures fell in through the shattered window and immediately turned their attention upon the open door to the well-lit room.

Dewey quickly put his head in through the door.

"Lock the door," he instructed before pulling it shut and disappearing into the garage. He heard Maude cry out after him to come back.

Instead, he trained his shotgun on the closest creature and fired.

The pellets tore into the torso of the oncoming figure, causing it to fall to the ground. It writhed and twisted on the ground as it screamed. The other creatures ignored it and pressed on through the store and toward the corridor.

He didn't have long before they would be upon him.

Dewey quickly turned toward the open area of the workshop and tried to think of a better position.

The first of the invading creatures moved through the corridor, passing the lunchroom door and directing their full attention upon the old man.

It was only a matter of time before they had him.

IX

"Anything?" Dawson said into his walkie-talkie as he moved along the northern corridor, checking the room overlooking the courtyard where he had placed the children. Five girls and three boys watched Sponge Bob on a television hitched to a trolley.

"We've just gone dark," Redhawke whispered into his radio as he peered through the binoculars and into the street outside. "All room and corridor lights are off. There's a large crowd of those things milling about out there, but they don't seem interested in us. They look this way now and then, but that's about it for now. How are things over there?"

"Kids are watching TV," Dawson replied. "We got blankets, crisps and movies for them to watch. Nothing we can do now except wait."

"Yeah," Redhawke replied. "Then you guys might want to keep the coffee coming this way."

"Working on it," Vaughn responded. "We just got the hot water thingy turned on."

"What?" Redhawke hissed.

"Everything was turned off for the vacation period," explained Vaughn. "It takes time to get things working again."

"Okay. Just make sure the southern sector is first on your..." Redhawke suddenly stopped talking.

Dawson stopped in his tracks. He stood outside of the door to a room where Agnes, Waring, Lilly Geddes the school principal and Barry Webster were resting. The sheriff could see that they were suddenly on edge as they were listening in on the conversation and were now waiting for a response from Redhawke.

The silence was horrifying.

A tense knot grew in Dawson's stomach, as he feared the worse. He turned to face Private Upton, who was standing at the southwestern corner of the corridor nursing her M-16 she had strapped over her shoulder in one hand and holding the walkie-talkie up to her ear with the other.

Waiting.

Waiting.

"Deputy," Dawson called softly into his radio. He waited for a reply. "Deputy, are you there?"

"Yeah," Redhawke hissed. "There's something out here. Just a minute."

***

Redhawke cocked his ear trying to home in on a noise he heard in the wind. The storm was too loud to pick a single noise out of. Trees cracked and rustled as the strong gale whistled between the leafless limbs. Thunder roared and lightning lit up the sky and yet, Redhawke thought he had heard something that wasn't part of the turmoil.

But there it was.

A soft hum was being drowned out by the surrounding blare.

Something in the air.

Something man-made.

He lifted the binoculars to his eyes and scanned the gathering crowd of creatures on the road. They all looked to the sky.

They heard it too.

He lifted the radio to his lips, "There's something flying around out there."

"You sure?" Dawson asked.

"Yeah," Redhawke answered. "I don't know what it is. But it has the attention of those things out there. They're all looking up."

Redhawke tuned his hearing into the sound. It was a metallic whirring that reminded him of a jet turbine.

It was growing louder and louder as if it was drawing nearer and nearer.

"I think it's a jet," Redhawke said to Miles Freeburg, who had just entered the room and crouched next to the deputy. "I think it's a jet," he said again into the walkie-talkie.

"A what?" Vaughn asked.

The noise was distinct. It was definitely a turbine engine, and it passed from the south, directly over them and to the north.

"Tell me you heard that?" Redhawke breathed.

"What the fuck was that?" Vaughn asked.

"I couldn't see it," replied Redhawke. "It's got to be a jet."

"I'm looking out the northern windows now," Upton informed them. "I heard it, but I can't see anything. It's too dark out there."

"Colin?" Dawson called to his deputy.

"Yeah, Boss."

"Are you watching the road?"

Redhawke quickly lifted the binoculars to his eyes and saw hundreds of pale faces glaring in his direction.

"Oh, shit!" Freeburg gasped.

One creature screamed a long shrill cry.

Others then responded with a similar call.

Then, as if of one mind, they moved.

Leaping, running and charging. Not like humans would, but like rabid animals, toward the entrance to the Long Valley High School.

***

"Here they come," Freeburg called over the radio.

"Shit," Dawson huffed before raising his walkie-talkie to his lips. "Okay, people. Get ready. Make sure you only fire your weapon when you have a clear shot."

***

The top portion of the high school's façade contained thirty-six windows. Bars covered each window, all of which were open with the muzzle of a fully-loaded M-16 A2 pointing through to the outside.

From the southwestern corner, along the southern corridor to the main stairwell were regular classrooms numbering 1 to 6. The latter was closest to the stairs. On the other side of the stairwell was a large storeroom followed by science labs 1, 2 and 3.

Redhawke had positioned himself in science lab 1. In the room with him were Jacob Sorenson, the snowplow driver, and Max Dooley, the owner-operator of the local bar.

The three men took a window each and aimed their weapons toward the oncoming horde.

"Ready, boys?" Redhawke asked.

"No," Dooley replied with a touch of nerves in his voice.

Creatures leapt onto and over the precariously parked vehicles in front of the building. They were rapidly making their way through and over the would-be maze of cars and pickup trucks toward the school.

Redhawke fired first.

He had seen the capability and aftermath of what one of these things had done to an orderly in the hospital. While it pained him that he was the one to put a bullet in poor Mister Quentin O'Brien's head, he did not want to see a similar fate to that of Kyle Yancy, the partially eaten orderly in the hospital.

The deputy had set his rifle to 'Semi', allowing a single round with each squeeze of the trigger. His first shot went wide of its target, a thin creature crawling over a car about halfway between the building and the road.

The bullet hit the windshield next to the writhing body of the beast. It glanced at the hole in the glass with disdain and continued forward.

Redhawke aimed carefully and fired again, hitting the individual in the top of the head. Its body slumped on the bonnet of the vehicle as blackened blood seeped from the bullet hole, over its whitened skin and onto the car.

The deputy took a deep breath to regain composure. His hands shook momentarily as O'Brien's face suddenly filled his mind.

"Hey," Sorenson called from beside him. "You okay?"

Redhawke snapped back to reality.

He could hear the bursts of gunfire from other rifles resounding from along the building's façade. Sorenson looked at him concernedly.

"I'm fine," the deputy answered. "That thing at the hospital just…"

"Can you do this, Colin?"

"Yeah." Redhawke nodded as he lifted the rifle to take aim. "I'm doing this."

***

The creatures moved forward like a wave. Automatic fire spat bullets into the air, riddling the oncoming invaders that relentlessly pushed forward toward their prey.

Bodies fell between and upon the mess of vehicles and upon one another.

Still, they came.

Fueled with the desire to feast.

Crawling over the dead.

Smeared with the dark blood of the fallen.

They pressed on toward their game.

X

They cowered in a corner as far away as they could from the sound of ripping, tearing and banging. The creature above was frantically trying to find a way through the floor to them.

The terrifying scraping noise signalled that the thing had torn its way through the clean, white woollen carpet that had neatly covered the hardwood floorboards. Now it scraped its claws along the wood trying to find a hold.

In frustration, and after many attempts, it thumped the floor in anger. Screaming a long high-pitched whistle, it smashed itself hard and heavily against the floor.

Dust drifted toward them as they looked to each other for any suggestions to the one impending question upon all of their minds.

How are we going to get out of here alive?

Stan looked at each one of them and saw the same fear that he felt in their eyes. At the same moment, he understood that they couldn't stay in the basement forever and would need to find a way out, if not fight their way out soon.

"We need to go," he said.

"Where?" Brad asked. "With that fucking thing up there, where do we go?"

"That thing will figure out a way down here and have us cornered," Stan replied. "Or we will die from the cold or thirst. Whichever comes first. We need to go now."

Brad stopped to think it through.

Stan was right. They needed to get out of there. But not without a plan.

"How do we do this?" Brad asked. "I think we need to get that thing before we leave."

"You mean kill it," Julia stated.

"Fuck, yes, kill it."

"Why not just run?" she sobbed.

"Because," Stan interjected, "that thing will chase us down and get at least one of us. Brad is right. We need to get it first. Before it gets us."

It thumped and thudded frantically from above them.

"Okay." Brad walked to the base of the stairs. "Let's get it."

They climbed the stairs as softly as they could. Luckily for them, the creature's ferocity in trying to break the floor masked the creaking that a few of the wooden steps made as they approached the basement door.

They huddled together at the top, gripping their golf clubs tightly in their hands. Stan slowly reached out his hand for the doorknob. His hand shook uncontrollably as nerves got the better of him.

He gently closed his fingers around the handle and twisted until he could twist no more.

Sudden silence invaded their ears.

The creature had stopped.

"Oh shit," Brad hissed.

They listened intently, waiting for the invader to make a sound.

Nothing.

"What do we do?" Tiffany asked fearfully. "Do we go?"

"I don't know," Stan replied. "Maybe it left. I think it le—"

It almost ripped the door from his grasp.

The creature had found them.

It pulled at the door with great strength.

Brad leapt forward and wrapped both of his hands around Stan's and pulled the door closed. The boys held it with all of their might, but the creature tugged and tugged, testing their physical abilities to the extreme.

"Get ready to hit it," Stan cried.

Brad stretched his arm out for his nine-iron, but it was lying on the floor by his feet out of his reach. Tiffany quickly realized his plight and retrieved the club for him.

There was no time for gratitude. Brad let the handle go, thus forcing Stan to do the same.

The creature fell backward and landed on its back in the kitchen.

"Now," Stan barked as he raised his club above his head and ran at the thing.

It opened its bloodstained, blackened mouth and screeched a long ear-piercing cry. The creature's white skin and hairless head looked like something from a nightmare and made Tiffany hesitate.

Stan and Brad, however, lunged and struck the thing over and over. Their aim wasn't precise enough. It cowered at first, raising its arms to protect its head.

After a moment, it had enough of being beaten and lunged back.

It gripped Brad around his ankle and pulled him to the floor.

Stan swung his club and missed the creature's head by an inch as it jumped onto Brad and sank its teeth into his leg. His club lodged into the wall.

Brad cried in shock more than pain. Instinct took over and Brad responded by punching the creature on the top of its pasty white head.

Tiffany and Julia suddenly snapped into action and swung their clubs overhead and directly down into the creature's skull.

At first, there was blood followed by a sickening crunch as Julia smashed her club through bone and into tissue.

The creature slumped onto Brad. One of its legs flailed as the nervous system reacted to the final blow.

Stan pulled the thing off his friend and pushed it into the middle of the kitchen floor where it continued to spasm.

"Fuck, it burns," Brad complained.

It took a moment for them to realize that he was talking about the bite wound from the creature.

"Let me see," Julia instructed.

Brad pulled his pants leg up to expose a large open wound. Blood had wrapped itself around his ankle and made it difficult to see the damage.

"Tiff, where do you keep bandages and shit like that?" Stan asked.

"Bathroom," she replied.

"Julia, use that dishcloth and clean that up," Stan ordered. "We'll get the bandages."

"No," Tiffany interjected. "Not the dishcloth. Here." She reached across the kitchen bench near the sink and tossed a roll of paper towelling to Julia. "This is cleaner."

Tiffany took a glass from a cupboard and filled it with water before handing it to Julia. "To help clean it up."

Julia nodded as she tore some paper from the roll and dipped it into the glass.

"We'll be right back," Stan assured them.

"Don't be too long," Brad replied as he looked across the floor to the creature. It had slowed its movement to an occasional leg jerk.

Tiffany and Stan moved into a corridor that led back to the bedrooms.

"This might hurt," Julia said before she applied the damp paper towel to Brad's wound. He winced slightly as she wiped the blood away.

Large teeth marks pierced the skin just above his sock. Blood slowly trickled out in places. The skin appeared to bubble yellowish pus around the immediate edges of the wound with darkened blood vessels branching outwards in all directions.

"What the fuck?" Brad whispered.

"I think the wound's infected," Julia said.

"Nothing gets infected that quick," he replied.

"What gets infected?" Stan asked as he and Tiffany returned with a first aid kit.

"Check this out." Brad pointed.

Stan leaned in close to see Brad's wound. He noticed the teeth marks instantly, then the pus.

"That's gross," he said as he continued to look. He then noticed the darkened blood vessels reaching away from the wound like roots of a tree.

As he watched, they grew slightly. He thought it was a trick of the brain at first. But when he noticed it pass a small scar on Brad's leg that he had got the year before when they were snowboarding, he knew something was terribly wrong.

Stan moved his eyes to the motionless figure in the room. It was white webbed with darkened blood vessels from head to toe.

XI

Dewey gripped the shotgun against his chest, as he remained curled up in the back of the firetruck's cabin. The vehicle rocked violently in all directions, like a small boat on a rough ocean, as the creatures clambered over and under the truck as they searched for a way in.

The yellow monstrosity still sat on the metal tracks that once held it high above the ground. Dewy had lowered it to floor level earlier, something he was thankful for. There were more than a few moments when he thought the truck would tip over. If he had left it elevated, the vehicle would have fallen to the ground.

A creature glared through the window at the old man. It butted its head violently against the glass over and over, harder and harder, until the skin on its forehead split open.

Blood sprayed across the clear surface as the fiend continued bashing its skull against the glass. It screamed an ear-piercing hiss in frustration as it furiously threw itself at the truck again and again.

Dewey knew that it would be some time before the things outside would break-in. The firetruck was sturdy, made to handle the heat, cold, high winds, extreme weather and harsh conditions. Surely, it could withstand this.

Still, the creatures showed determination to get to him.

He heard thudding from above and scraping below as they frantically tried to claw and beat at the panels of the vehicle. Something drew his attention to the front of the cab where open hands slid and smacked upon the large windshield.

More of the creatures had arrived and made their way into the garage since he had first climbed into the truck. Just how many he could not be sure of.

Craning his neck, he attempted to see if the things had broken into the lunchroom. White faces, yellow teeth and clawing fingers obstructed his view.

It would not have mattered if the beasts were not there anyhow. He would not have been able to see the door to the room from his position.

He hoped the others were okay.

***

Farris shook frenetically as fear gripped him. He huddled against the far wall with his knees up near his chest. The.357 Magnum rattled loudly in his hands. His teeth chattered, and he moaned softly with each exhaling breath.

"Are you cold?" Maude asked sympathetically from her chair at the table.

"Shhh!" Saul hissed from his position near the door. He held the three-oh-three steadily in his hands and listened to the uproar occurring outside the lunchroom.

"I'm trying to help," Maude shot back loudly.

"You're gonna get us killed if they hear you," Saul snapped back in a loud whisper. "Now shut up."

Maude sat open-mouthed, shocked at being spoken to like that by someone she had known since his childhood. How dare he?

"How dare you?" she barked, rising to her feet and making the metal legs of her chair scrape against the cement floor. She placed her hands on her hips and pointed to Farris. "This boy needs our help and you're worried about that noise. We're here. Locked safely in this room. They can't get to us."

Saul couldn't believe what he was seeing and hearing. Imminent death was outside the door and this fat bitch of a woman wanted to make a fucking point.

"Dewey's out there," she continued. "He's out there on his own and you're in here safely locked inside. He saved our lives and you show how much you deserve to be saved by telling me to shut up. What sort of man are you?"

Farris moaned louder and louder with each breath.

"Well?" Maude cocked her head. "I'm waiting for an answer. Do you treat all yer women like this? Are you always such an asshole?"

THUMP! THUMP! THUMP!

Saul stepped back from the door and trained his rifle upon it.

Farris' moans turned into yelling.

"Now you've done it," Saul snapped. "I told you to shut up."

THUMP! THUMP! THUMP!

CRACK!

The door bent slightly in the middle.

"Fuck!" He moved around to the far side of the table. Quickly, he slung the rifle over his shoulder and tilted the table over onto its side. Its contents of plates, cutlery and condiments spilled to the floor with a smash. The table now stood as high as he was, just slightly shorter than the entry to the room. He pushed it forward so that the tabletop was flush with the door.

"What are you doing?" Maude cried over the loud thudding and Farris' screams.

Saul ignored her and unplugged the fridge. It was large and heavy but he managed to twist it and turn it so it walked to the door. He jammed it against the table to act as a weight, hoping to slow the creatures' attempts to gain entry into the room.

The thumping continued.

The fridge rattled with each blow.

Farris screamed over and over and over.

Maude sat back in her chair wearing a look of dismay.

Saul trained his three-oh-three back upon the door.

It was only a matter of time before they would all be dead.

XII

Blood sprayed over the chassis and windows of parked vehicles and formed small puddles in places across the snow-covered ground. Bodies lay strewn across cars in awkward positions as gunfire mowed them down.

Still, they came.

"Shit," Freeburg whispered as he pushed his face against the bars covering his window to see the ground near the front of the building. He stood toward the western end of the corridor where there were seemingly fewer invaders approaching than at the rest of the school's façade.

Below him were some creatures pressed against the wall. One had climbed onto a protruding windowsill on the level below him and was reaching up the wall with its long white fingers.

Suddenly it sprung up from the ground and could almost reach the window at which he stood.

He angled his rifle straight down and fired. A three-shot burst met its target, opening the creature's head like a canoe. Dark liquid splashed onto the snow below moments before the body hit the ground, twisting and convulsing in spasm.

The other nearby creatures noticed the structural weakness and speedily made their way to the protruding windowsill, ignoring their fallen comrade.

"Redhawke," Freeburg called into his walkie-talkie. "You copy?"

***

Deputy Colin Redhawke was taking careful aim and knocking down targets that were less than twenty yards out. There weren't many as most of the gunfire was keeping the infected about fifty yards out. He had just popped a bullet between the eyes of a screaming creature that was half hiding behind a tree, staring straight at him, when the call came over the radio.

"Redhawke," he replied into the walkie-talkie. "Who's this?"

"Miles Freeburg. Can you see beneath my window from your location?"

Redhawke craned his neck, turning his head to the right and pressed the side of his face against the bars. He saw a gathering of infected people on the ground just outside the building.

"I see them," Redhawke said. "If anyone is listening, we have about five of these things on the ground just below Freeburg's position. I can't get a bead on them at this angle. Looks like a protrusion under one of the first level's windows. The infected are climbing onto it as I speak. We may need additional defence in the southwestern sector."

"Copy," Dawson replied. "I'm sending five men to assist."

"I'm doing the same," Vaughn informed them. "But I may need to recall them if any get past you, Redhawke."

"Understood," Redhawke responded. "Let me know when they get there, Miles."

"Will do," Freeburg called back before lowering the walkie-talkie and aiming his rifle back out of the window and toward the ground below him.

Five fully armed men ran from the northern corridor, through the western sector toward Freeburg's position. Another five men ran from the eastern sector toward the same location, dodging people who were moving supplies into rooms nearby.

Freeburg and two other men aimed low and squeezed off rounds into the infected that had made it to the protruding ledge. The men momentarily thought they had a handle on the situation until they noticed several creatures approaching from just inside the tree line that ran along the border of the school's property to the west.

"We're here. Where do you need us?" announced one man.

"Uh," Freeburg grunted as he quickly turned to acknowledge the newcomers. "We have a situation directly below us that we are taking care of at the moment. But there are some others coming from the trees over there." The firefighter pointed with his chin toward the encroaching creatures to the west.

The men raced to the windows to assess the conditions outside.

The sight of the infected horde was overwhelming. They moved like a heaving, pulsating mass with one focus. Individual beings broke from the crowd and leapt over vehicles toward the building, only to get torn into by bullets before crashing to the ground in a bloodied heap.

Directly below the window was a small group of animals peering up toward the onlooking men. They would scamper onto the protruding window ledge and spring toward them, attempting to grab the bottom of the window ledge at which the men stood watching. Freeburg, or one of the other men in the room, would reward the creatures' attempts by blasting their faces open with an M-16.

The men then turned their attention to the tree line.

Numerous invaders were moving from the road and into the cover of the forest to get around the onslaught of bullets. They had found a weakness below the southwestern section of the building and looked as if they were about to try to exploit it.

"Well," one of the men started. "We gonna shoot 'em or what?"

"Can't," answered another. "We'll be wasting bullets. They have the cover of the trees and they're moving toward the building at an angle we can't reach from here."

"So, we just wait for them to get to the ground below us?" the first man asked.

"No," Freeburg replied. "We need some people in the room next door to shoot those bastards as they come out of the tree line." He pointed toward the western corridor as he spoke.

"That's our job," one of the newcomers answered. And with that, the ten men left the room.

"Sheriff, you there?" Freeburg inquired into the walkie-talkie.

"Dawson here."

"The men have arrived. I've positioned them in the room closest to me in the western corridor. We have some of these things using the trees for cover."

"Copy that," Dawson replied. "Good call, Miles."

XIII

The intensity of each blow against the door had increased. The refrigerator slid little by little back toward the three gas station workers. The table rocked on its end as the door opened wider and wider.

Farris had fallen silent and was staring at the floor. Saul had called to him on several occasions but received no response.

Maude had turned to bawling her eyes out. She had come to grips that this was the end for her. She understood that she was neither fit enough nor equipped with the skills to escape.

Saul let her cry.

It was no use trying to be silent now. They were breaking in. So, let her cry.

It's her fucking fault they found us.

The door opened wider as the things smashed against it with all their weight.

White hands with blackened fingernails reached into the room through the widening gap, gripping the edges of the door and surrounding wall.

Wider and wider the door opened.

Forearms, elbows and shoulders gradually became visible.

Suddenly a face glared into the room. Its ghastly white eyes and yellow teeth were enough to set Farris off screaming again.

BLAM!

The creature's head disappeared, leaving a spray of blood on the wall and door. Saul slid the bolt, ejected the spent shell and reloaded the three-oh-three.

It wasn't enough to persuade the others to quit.

The door continued to open farther and farther.

Maude reached for the Magnum in Farris' hands. She grabbed it by the barrel and tried to take it from him. He reacted by gripping it tighter and pulling it back toward himself.

"No," he cried. "No."

"Give it to me," she barked as she yanked and yanked.

"No," he screamed. "No. No."

BLAM!

Saul hit the wall behind another intruding face. He slid the bolt and took another shot. The bullet hit the creature in the neck, and a pulsating spray of blood squirted into the room as the beast fell.

"I need it, Farris," she shrieked. "Give it."

He continued to struggle against her, grunting and yelling in her face.

BLAM!

Saul slid the bolt ready for the next target.

"No!" Farris bellowed as he pulled the trigger.

Maude stepped back in surprise.

She raised her hand to the smoking hole in her chest. Her mouth was wide open as she turned her gaze to Saul.

"What just happened?" she asked before falling on her side.

The door slid farther open.

White grimacing faces appeared.

"What the fuck did you do?" Saul glared at Farris.

"No!" Farris blared at Maud.

She moved her eyes to him as she tried to suck air into her lungs.

He pulled the hammer back and shot her again, hitting her in the neck. A hole the size of a fingertip seeped a thin line of blood onto the ground.

"Fuck!" Saul shouted. "Farris? What the fuck?"

"No!" he screamed as he trained his weapon upon Saul and fired.

Saul fell onto his rear, back against the wall. The bullet had hit him in the stomach and burned like hell.

"Farris?"

The.357 Magnum fired again.

Blood ran from above Saul's left eye, down along his nose and dripped from his chin to his lap.

"No," Farris cried as he placed the hot muzzle against his head.

***

Dewey had heard the gunfire but couldn't see the commotion. The creatures had thinned out from around the truck as whatever was happening drew them away from him momentarily.

He saw this as an opportunity that he couldn't waste.

Quickly as he could, Dewey climbed into the driver's seat and pressed the ignition button on the dash.

The truck immediately roared to life.

At that same moment, the creatures suddenly returned their attention to the yellow fire truck.

They leapt and crawled across the vehicle, screaming and thumping at the windows.

The old man knocked the truck into reverse and hit the accelerator. It lunged backward and tore through the large metal roller door at the front of the workshop.

Some white figures fell from the vehicle, injuring themselves on the broken door as they desperately attempted to keep hold.

Dewey could see a trail of liquid in the truck's wake as it crossed snow-covered ground. Something had torn through the tubes under the vehicle.

He couldn't be sure if the damage was from the door he had just broken through or from the creatures that had been trying to break in earlier.

The creatures speedily made their way out of the garage through the ruined workshop door and focused on the truck.

Dewey kept his foot planted, unable to see where he was going. He eventually smashed rear first into a parked car just a few yards outside of the workshop.

The creatures were all over the vehicle again.

He could see others in the road also running directly for him.

Too many to count.

There was no movement from within the garage. From his position, he could see the door to the lunchroom. It was broken from its hinge and spattered with blood.

His heart broke as he thought about what might have happened to Maude and the boys.

"You bastards," he whimpered, and he stifled his tears.

He needed to decide to either hightail it towards the highschool or do something stupid.

He pushed the stick to drive and planted his foot again.

The truck lurched forward as he turned toward the gas pumps.

The creatures bashed and slammed themselves against the exterior of the vehicle.

Dewey hit the first of the gas pumps with the truck and slammed his foot on the brake. The truck slid forwards, taking out the adjacent pump before coming to a complete stop.

Fuel spurted up from the ground beneath the fire truck and spread across the ground in all directions. A great puddle of gas formed.

The creatures seemed impervious to this as they continued to clamber over the cabin of the vehicle.

Dewey took a deep breath as he reached into his coverall pockets. He produced a packet of cigarettes and a lighter.

The cab rocked from side to side.

The old man placed a cigarette between his lips and lit it. He drew back, deep and long.

Several creatures screeched a loud cry as more and more of their kind bolted toward the gas station.

He exhaled a thin band of bluish smoke into the cab and smiled as tears welled in his eyes.

"I hope you're ready for this, boys," he said to the figures outside of his window.

Pasty faces with dark lips glared back at him hungrily.

He took one last long drag on his cigarette.

"Here we go," he announced.

He lifted the handle on the driver's door and pushed with all of his might. The door reluctantly opened as three figures clung on, trying to reach over the door to get to the old man.

Other creatures to the side of the door grabbed him with their claws and dragged him from the cab. One reached in with its gaping mouth and sank its yellow teeth into his arm, drawing blood.

The pain was excruciating.

He winced in agony.

But in moments, it wouldn't matter.

Dewey spread his fingers wide, allowing the lit cigarette to fall.

It bounced off his knee, against the torso of a creature and onto the step below the door. There it stayed, teetering as if making a hard decision as to cling to life or fall to impending death.

The creatures ripped the old man from the truck and dragged him to the ground.

The truck rocked violently.

The lit cigarette tilted.

Tilted.

Fell.

XIV

"Cheese and crackers!" Andy bellowed as the fireball rose into the sky. "Did anyone else see that?"

Timothy and Justin, bag boys from the grocery store, suddenly turned and saw the dying glow of the orange orb of flame. The three boys pressed their faces against the classroom window and peered into the night beyond the glass. Until that moment, the three young men were talking about cars, video games and music. Things that really mattered.

"I think that was the gas station," mumbled Paul Harris, the elderly caretaker of the church, as he carefully crossed the classroom to the window next to the boy. He pushed his thick glasses up to his eyes and tilted his head back to view through the magnified bifocal section on the bottom of his spectacles. "Something hit the tanks for sure."

Deputy Vaughn lifted the walkie-talkie to his lips as he peered through the glass, "Looks like the gas station just blew up, boss."

"Copy that," Dawson replied. "How are you guys holding up over there?"

"No trouble as of yet," Vaughn replied. He pressed the side of his face against the window. The cold surface sent a quick shiver into his body as he saw the edge of the horde outside moving toward the southern sector. Gunfire resonated through the corridor outside of the room as he witnessed several creatures falling into the snow as bullets ripped into them. "Request permission to help the guys at the front of the school."

Betty Sue suddenly looked to Vaughn. Her eyes told him she wanted him to stay right here. Everything in her willed and wished for Dawson to deny the deputy's request. Vaughn read her face and cursed himself silently for saying those words.

"Negative," the sheriff answered. Betty Sue was relieved to hear those words. So was Vaughn. "I need you where you are in case they make it around to the east."

"Understood, boss."

"You asshole," she hissed as he made his way to her. She lifted herself from the lounge she was sitting in and thumped him on the chest as he wrapped his arms around her.

"I'm sorry, baby," he said as he held her tighter.

"Don't ever do that again," she ordered. "What were you thinking?"

"I wasn't thinking," he replied. "I'm sorry."

She buried her head into his chest and wept.

Vaughn glanced around the room and saw every eye focused on him. Andy and the boys, old Mister Harris, the three checkout girls from Stop N' Save and Carl Mason who was standing near the door.

"And when were you going to fill me in about this little relation-ship?" Mason grunted.

"I'm sorry Mister Mason," Vaughn started. "It's just that..."

"Daddy," Betty Sue said as the deputy was still speaking. "I was going to tell you but..."

"Oh, shut up the both of you," Harris chuckled. "The whole town knew about you two. Your dad's just funnin' with you."

Mason let his composure fall as a wide grin grew on his face. He sauntered over to the window and rested the butt of his rifle against the sill as he peered into the darkness beyond.

"Hey look," he said with a hint of cheer and sarcasm. "It's snowing."

XV

Donald Gibb crossed between the loading dock and the house. The gravel and snow crunched under his feet as he drew nearer to the fence-line that bordered the yard and the nearest northern field.

Thunder rolled through the valley as sheet lightning flashed above the mountain peaks to the south and east. It was what he thought was the thunder that drew his attention toward the town sometime earlier.

After several minutes of staring into the darkness, his eyes focused on something that now had him transfixed. He moved from the dock and headed for the fence to see if the angle of view was better.

Some cows had gathered near the fence during the height of the storm and snorted softly as he approached them. Ignoring them, he rested his elbow on top of a fence post and peered back toward the town.

Anthony Gibb sat in an old rocking chair on the front porch watching his son with curiosity. He took a sip of his steaming coffee that his wife Sallie had just handed to him before she returned inside to get out of the cold.

She never understood how a man could sit out in such freezing conditions for what she deemed a long time. Inside was warmth from a fire and TV cooking shows. For her, that was ideal.

For him, cooking shows were a sure sign of the end to come.

"What's going on, Donny?" he called.

"Town's on fire," the younger man replied.

Anthony rose to his feet and strolled toward his son. As he walked, his eyes followed the straight line that was the main road. It led his gaze to the low clouds moving quickly above the town.

A bright orange glow resonated from the ground and reflected off the clouds above. A rise in the terrain blocked any view of the town itself, but both men knew that something was definitely ablaze.

"Lightning strike?" Anthony asked.

"Been hearing thunder all night," Donald replied. "Could be just that."

"Maybe we should take the truck to see if they need help," the older man suggested.

"Wait," said a voice behind them.

Both turned to see Jerry, one of the farmhands, holding a pair of binoculars to his eyes.

"Someone's coming," he informed the others.

"Where?" Donald asked.

"On the road," Jerry replied. "Two. No. Three, I think. Too far and too dark to see exactly. Can just make their shadows out against the glare."

Jerry handed the binoculars to Donald. The younger Gibb held the glasses to his eyes and moved the sites back and forth across the horizon.

"Where?"

"Go to where the road goes over the rise and follow the road back toward us," Jerry instructed.

Donald scanned until he found the road. He didn't see any people there. Slowly, he followed the road back toward them until he saw movement.

At least three figures were running in the snow.

Suddenly they disappeared into the shadow being caused by the rise in the terrain blocking the glare of the fire.

"Shit," Donald lowered the binoculars. "I lost them."

"Three, right?" Jerry asked.

"At least," Donald replied.

"Kane and me will take the truck and see if they need help," Jerry offered, "if you want us to, Mister Gibb."

"Sure," Anthony agreed. Send Mike and Adam out here before you go, please Jerry."

"Yessir," Jerry jogged toward the loading dock and vanished inside the building.

"What are you thinking, Dad?" Donald asked as he scanned the road with the binoculars again, unsuccessfully.

"I'm thinking we need to get the boys locked and loaded," Anthony Gibb retorted. "Something just ain't sittin' right about this."

XVI

They moved Brad to the couch where he lay covered in blankets. He constantly complained about how cold and thirsty he was. Tiffany checked his temperature with the back of her hand.

"You're roasting," she informed him. "You have a fever."

"What's wrong with him?" Julia asked.

Stan closed the basement door, passed through the kitchen and entered the living room. He had just dragged the creature's body down the stairs and left it slumped against the washing machine. "How is he?"

"He's boiling," Tiffany replied. "He keeps asking for water and says he's cold."

"I *am* cold," he barked. Stan watched as his friend shivered under the thick blanket he had pulled up under his chin. Brad's face had lost its color and dark rings had formed around his eyes. "I think I need a doctor."

"I do too," Stan agreed. He crossed the living room to a phone that hung on the wall near the kitchen. He lifted the receiver and began dialling.

"I need water," Brad wheezed.

"Who are you calling?" Julia asked as she handed Brad another glass of water.

"The hospital," Stan replied as he listened to the dial tone. "They might send someone."

"I don't think so, my friend." Brad shook his head. "We saw a lot of those things running up the street. That's why we came to get you earlier."

"What do you mean?" Tiffany looked from Brad to Julia.

"We heard a crash outside when you two were sleeping on your mom's bed," Julia explained. "We looked out through the blinds in your room and we saw them. I just thought they were people, but there were some who were naked, and they didn't move like people."

"That's when I came to get you," Brad interjected.

"So, we can't leave?" Stan inquired. "There may be more out there?"

"There *are* more out there, man." Brad tried to sit up but failed. He almost spilled the near-empty glass of water he was holding onto himself. "I think the whole town has been taken over by them."

"No answer," said Stan as he placed the receiver back into the cradle.

"What do we do?" Tiffany asked.

"I don't know," Brad replied. "But whatever it is, you better think of something quick. Judging by this, you don't have much time." He held up his hand that held the glass. Dark lines had spread down his arm, across the back of his hands and along the length of his fingers. "I think, soon you'll have another one of those things to deal with."

XVII

It crept on its hands and toes, keeping the silent vehicles between itself and the large building.

Thunderous claps and muzzle fire continuously streamed from the upper windows.

It cowered as bullets hit, bounced and zinged on the chassis of the wagon it hid behind.

Snarling, it lunged over the vehicle and bolted upright toward the building. Snow and mud kicked up all around it as ammunition ripped into the ground.

Blood sprayed against its bare chest as another beside it copped a hit in the face.

It didn't matter.

The urge to feast was too strong for fear to dictate any form of self-preservation.

It darted to the left and then the right as it avoided more parked vehicles and merged with a thronging crowd of ravenous creatures.

Something urged it to move to its left and ignore the reward of flesh in the windows above.

It didn't care that the guns were slaughtering others like itself, as they grew closer to the building. The fear of death had no hold.

But the urge...

Oh, the urge held too much power to resist.

It quickly ran through the horde, moving toward the tree line to the side of the building.

Muzzle flares and the terrifying crack of gunfire were here too. But they focused on the trees. They shot away from the side of the building.

It was darker here.

The ground slightly sloped upwards and a downpipe near the first open window would make a perfect aid to climb the wall.

The creature slunk into the shadow between the building and the tree line and moved along the wall until it reached the downpipe.

Carefully, and precariously it climbed, keeping the blaring muzzle of the assault rifle above in its sights as it moved hand over hand.

Higher and higher.

***

His Red Socks cap was slightly askew as he popped shot after shot into the tree line, picking off the creatures one by one. Carefully and deliberately, he waited until each target was in sight before squeezing the trigger. Each shot was rewarded with a direct hit.

He saw another bald-headed monster running between the neatly planted rows of trees and took aim. His finger squeezed the trigger and...

Nothing.

"I'm out," he called over his shoulder.

"I'm up," replied another gunman wearing a baseball cap, Yankees.

Red Socks lifted himself from his crouching position and moved back into the classroom toward a small ammunition cache the men had set up near the door to the room. Yankees positioned himself where Red Socks had been and took aim.

"Where are we?" Yankees asked.

"Go to about somewhere between twelve and one," Red Socks replied. "You see him?"

Yankees aimed his M-16 and panned to the right slightly and saw the creature moving between the trees. "Yeah, I got him."

BANG!

The creature fell to the ground as blood sprayed from its neck. Yankees panned back and started to target another creature.

It was moving to the right, keeping the trees between itself and the building. Yankees could not get a clear shot and was willing the creature to take a more direct route toward the building; one that wouldn't take it behind another tree.

"Come on," Yankees urged. "Come on."

The creature paused momentarily.

It was an open target.

Yankees squeezed on the trigger slightly.

The creature moved to the right, behind another fucking tree.

"You bitch," Yankees snorted.

The creature paused again and seemed to sniff the air.

Yankees waited and watched. His finger rested on the trigger.

It turned toward the building and made its way forward. Directly toward Yankees.

The gunman smiled as he carefully squeezed the trigger.

"Now I got you," Yankees whispered.

A creature lifted itself through the window, wrenching the assault rifle from his grasp. It tossed the M-16 to the floor as it pounced upon Yankees and sank its teeth into his face.

Red Socks snapped his head around to see what the commotion was.

Yankees was screaming a high-pitched wail as the creature wriggled its face back and forth, using its teeth like a saw to dig into the flesh of its prey.

"Fuck me," Red Socks bellowed as he slammed a new magazine into the assault rifle. "Fuck me."

Blood sprayed across the room as the creature pulled its face away from Yankees, clenching a large sheet of flesh in its teeth.

Red Socks almost choked on his own bile at the sight of his friend. The creature had torn the skin away from Yankees' lower lip to the collar. White bone and teeth protruded grotesquely from pulsating dark, wet flesh and stringy sinew.

"Fuck me," he called again.

The creature dropped the body to the floor and turned its attention upon the other gunman in the room. It opened its bloodstained mouth and shrieked.

Red Socks lifted the rifle and fired a three-shot burst into the creature's chest. It fell instantly and writhed a little before coming to a rest.

"Fuck me," the gunman called once more before he heard another voice beside him.

"Let's go," the voice ordered. "Now. Snap out of it and move."

Red Socks refocused and saw a man in army fatigues standing next to him. The soldier had his hands on the gunman's shoulders and was pulling him toward the door. On the soldier's chest was a nametag.

SHARPE.

"Come on," Sharpe yelled.

His legs started to move toward the door as he took a quick glance back to his friend on the floor. A pool of blood was forming around Yankee's head and torso.

It was then that he noticed the other figures climbing in through the window.

Reality kicked in and he darted through the door.

Sharpe pulled the door shut behind them and held the handle tight.

THUD!

One creature rammed itself against the door.

Red Socks grabbed what he could of the handle and pulled back with his weight.

THUD!

THUD!

Sharpe noticed a keyhole near the handle he was holding onto for dear life. He reached with one hand to retrieve the walkie-talkie clipped into his belt.

"Does anyone know where the groundskeeper is?" he called into the radio.

"He's with me," Dawson replied. "Who's this?"

"Sharpe," the soldier replied. "I need him to come and lock a door. Some of those fuckers made it up the side of the building over here."

THUD!

"Fuck!" Sharpe cried. "Room forty-nine," he shouted into the walkie-talkie. "Room fucking forty-nine."

***

Running as fast as she could, Sandra Upton bolted westward along the southern corridor with Dawson in tow. She raised her M-16A2 to shoulder level as she rounded the corner to the left.

"All available guns to the south-west now," Dawson bellowed into the walkie-talkie as he desperately attempted to keep up with the young private. Some curious faces peered out through doorways as he ran by. "Back inside. Back inside," he instructed.

The footfalls of Barry Webster, the school's groundskeeper, were falling away behind him. He saw Sharpe and another man in a baseball cap holding the door shut at the far end of the long passage.

Swiftly, Dawson clipped the radio back onto his belt and lifted the assault rifle to his shoulder. Upton levelled her rifle on the door as she pulled up to a stop next to Sharpe and the other man. The sheriff was still about halfway along the corridor at this moment. Webster had just made his way around the corner from the southern passage into the western sector.

The groundskeeper frantically fumbled through his keys as he ran. His slightly overweight build made him slower than Dawson would like him to be. In saying that, the sheriff respected the effort and had to acknowledge that the man was moving faster than most people in his condition.

THUMP! THUMP!

Dawson almost skidded to a halt next to Upton and pointed the muzzle of his M-16 at the center of the door. He breathed in deeply through his nose and out through his mouth, attempting to silence the loud beating of his heart that pumped in his ears.

"You okay, Chief?" Upton asked.

"Getting old, Cadet," he replied with a wry smile.

Webster finally caught up with the key ready in his hand. He ducked and squeezed himself between Sharpe and Red Socks and slid the key into the lock. With a twist to the left, the door locked.

THUMP!

"Shit!" The groundskeeper fell backward, landing on his posterior.

"You sure this is locked?" Sharpe asked the wide-eyed man sprawled on the floor.

"Huh?" Webster moved his eyes from the door to the soldier gripping the handle. "Yeah, yeah. It's as secure as it's going to get."

Sharpe let go of the handle and instantly trained his weapon on the door. Red Socks took the action as silent instruction and did the same. Both men stepped back in line with Dawson and Upton.

"Now what?" Upton asked.

"How many are in there?" Dawson asked.

"They were still climbing in through the window when we closed the door," Sharpe replied. "I counted three. Could be more by now."

"Barry?" The sheriff directed his attention to the groundskeeper who had lifted himself back onto his feet.

"Yeah," he wheezed between heavy breaths.

A few men from the southern sector had gathered around, answering the call for support that Dawson had made moments earlier.

"I need something heavy to block this door. What do you suggest?"

"Lockers," he panted. "The student lockers in the southern corridor are freestanding. They're metal, about six feet high by eight wide, and full of the students' belongings."

"Perfect," Dawson stated. "You men help Barry move those lockers here and put two of the heaviest ones against this door."

THUMP! THUMP!

"And we're on a time limit here, gentlemen," the sheriff explained as the men moved away.

"Dwight, you there?" Sharpe called into his radio. A momentary silence passed for what seemed an eternity. "Dwight, come back."

"We're a little busy right now, Frank," Krane replied. "We've got fuckers in the tree line and fuckers climbing the wall out here."

"We know," Sharpe informed. "They have breached the building. Concentrate as much fire as you can on those fuckers climbing the wall. They're getting in through a window here."

"Already ahead of you."

The corridor suddenly filled with the sound of loud scraping and metallic rattling as Webster and a group of five men pushed a large, tall gray box around the corner from the southern sector into the western passageway.

Eventually, the men placed the locker unit across the door to the classroom, covering the access entirely. They quickly retreated to collect another unit from the southern corridor.

"I want someone armed out here watching this at all times," Dawson instructed Sharpe.

"I'll do it," Red Socks volunteered.

"It'll be in shifts," Dawson put in.

"And I want the doctor to check you over," Sharpe instructed.

"What the hell for?" Red Socks appeared offended.

"Shock," the private answered.

"But I'm fine," the gunman insisted.

"It's not a debate," Dawson said. "Go get checked, now. Rejoin us as soon as you can."

XVIII

Jerry crawled the pickup truck along the middle of the road as Kane, standing in the tray behind the cab, swung a hand-held spotlight from left to right. The bright beam of light broke through the darkness in a widening beam before it exploded in a large circle of white light on the snow-covered ground.

The wind had picked up, bringing with it stinging wisps of snow that struck Kane unforgivingly on his bare skin. He pulled his hood tighter around his head, adjusted his goggles and turned the light from the right side of the road back toward the left.

"I don't see nothing," he called over the howl of the wind. "It's fuckin' cold out here, man."

"No shit," Jerry replied. The window was down to hear Kane, but he sure as shit stank wished he had it wound up. "Can you still see the house?"

Kane turned his head to look behind the vehicle. Lights from the house and the surrounding buildings were visible. He could make out the figures of four people on the porch gathered near the door. In all the time it took to sweep the light back and forth, back and forth, they had moved about half a mile at best.

"Yeah," he replied.

"Okay," Jerry called. "I think we're about halfway to the rise. We'll go there and then turn around. What do you think?"

"I think I want to turn around n—" Kane suddenly stopped as he thought he saw something cross the road about ten yards in front of them. Jerry must have seen it too as he pulled the car to a complete stop.

"Did you see that?" Jerry called.

"Yeah," he responded. "It went over there." He held the light in an area to the right of the road. He moved it a little to the left, aiming it at the fence-line parallel to the road, and then moved it slowly back to the right.

Nothing.

"Where did it go?" Kane called.

He sustained his slow sweeping of the light toward the right.

"Call out," Jerry instructed as he climbed out of the cab, leaving the engine running. "Maybe they need help."

"Hey," Kane called as he continued to move the light slowly to the right. "Anyone there?"

The light moved across an area just to the front right side of the pickup truck. Kane directed the beam from the side of the road, to the fence-line and back, all the while moving it slowly to the right.

He continued this motion as Jerry moved in front of the vehicle, his frame squarely in the beams of the headlights.

"Hello," Jerry called.

"Do you need help?" Kane bellowed.

Blank snow with bony wooden posts lined up in a long row stared back at Kane.

There was nothing.

Nobody.

He felt his teeth chatter.

"Hey," Jerry screamed.

Kane was about to call again. He wasn't about to let Jerry get the better of him. He needed to demonstrate his ability to withstand the cold longer than the other man.

Can't go back a pussy!

Movement to his left made him pause momentarily.

He snapped his head toward the front of the vehicle.

Jerry was gone.

"Jerry?" Kane called. "Jerry? Where the fuck did you go?"

Kane swung the spotlight to the left. The beam crossed those of the headlights and moved over the road's surface.

There in the ditch that lined the left side of the road lay Jerry.

A white figure in jeans and a plaid shirt had its face buried into Jerry's neck. It shook its pasty, bald head as it opened and closed its jaws, spilling blood onto the soft, clean white surface of the ground.

"Shit!" Kane dropped the spotlight onto the tray with a loud clank. "Fuck!"

Jerry writhed and twisted in the darkness as Kane dropped to the ground and moved toward the figure intending to help his friend.

The figure stopped and turned toward Kane.

Hunkering over its kill, it bared its blood-soaked teeth as it shrieked loudly before returning to feed.

The blood was dark and thick. It drifted across the ground as the figure chewed and crunched bone and sinew from Jerry's neck.

Kane turned to see another two bald, white figures standing on the side of the road to the right of the vehicle. Their hunched bodies stood motionless as they cocked their heads, eyeballing Kane as he used every ounce of being to stifle a scream.

Quickly, Kane leaped into the pickup truck and slammed the door closed behind him. He pushed the stick into reverse and slammed his foot onto the gas.

The tires spun for an eternity as they sought traction on the icy surface of the road.

The two creatures moved. One ran around the front of the vehicle toward the driver's door, and the other leaped onto the roof, causing the pickup truck to bounce.

The pickup truck slid backward little by little.

Kane reached for the window handle and frantically turned. The window began to rise.

The creature climbed over the hood and thudded against the windshield.

"Fuck," Kane called as the vehicle suddenly lunged backward.

The creature fell from the front and landed spread-eagled on the ground.

Kane continued another ten yards in reverse before turning the truck at an angle. He now had the rear of the vehicle pointed toward the right side of the road.

With a glance back down toward the mayhem that had just occurred, he pushed the stick into first gear. Jerry was still being consumed by the first creature on the side of the road. The other was rising to its feet.

Kane accelerated and started to turn back toward the farm.

Something suddenly blocked his view.

A white hand with black claws grabbed him by his face and pulled him toward the partially open window.

Kane struggled to escape the grasp of the creature. It was too strong for him.

He reached to the handle with all of his might and started winding the window with his left hand while hitting at the figure's face with his right.

The creature let go of Kane's head and grabbed his right hand instead.

Within less than a second, his fingers were in the creature's mouth. It bit hard and held tight.

Kane heaved with all of his might as he screamed in agony.

Bones cracked and flesh split as he got free from the grasp of the thing outside. He quickly wound the window the rest of its way closed and moved the car forward as the creature bashed itself against the door.

Kane suddenly felt hot.

His vision blurred slightly, and he started seeing double.

Two farmhouses. Two loading docks. Two steering wheels.

He pulled the pickup truck to the right and slammed into the ditch.

What is happening?

The heat was unbearable.

He looked at his hands. The skin was turning pale, dark veins formed like spider webs and his fingernails were turning black. Dark blood oozed from where his two missing fingers once were.

God help me!

His throat was itchy and forced him to cough violently.

Blood sprayed across the windshield.

His forehead burned with intensity.

Why?

He pulled his hood off and wiped at his brow. Hair fell in clumps onto his lap.

Hunger engulfed him.

He needed to feed.

XIX

The man in the Red Socks cap lay as stiff as a board on the table in the science lab. Vanderberg aimed a pen-sized flashlight into the man's eyes and flicked the light away repetitively.

"What's your name?"

"Frank," Red Socks replied. His voice shook with fear. "Frank Levinson."

"You're all right, Frank." Vanderberg smiled. "I'm just making sure that you haven't suffered any substantial wounds or are being overcome with shock."

"Am I?"

"Are you what?"

"Wounded and going into shock?" Frank asked, following the doctor with his eyes as he moved across the room.

"No shock," replied Vanderberg as he lifted a small self-adhesive bandage from the bench near the windows. "But you do have a small wound."

"Wha..? Where?" Frank tilted his head this way and that in an attempt to see.

"Just a slight graze that you probably got scraping against the floor or doorframe. I'll treat it and you'll be right to go."

Vanderberg placed the bandage over a tiny red mark on Frank's hand.

"There." He nodded. "All better."

"Would you wike a fuckin' wowwy pop?" Burkley grunted from his seat behind a desk.

XX

Andy sat on the floor of the teachers' lounge with his back against the wall. He chewed on a large piece of salty beef jerky as he tried not to watch Deputy Vaughn and Betty Sue Mason making out on the couch across the room from him.

It made him feel uncomfortable, just like when Stan and Brad would play tonsil hockey with their girlfriends right in front of him. They seemed to enjoy taunting him with their successful relationships. Slapping him in the face with their expressive emotions compiled with excessive hormones and pant-stretching boners.

Fuck them.

He shook the thought away and chewed harder on his jerky before swallowing a mouthful of salty saliva.

The others had found a place around the room to sit and ponder things for the moment. The bag boys from Stop N' Save snuggled against a wall with two of the checkout girls. Evan Putney, the manager of the grocery store, sat at the table nursing a steaming cup of coffee while he talked to the other checkout girl. Carl Mason stood near the window as if waiting for something to happen.

"What's wrong, son?" asked Paul Harris, the elderly man from the church.

Andy turned his head to face the old man who sat in a large armchair in the corner nearby. Harris' eyes were deep and slightly wet. The boy wasn't sure if the old man had been crying or whether it was just something that happened when one got older. He had seen many old people with watery eyes and had never given it a thought before.

"Nothing, sir," Andy replied. "I just wish the night was over."

The old man shook his head slightly and closed his eyes.

"I don't think the sun's rising will stop those things out there, boy."

Andy kept his gaze on the old men, but in the corner of his eye, he could see the girl at the table turn her face toward Harris.

"What do you mean?" she asked.

The old man just shook his head and let out a soft sigh.

"Please Mister Harris," she begged.

"I'm an old man and not long for this world anyway," he replied. "But I don't believe any of us will make it out alive."

She moved her gaze from Harris to the boy nearby on the floor chewing jerky. Her eyes darted to Vaughn and Betty Sue, to the other girls and the bag boys and back to Andy.

"Right," she said.

She rose to her feet and crossed the small section of floor between her and Andy. Stooping slightly, she grabbed Andy's hand and pulled. Andy instinctively rose to his feet and let her lead him out the door of the teachers' lounge.

"The room directly across the hall is available," Mason called without taking his gaze from the window.

They crossed the corridor and entered the room. He closed the door while she turned on the light.

She immediately started unbuttoning her blouse. Andy was speechless as she undid one button, then two, three. Her cleavage was showing. She opened her shirt, revealing a frilly white lace bra cradling her shapely breasts.

"Wait," he interrupted. "Please."

She stopped. Her face wore an expression of confusion.

Andy looked at her intently.

She was beautiful.

"What's wrong?" She tightened her eyebrows, causing a soft wrinkle on her forehead.

"I..." Andy swallowed the beef jerky. He could feel the lump sliding down his throat slowly. "I don't know your name."

She smiled and slowly walked to him. Taking him in her arms, she reached up to his forehead with her lips and kissed him there.

"I'm Tina," she said as a tear fell down her cheek.

"I'm Andy," he replied with a smile before softly pressing his lips against hers.

XXI

"How many are out there?" Redhawke called to the men in the room with him.

"It's the whole town, Deputy," replied Harry Rourke. He took aim with his M-16 and fired.

"We can't keep this up." The deputy shook his head and lifted the walkie to his lips. "Sheriff, you there?"

"Yeah," Dawson responded.

"I think we need to use some artillery on these things," Redhawke suggested. "There's just too many and ammo is getting low."

A vast crowd of creatures sprang over the bullet-riddled vehicles, crawled across the bloodstained snow and continued toward the high school.

Max Dooley, the barkeeper, took up the position on the window alongside Rourke and started firing into the crowd. Both ex-marines were relentless. They levelled the closest invaders first before targeting others farther back.

But the creatures were cunning.

They had used the vehicles as cover and waited for the gunmen to reload or ease up before advancing.

"You should have a launcher in one of the crates in the corridor," Private Sandra Upton announced through the walkie. "Look for *RPG* stencilled on the side."

"I'll check," Redhawke replied as he exited the room.

Various sized crates were piled against the far wall of the corridor. He scanned with his eyes for the letters *RPG*. He saw numbers and letters for many other things and uttered, "RPG, RPG," repeatedly as he searched.

Finally, his eyes landed on them. They were on a larger crate underneath a few others. He moved them onto the floor nearby as quickly as he could. After clearing the crate of obstruction, he unhinged the clips and opened the lid.

A long tube-like object with a trigger mechanism lay neatly surrounded by moulded padding inside. It was the only thing inside the box. He couldn't see any ammunition.

He lifted the walkie to his mouth and screamed, "There're no bullets."

"It's fully loaded," Upton replied. "One shot only."

"One shot?" Redhawke grunted to himself. He lifted the launcher out of the box and ran back into the room. "Only one shot," he announced.

"Then we better make it matter," replied Rourke as he rested his rifle against the wall below the window. "Give it to me."

Redhawke handed the tube to the ex-marine. Rourke rested the tube on his shoulder and pointed the RPG launcher out the window. He scanned for the best target that would make the most damage.

"Gotcha," he sneered as the crosshairs landed in a small red bubble-shaped vehicle; a small Chevrolet Sonic sitting in the middle of a large crowd of creatures.

Rourke pulled the trigger.

A long orange glow flared across the air, trailing smoke behind it like a falling meteor. It hit the side of the Sonic hard. A large fireball ensued, swallowing up at least fifty of the creatures that were surrounding the vehicle.

"Gotcha," Rourke roared into the night.

A chorus of high-pitched screams resounded through the darkness as if to say, *we're still here.*

"We need a few more of those rocket launchers if we're going to make a dent in them fuckers out there," Dooley muttered.

XXII

"What are we going to do?" Mayor Harold Waring moaned as he sat in a large office chair.

"Snap out of it, you old fool," retorted Agnes as she paced back and forth across the room. "There's not a thing you or I can do."

"I should have seen this coming," Waring whined. "I should have done something."

"No one saw this coming, Harold," she barked.

Waring closed his mouth, placed his head in his hands and sobbed.

"This is not the time to place blame," Dawson announced. "Especially on ourselves."

He turned to Lilly Geddes, the school principal.

"Any ideas or input would be appreciated," Dawson urged.

"I don't know what I could tell you," she replied.

"What about a contingency plan?" he asked. "If we need to get out of here, what would you recommend?"

She turned to Barry Webster, the groundskeeper. Her eyes pleaded for him to suggest something. He thought for a moment.

Suddenly a light inside his brain switched on.

"The bus," he stated.

"What?" Dawson quizzed.

"If we need to get out of here," he continued. "We could climb out through this window, drop onto the top of the carport below. It's a bit of a drop, but not enough to get hurt. The school bus is parked inside. I got the keys," he said fishing his keys from his pocket.

"Okay," Dawson nodded. "We take the children first, then the women."

"Hey," Agnes snorted.

"I won't argue about women's equality with you, Agnes. Women and children first," Dawson insisted.

"Fine!"

"Who goes after that?" Waring asked.

"Barry drives the bus, Vaughn and the soldiers with the kids."

"What about the rest of us?" the Mayor questioned.

"We do what we can," Dawson said.

Silence fell across the room. It was a lot to process.

Webster cocked his head.

"Where do I take them?"

XXIII

Julia was hyperventilating, shaking uncontrollably and crying. Tiffany held her tightly as they stood near the front door of the house, at a distance from Brad. Stan kneeled beside his friend, holding a glass of water at the ready.

Brad convulsed violently. He had kicked the blanket off and it now lay in a tangled mess on the floor. Stan instinctively wanted to hold his friend down so he didn't cause damage to himself, but he knew that he would be in danger if he did so. Instead, he moved away slightly to allow Brad room to flail.

"What's happening to him?" Julia screamed. Tiffany held her tighter.

Suddenly, the convulsions stopped.

Brad opened his eyes slowly. All pigmentation had gone. Only small black pinhole pupils remained in two bloodshot seas of white. His hair had fallen away from the sides of his head, leaving tiny patches and small tufts around his ears and on the top of his scalp.

"You need to leave," Brad slurred as foamy blood frothed at the corners of his mouth.

"I need to help you," Stan assured.

"It's too late." He grinned. His teeth were stained red and his gums had blackened. "I'm getting hungry. I can only fight it for so long, Stan. Take the girls and get out now." He started to cough, spraying blood across his chest.

The convulsions started again.

Stan rose to his feet quickly and crossed the floor to Tiffany and Julia.

"We need to go," he stated.

"I'm not leaving him," Julia cried.

"Julia." Stan grabbed her by the shoulders and looked her directly in the face. "He is changing into that thing downstairs. If you stay, he will kill you or change you. I know you love him, but I cannot stay and I'm not leaving Tiffany. Either you come or you don't. I would prefer it if you did."

She watched her boyfriend.

Convulsing.

Twisting.

Arching.

"He's in pain," she bawled.

Brad looked at her. He had heard her. His piercing eyes burned through her.

"He needs me," she sobbed.

His mouth opened and let out an ear-piercing screech as blood slowly dribbled down his chin and dripped onto the floor. Pasty hands with dark web-like lines and black fingernails stretched toward her.

"We need to go." Stan took Tiffany by the arm and headed for the door.

"Julia," Tiffany called. "Come on."

Brad dropped to the floor and crawled on his stomach toward them.

Drooling.

Reaching.

Closer.

Closer.

"I'm staying with him," she said. "He won't hurt me. He loves me. I love him. I'll be fine."

"We need to go, Tiffany," Stan said again. "I'm not staying for this."

He opened the door and the cold night air hit with ferocity. The wind tossed Tiffany's hair across her face.

"Julia, please come," she called one last time.

Julia smiled and turned away from her friends to face Brad who was edging closer and closer.

Stan shook his head as he pulled Tiffany into the night and closed the door behind them.

Brad's eyes fixed upon the door as he crept forward.

"I'm here, Brad," Julia said. Her arms stretched toward him as she crouched down nearer to his level.

The pinhole dots flicked back to her. Slowly he pushed his body higher from the ground. He moved his legs under his mass and lifted himself upright.

He now stood above her.

Glaring.

Snarling.

Salivating.

Now she understood.

He had loved her, but this was not him. Not anymore.

He readied himself by tightening the muscles in his legs and stretching his fingers toward her.

Her arms dropped to her sides as her heart broke. She lowered her eyes to the floor and allowed a single tear to fall.

"I love you, Brad."

He pounced.

XXIV

Mike had been observing the idle pickup truck through the binoculars for a long time. The headlights beamed off into the field to the left of the farmhouse. Puffs of vapor rose into the air and passed through the beams of light.

"What's happening?" asked a young man standing next to Mike on the front porch of the Gibb house.

"Engine's still running," Mike replied. "I don't see anything else."

"No Jerry or Kane?" Donald Gibb asked as he crossed the porch again, rifle slung over his shoulder.

"You keep walking up and down that porch, you gonna wear a hole right through it," Sallie Gibb stated from inside the house. She had wrapped a blanket around her and shivered in the doorway.

"You should get back inside, Mom," Donald suggested. "It's too cold out here."

"Wait," Mike interjected. "I think I saw something move."

"Where?" Adam raised his rifle's scope to his eye and aimed toward the pickup truck.

"Behind the truck," Mike replied as he scanned slightly to the right of the vehicle. "I saw a couple of red flashes. Something moving past the taillights I suspect. It was quick."

"Anything?" Anthony Gibb asked Adam as he passed by his wife and exited the house to stand on the porch with the others.

"Nothing, boss," Adam answered. "Too damn dark." He suddenly remembered who was in his company. "Sorry Missus Gibb. My mouth shoots off before I think things through sometimes."

"Quite all right, Adam," she replied with a smile. "Understandable in the current situation."

Mike continued to sweep the binoculars to the right, seeing nothing but a darkened and bleak landscape.

Everything appeared gray or black and any movement was hard to pick up as wisps of snow continued whirling in the wind. The long flat surface of the road and the regular black posts from the fence were the only recognizable and stable objects Mike could identify. Everything else, including trees and small tufts of plants exposed in the snow, moved and swayed as the storm picked up.

Sudden lightning illuminated the area in front of the farmhouse. The light vanished in an instant, but it was long enough.

Mike dropped the binoculars. They fell to his chest where they dangled from the strap that looped over his neck.

Thunder erupted loudly and momentarily echoed back as it reached the mountains surrounding the farm. Mike reached behind him to the rifle he had rested against the house's wall. He slid the bolt, loading a round into the chamber and aimed the rifle toward the road.

"What is it, Mike?" Anthony Gibb asked anxiously.

"Four men coming up through the field," Mike replied. "'Cept they don't move like men. Something's wrong with them."

"I think you and Mom should get inside, Dad," Donald suggested to his father.

Anthony Gibb stood motionless as he weighed his son's words. He stared toward the dark field, and his eyes met the headlights of the motionless pickup truck.

"Your wife's in there," Anthony reminded his son.

"So is yours," Donald replied.

Anthony nodded. He was an old man compared to the three men surrounding him, all in their twenties. More agile, more athletic than he ever could be at sixty-four.

"Be careful, Donny," he said before retiring to the interior of his house with his wife. He closed the door behind him and moved into the kitchen with Sallie.

Melissa Gibb, Donald's wife, was standing over a pot of stew on the stove. She stirred at the contents as she turned and smiled at the elderly couple. With a twist of her head, she flicked her hair from her eyes and continued stirring.

"Won't be long now," she informed them, oblivious to what was happening outside.

"Smells delightful." Sallie smiled back.

XXV

Sheriff Tom Dawson strolled along the lengthy corridor on the northern side of the high school. His M-16 was slung over his shoulder and he held a large thermos in one hand and a sandwich wrapped in brown paper in the other.

Private Sandra Upton had been standing near the northwest stairwell but now made her way toward him. They eventually met each just outside the Girls' bathroom.

"It's not much. Hot coffee and a ham sandwich," Dawson offered.

"It'll do." She took them with a smile. "Thanks."

"How you holding up?" he asked.

"Tired," she admitted. "I don't feel like I'm doing much. All the fighting is on the other side of the building."

"You're doing plenty," the sheriff informed her. "We've got kids here. We need you here."

"I know," she said sheepishly, still wishing she could be among the action. She understood that she was the last line of defense between those things trying to get in at the other end of the western corridor and the children in the rooms nearby.

"You want some company down here?"

"No," replied Upton sharply. "I do better on my own."

XXVI

Doctor Neville Edry sat in Lab 5, the room next to the makeshift medical facility, and stared out of the window into the darkened courtyard below. Snow had built into little mounds on the tree branches and gardens. Small spiraling wisps of white spun in circles where the breeze got trapped.

His thoughts ventured between several places as he sat and watched the scenery below.

The gunfire drew his attention momentarily and in his mind's eye he saw the creatures advancing. Eventually, they would get in. There was just too many for them to handle. Ammunition would run out, leaving them with no option but to flee.

He remembered the many test subjects and samples he had laid his hands on. Experiments that he had conducted, supervised and successfully performed. Faces of his test subjects flooded his thoughts.

He squeezed his eyes shut as tightly as he could, wishing the thought away.

It didn't leave him.

He believed he was doing the right thing. They all believed they were making a difference. This was advancement for the protection of their nation. This was protecting the American way.

Now it had come for him.

For all of them.

He shook his head and opened his eyes.

Wisps of snow danced in the courtyard at the base of a large tree.

XXVII

"How are you feeling?" Donna Leggett asked Frank Levinson who now sat in a chair sipping on a juice box. He still wore his Red Socks cap and looked wide-eyed and bewildered.

"Fine, sweetie." He smiled.

"Do you think you're able to go back out there?"

"I think I need to use the restroom first," he stated as he held up the juice box for her to see. "I've had four of these."

She smiled and nodded.

"It's just across the hall, Mister Levinson."

"Okay." He lifted himself to his feet and strode to the door where he dropped the empty juice box into the trash bin. He retrieved his gun that was leaning against the wall near the door and turned to face the nurse. "See you 'round."

He walked with confidence as he left the room. As soon as he was out of view, he picked up the pace.

"Man, I'm busting," he muttered as he briskly moved along the corridor toward the nearest bathroom. "Why did they give me so much juice?"

The surrounding gunfire was rapid and unrelenting. He imagined waves of those things outside rushing for the building like waves in the ocean crashing against rocks.

He hoped the shooters were doing well as he ducked into the bathroom and started unzipping his fly.

Bolting now, he let the snake loose as he homed in on the nearest cubical. He pushed the door open and released as he leaned his gun against the wall.

It splashed across the seat before he could correct his aim. It was almost orgasmic.

A long sigh escaped his lungs.

He felt relief begin to overcome the discomfort he was experiencing.

I have opened the floodgates; he thought as a smile spread across his face.

A cold breeze brushed over the back of his exposed neck. He turned his gaze toward the windows above the cubicles along the adjacent wall. Glass slats, which were all closed tightly, covered them. Or at least the ones he could see from his position.

Still, it took only one missing panel, or a crack in the glass to let in a breeze.

He returned his attention to draining his bladder. It seemed to go on and on.

Damned juice boxes.

Finally, the flow slowed and turned into a trickle.

More than three shakes and you're a wanker, he heard his father say in a childhood memory.

"One, two, three, four." He chuckled before zipping up his pants.

He straightened his shirt and jacket before he grabbed his M-16 with one hand and pushed the button on the cistern with the other.

A loud flush erupted from the toilet as he turned.

It glared back at him with mouth agape, drooling dark saliva across its chin. The clothes it bore told him it was a man, possibly caught unawares in their home when attacked. It wore jeans and a t-shirt, but its feet were bare.

The skin was a pasty white and teeth a dirty yellow.

Its bloodshot eyes with its pinhole pupils bored into his.

Levinson was transfixed.

His muscles locked and his mind seemed to stop thinking.

It lunged and drove him back into the cubicle. Levinson fell hard against the wall as it dug its teeth into his shoulder.

A tiny yelp fell from his lips.

The creature released its hold. Levinson suddenly snapped back into reality.

He raised his assault rifle and fired toward the creature.

It was gone.

Shit!

Levinson's eyes scanned the area, but he could see no sign of the intruder. His eyes eventually landed on a section of the windows, on the opposite side of the room, where some glass panels were missing.

Tiny snowflakes drifted in through the breach as the wind blew in and lightning flashed.

Levinson felt himself slipping, slipping.

A sudden heat flowed through his body in the same way that he had experienced relief just moments ago. This time, there was pain.

His stomach turned like a churning tempest and he winced.

He called for help but knew that it was in vain. The gunfire outside was too loud for anyone to hear his cries.

He closed his eyes as his head began to swim.

Slipping, slipping.

Slipping.

XXVIII

Tiffany and Stan huddled behind a fence bordering the sides of two yards. They had made it to the end of the block before the need to hide presented itself.

Stan risked a peek over the fence and up the street where he saw several creatures running through a cross-section in the road. Even in the darkness and with the storm kicking up snow and mist, he could see the translucency of the white skin.

One stopped in the center of the intersection and turned its head in his direction. He quickly ducked and placed a finger against his lips. Tiffany nodded. At least he thought she did. It was so damn cold he couldn't tell if she was gesturing or shivering.

He slid his eye over the fence again and saw the creature sniffing the air. The wind was blowing in from behind the beast. One thing Stan understood from hunting with his father was the need to keep downwind from your prey.

It lowered its head and quickly moved on after the others.

Stan saw their chance to make some ground.

He grabbed Tiffany by the hand and ran onto the street where the ground was easier to traverse. They edged toward the intersection carefully, looking in both directions for any sign of danger.

The creatures were nowhere in sight.

"Let's go," Stan said. They ran as hard as they could in parkas, boots, gloves and woollen caps. It felt awkward and slow.

Their heads kept turning, snapping around to listen and see what lay in each darkened patch of the landscape.

"Where are we going?" Tiffany asked through chattering teeth. She was wide-eyed and petrified.

"I don't know," Stan replied. "I'm hoping to find someone who can help us. Or a place where we can hide away from these things."

The wind howled through the leafless trees that lined the road. Their gnarled limbs reached like bony fingers into the black sky.

Stan trudged on, still holding Tiffany's hand as they made their way along the icy road before them. The houses thinned out on either side of the street, giving way to patches of bare ground and the occasional encroaching pine tree.

It was then that Tiffany realized they were heading away from Main Street.

"Do you know where we're going?" she asked.

"I got lost," Stan admitted. "We've been ducking in and out of yards for so long I forgot which direction we were going."

"We're heading for the forest." She pointed along the road.

Stan looked to where she was gesturing. It was too dark to see and the mist-like snow all but concealed everything more than a few yards in front of them.

The wind howled in their ears.

"We'll run out of houses soon and then the road," she informed him. "We need to get inside now."

He nodded. She was right.

The howling grew louder.

He glanced around for the nearest house and let his eyes fall upon a neat brick cottage with storm shutters covering the windows on their left just a little farther along the road.

"There," he pointed.

The howling wind called from behind them.

They started forward again. Stan wrapped his arms around Tiffany to keep her warm. Her body was shaking intensely.

The wind howled to their right making Tiffany turn her head.

Just inside the tree line of the pines stood a lone figure, staring through the darkness with yellow eyes.

It slowly moved forward into the clearing.

A wolf.

"Oh shit," she hissed.

Stan snapped his head around to see the monstrosity. It was larger than any wolf he had ever seen.

There was not much they could do but keep moving. The house was only a few yards away. They could beat it there and be inside before it reached them.

It lifted its head to the sky and howled a long whining call.

"Come on," he said to her softly. "We're almost there."

She moved with him.

Another answered the howl.

Behind them.

Much closer.

Both Tiffany and Stan turned to see another wolf.

Snarling.

Drooling.

It bared its long yellow teeth, snarling as it lowered its head and crept toward them.

XXIX

A loud sound near the fence caused the two young men to turn toward the field. The cows that had gathered there started to bolt further into the open area, running toward the town, away from something.

"I don't see anything," Adam stated as he kept his eye fixed in the scope of his rifle, scanning the area.

"They're not going for the cows," Mike replied as he walked along the porch toward the commotion. With his rifle at the ready, he stepped off the porch and onto the ground, facing toward the bolting cattle. The sound of their thundering hooves was almost drowned out by the roaring wind.

Stinging snow swept across the bare skin of his face. He squinted as he attempted to find the men he had seen earlier.

Nothing.

A flash of lightning illuminated the sky directly above the farmhouse.

For an instant, Mike saw the backsides of the cows running away. He could see their trail in the snow-covered ground. The neatly spaced posts of the fence-line stretched in either direction, holding the steel lines that kept the livestock in their designated area. Something moved to his left.

Darkness fell again.

Thunder rolled.

Mike spun to face the rear of the house. He raised the rifle and pressed the stock against his shoulder.

Adam moved toward him. Mike held up his left hand. *Stop*. He then signalled for the other to go around the left side of the house.

Adam understood.

The intention was to trap the invaders between them.

He turned and moved to the other end of the porch, checked his weapon and lowered himself to the ground.

Keeping his rifle pointed in the direction he was stepping he constantly checked his peripheral vision for any movement to his left.

Slowly he crept toward the rear of the house. He planted each footstep carefully and as quietly as he possibly could. It was not an easy task as the constant barrage from the oncoming wind kept rocking him off balance.

The roar of the gale smashed into his ears and the sting of snow felt as if it sliced into his face.

He made his way to the back corner of the building.

Cautiously, he moved around and saw Mike standing at the other end of the house.

No one else was here.

The two men moved toward each other, keeping their rifles aimed away from the house.

"Must've run off toward the river," Adam speculated.

"Or they got around us," Mike responded. He swept the area behind the house with his eyes. The light emitting from the windows reached a few yards beyond where the men stood. After that was darkness.

The silhouette of the surrounding mountain range towered over everything else like giant jagged teeth. Sheet lightning flashed inside the clouds that surrounded and lapped at their peaks.

"You go back the way I came from and get back to the porch," Mike instructed Adam. "I'm going to the slaughterhouse. Maybe they got in there."

Both men turned to go their separate ways but suddenly stopped in their tracks.

Adam stood, mouth agape, staring at the house.

Mike reacted instantly by lifting his rifle back against his shoulder.

The back door to the house rested upon the porch, torn in half and ripped from its hinges.

The invaders were inside.

XXX

Gripping his gun by the muzzle and dragging the butt along the floor behind him, he stumbled into the corridor. The unbearable noise of unrelenting thunder surrounded him. He placed a hand against the wall and slid it along the smooth surface as he sluggishly moved toward the science laboratories.

Movement ahead of him caught his attention. Something white crossed his view. He tried to focus his eyes, but they swam in and out of clarity as he staggered and waddled along the passageway.

The white object made a sound that bounced incomprehensibly around in his head. It sounded like echo after echo through a deep tube that went on forever.

"...inson. You all ri..."

He dropped to his knees and pushed his palms against his ears. His rifle fell to the floor with a clatter. Inside his head, he heard a wrecking ball smashing the world apart. He shut his eyes tightly and tried to gain some control.

"...ister Levinson. Are you all ri..."?

He opened his eyes and locked onto the white object before him. It was close to him now.

She was close to him now.

Her face shone radiantly like an angel. The white nurse's uniform she wore burnished brightly like a vision from on high. The screams she made pierced his ears and flared his urge.

He had to silence her.

In one swift movement, he had his teeth buried deep in her neck and ripped her larynx out. She fell suddenly silent as he began to chew the flesh in his mouth.

"Donna?" Another object entered his view. This one's sound was deeper, and it stood differently. Taller.

He hissed a warning.

This kill is mine.

"Oh, dear God no," Vanderberg whispered.

Donna Leggett lay in an expanding pool of blood. She tried to breathe but could only make sickening gargling noises. Her eyes darted back and forth, not understanding what had just happened to her.

Private Frank Sharpe stepped out of a room farther along the corridor. He instantly trained his M-16 on Levinson who had turned a pasty white and still had fresh flesh dangling from the corners of his mouth.

Levinson locked eyes with the newcomer and hissed. He recoiled, creating some distance between himself and the fallen nurse.

Vanderberg didn't hesitate. He dropped to his knees beside Leggett and placed his hand over the wound. It would be in vain and her eyes told him she knew so.

"I'm so sorry, Donna," he sobbed. "I'm so sorry."

Her eyes rolled before they closed. The gargling stopped and her body lay still.

Vanderberg kept his hand over the wound and cried.

Sharpe squeezed the trigger.

Levinson's head opened up and sprayed blood against the smooth wall beside him.

XXXI

"We lost two, Tom," Walter Burkley's voice crackled over the walkie.

Dawson, who was half asleep in a soft office chair behind a large desk, suddenly found himself on his feet. He looked around the room at the faces of the people nearby. Their eyes were all on him, waiting for more news.

"Who are they?" he asked.

"Donna Leggett, one of the nurses, and Frank Levinson," Burkley replied. "You know, the guy who always wears that Red Socks hat."

Dawson knew the guy immediately. Frank Levinson had visited the town lockup a few times for drunk and disorderly behavior. He had found Levinson to have always been a polite and well-mannered guy, even if he liked to chase cats and kick them in the ass when he had downed a few beers.

Donna Leggett was someone he didn't know too well. His interaction with her was always work-related. He had only ever spoken to her at the hospital and he never saw her anywhere else in the whole time she had lived in Long Valley.

Still. It was such a shame. Both were young and had their whole futures ahead of them. That was, until tonight.

They had their futures taken from them. Stolen.

Now was not the time to lay blame.

Fucking army.

Now was the time to focus on how to survive.

"What happened, Walter?"

"Frank turned," Burkley explained. "We don't know how yet. He attacked Donna in the corridor and killed her. Then Frank shot him."

"Frank turned and shot himself?" Dawson quizzed.

"Sorry," the doctor apologized. "Frank Levinson turned into one of those things. Frank Sharpe shot him."

"Got it." Dawson understood now.

"Frank killed Frank," Waring muttered. "Weird!"

"We need some people over there to search for a breach," Dawson instructed. "Can you pass that on?"

"Already ahead of you. Frank..." Burkley paused. "Frank Sharpe, that is, is searching the rooms nearby at the moment. Dwight is with me right now in the lab but intends to join the search.

"Thing is, Tom, we have at least two or three people in each of those rooms all the way along the hallway. We've barricaded one room, and we checked there first. Nothing has gotten through. Someone would have seen something."

"Understood," Dawson said. "Keep looking. Something got in somewhere. Levinson wasn't infected when he arrived. It had to have happened here."

Dawson lowered the walkie and placed it onto the desk.

"We need to evacuate," Waring stated.

"Agreed." The sheriff nodded. "If those things have found a way in, we need to get out." He shifted his gaze to Barry Webster, the groundskeeper. "How much time do you need to get that bus of yours operational?"

"Just a turn of the key," he answered. "She might be cold, but she usually starts straight up. Thing is, time to warm up. She can be a bit sluggish or can stall if she isn't warm."

"How long does that take usually?"

"Two or three minutes," Webster replied.

"Two or three minutes can be a long time," Dawson affirmed. "Okay, so we load the kids and the women in first before you turn the key. We get a few guys out there with guns to plug those things if they try anything. In the meantime, we keep guns blaring at the front of the building hoping most of those things focus their attention there." He looked to each one of them for advice. "Now's the time to speak up."

"As good a plan as any," Webster put in. "Just, how do we get to the bus?"

"Through this window." Dawson pointed.

"Well." Agnes got up. "If we're going to be climbing out windows and helping kids down, we better get some other stuff done first." She turned on her heels and headed for the door.

"Where are you going?" Waring asked.

"I need to use the restroom," she answered delicately.

"Not on your own," Dawson instructed.

"I'll go with her," Lilly Geddes offered.

"I need to take a shit," Agnes spat. "I don't think anybody wants to be around when that happens."

They all stood dumbfounded, blankly gawking at each other as Agnes continued toward the door.

She placed her hand on the doorknob and suddenly stopped before opening it. She turned around and picked her handbag from off the floor beside the table. Slinging it over her shoulder, she shot everyone a quick look of contempt before returning to the door.

"My bag has my phone in it," she explained. "I might play some Angry Birds while I snap one off."

With that, she was gone.

XXXII

Stan pressed Tiffany against the door with his entire body to protect her as he twisted the handle, hoping it was unlocked.

It was not.

He took a quick glance behind him and saw that one wolf was standing at the edge of the yard. The other was just across the road. Both were watching intently.

Tiffany started to press her body against the door rhythmically as she turned the door handle. Stan joined her.

The closest wolf cocked and twisted its head, confused by this new strategy.

Stan heard the door creak a little. Something was giving way.

"Harder," he breathed in her ear.

They both worked in unison. Pushing, pushing, pushing.

The door gave way a little more emitting a louder crack.

The wolf growled. It suddenly understood and ran forward.

The other saw the motion and started bolting toward the prey.

"Shit," Stan hissed. "Shit. Shit."

"What?" Tiffany cried as she pushed with all her strength.

The door flung open and both of them fell onto the floor.

Without hesitation, Stan jumped to his feet and slammed the door closed and pressed himself against it.

THUD!

The wolf hit the door at a bad angle and bounced against the wall with a yelp.

"Get something heavy," Stan barked.

Tiffany noticed a two-seated sofa nearby and pushed it toward the door. Risking a chance that the wolves would try again, Stan let the door go and helped her. They pushed the back of the sofa against the door as hard as they could and stepped back.

"Will that be enough?" Tiffany asked.

"No," he replied as he peered into the darkened cottage to see what else they could use to hold the door.

XXXIII

Mike stepped over fallen bric-à-brac and broken furniture with care. His boots softly squeaked with each gentle placement of his feet as he moved through the kitchen of the farmhouse and into the dining room.

Adam stood by the broken door at the back of the house with his rifle raised and ready for action. In all seriousness, he wanted to hightail it to the mountains so he could try to find a way out of the valley.

After a small debate, Mike entered the house to see if he could help anyone. He slowly made his way through the dining room and through an arch into the living room.

A trail of smeared blood stretched over the polished wood floor, leading toward the front door. Mike wished he hadn't seen the grotesque mess as his heart skipped a beat. He wished that the lights were off and that he was in pitch darkness instead of a well-lit house.

He had worked in the slaughterhouse for most of his adult life, so the sight of blood wasn't unnerving. Knowing that this blood didn't belong to a cow, but that it once ran through the veins of someone he cared about, was gut-wrenching.

The trail ran past the front door and toward the stairs that led to the bedrooms. He followed the deep red smear with his eyes.

A tiny thud from the floor above caused him to turn his head slightly.

Something was still up there.

Tiny ribbons of blood trickled down the front side of each step, pooling together on the surface of the next one down.

He lifted his rifle and aimed toward the top of the stairs as he forced his legs to ascend slowly. His heart pounded in his ears so loudly that he thought others would surely hear it.

Step by step, he slowly climbed. The wooden stairs creaked with each tender footfall.

The top of the stairs opened into a small hallway. The bathroom was straight ahead and the main bedroom to the right.

The blood trail swept to the left and deep into the hallway toward the room at the farthest end.

Now Mike wished for the lights to be on here.

The hallway was long with two rooms on each side and one at the end. The doors were open, revealing darkened rooms inside.

Mike stepped into the hallway and quietly moved toward the first room. The blood trailed past the nearest rooms and disappeared into the farthest open door.

It seemed to stare back at him.

Beckoning.

Summoning.

Calling him to come.

He kept his rifle trained on it.

The blood led into that room. Something had to have dragged its prey in there to devour it.

It had to be in there.

The dark open door was a gaping mouth.

Mike felt bile rise in his throat. The stinging sensation caused him to wince.

He swallowed and tried to breathe his fear away.

In through the nose. Out through the mouth.

The sting from bile lingered.

Carefully, he passed the first two open doors; one on the right, one on the left.

He glanced quickly into each room as he passed and saw nothing. Like the doorway before him, they were both dark inside.

His knees started to feel weak and small spasms ran up and down his thighs as he approached the next two open doors.

Closer and closer he drew toward the gaping mouth that called him.

THUD!

He stopped.

The rifle suddenly felt heavy as his heart exploded in his chest. His breathing became shallow and his head felt dizzy.

Something moved.

Mike heard it but couldn't tell whether it had come from the room to his left or from the room into which the blood trail led.

He froze in place.

Waiting.

Waiting.

The thing inside could have him at any moment.

It would have him if he didn't act first.

He collected his courage and darted into the room to the left. Quickly he crouched and aimed his rifle at the far door.

A sudden movement to the right drew his attention.

A creature vaulted from the darkened room directly across the hallway from his position.

He swung his rifle toward his attacker and pulled the trigger.

BLAM!

The figure fell to the floor in a writhing, twisting heap as blood sprayed from its neck.

But it was too late.

No sooner had he made the shot, than another creature reached out from the darkness in the room where Mike had entered. It dragged him deeper into the darkness and sank its teeth into his face.

"Mike?" Adam called from downstairs. He stood near the broken back door. The sudden gunfire caused him to jump in fright. "Mike?"

A screeching cry echoed throughout the house, quickly chorused by others inside.

Adam didn't stay to find out what had made the terrifying sound.

Instead, he bolted toward the slaughterhouse as fast as he could.

He could hear tumbling, crunching and smashing behind him as several things moved through the farmhouse, making their way to the ground floor.

The area between the house and the docking bay seemed to have grown larger. Adam ran for what seemed forever across an expanse of space that took seconds on any other day.

Light was emitting from a small gap between the slaughterhouse door and its adjacent wall. He must have left it a few inches open when he attempted to slide it shut behind him in the late afternoon before dinner.

Still, it was now a beacon of hope as he ran for his life across the snow-covered patch of ground between the house and the loading dock.

He had reached the edge of the ramp to the side of the dock when he heard a horrific screech behind him. The sound resonated across the fields around the farm and seemed to linger in the air.

Adam turned to see seven creatures standing at the back of the house glaring toward him.

"Shit," he whispered. He recognized some of them. Anthony and Donald Gibb. Melissa, Donald's wife. One he thought might have been Kane and two others that he hadn't seen before.

Their pale skin and blood-streaked clothing were enough to persuade Adam to move. He dashed for the door and slid it open in a swift motion with one hand while he gripped his rifle in the other.

His feet slipped on the icy concrete as he attempted to balance himself due to the sheer weight of the door. It was heavy and made so to keep the temperature inside the slaughterhouse low enough to preserve the beef inside.

His knee smacked against the hard surface and his rifle escaped his grip. It fell off the edge of the loading dock and into a deep pile of snow.

"Fuck!"

Adam shot a quick glance back toward the house.

The pack of creatures was halfway across the area between the house and the dock and moving swiftly.

He lunged inside the door and pulled the door closed. It rumbled as it rolled along the rails above and below until it shut with a loud CLANG!

Adam pushed a large pin near the handle to lock the door.

THUMP!

Something outside rammed into the door.

Adam jumped back away from the door as the others joined in.

The noise was horrifying.

For a moment, he stood there staring at the door, wondering what to do.

His brain eventually kicked in when a new fear suddenly took control.

What about the other doors?

There were two, one at the rear of the building and another at the far end facing the barn. Both were small and usually closed at all times. In fact, Adam could only remember opening the doors himself when he needed to take a leak out the back.

He had hoped the boss never knew he did that. A discussion about hygiene and washing of hands after draining the lizard was something he saw old man Gibb conduct with other employees. Adam managed to get away with it somehow. And yes, he had loaded cow carcasses onto trucks without washing first.

Right now, he didn't give a shit.

He ran through the first room of the slaughterhouse, pushed the large rubber curtains that covered the access corridor aside and promptly made his way to the door at the end. His hand gripped the handle.

He gave it a twist.

It didn't turn.

He gave it a shake.

It didn't open.

Content that he'd locked it, Adam spun on his heels and ran back the way he came. He passed through the curtains and glanced at the door to the dock.

The things were still thumping against the heavy entrance.

Adam turned to his left and headed for another large access, covered with two large black rubber curtains. He pushed in the center of the curtains, forcing them apart.

The room's most noticeable feature was the rail that snaked across the ceiling. Along the rail were large meat hooks. Some hooks held beef carcasses, skinned and cleaned to prepare for butchering.

Long stainless-steel benches, set in three rows, allowed the hung carcasses to pass between them. The rows sat parallel to the door where Adam had just entered.

Around the edges of the room were a variety of circular saws and band saws. The workers used these for cutting through meat and bone, enabling the packaging and shipping of manageable portions of produce.

His heart stopped momentarily, skidding to a halt.

A creature popped its head up above table height to see what had just come into the room. It gave a soft hiss before lowering itself out of sight behind the second row of benches. Adam heard loud crunching and slapping sounds.

He scanned the area frantically. His gaze finally fell onto a large knife on the nearest bench. The blade looked to be twelve inches long. Adam had no idea what they used the knife for, but he had a use for it now. He grabbed it as quietly as he could.

The thing hissed disapprovingly.

Adam cautiously made his way around the edge of the first bench. He knew he would have to deal with this one if he was to have any chance of surviving.

The creature sensed Adam's approach and hissed louder.

He gripped the knife tighter in his hand. His knuckles turned white.

Adam could see the source of the crunching sound. The creature had pulled one carcass to the floor and was feasting. Its eyes locked onto him as he made his way down the aisle toward it.

It lifted itself and moved over the carcass where it paused, almost straddling the dead cow. It was as if protecting its kill. It hissed a warning.

Moving the knife between himself and the creature, Adam readied himself.

The thing growled and lunged.

It was fast.

But not fast enough.

Adam swung his arm upward, right into the soft flesh behind the creature's chin. He felt the crunch as the knife pushed through bone.

Its arms drooped by its sides and its legs gave way. Adam allowed it to fall in a heap on the floor next to the beef carcass.

THUNGK!

Adam's head snapped back toward the main room of the slaughterhouse. He raced back around the benches and to the large rubber curtains.

Carefully, he opened the curtains just enough to peer through.

The large door had come off its rail at one end. The creatures were breaking through. It was only a matter of time.

Adam had no choice.

He needed to get to the back door. A sudden desire to piss overcame him, but that was not the purpose of the door tonight. It was his means to escape.

He believed he needed to create a distraction, which would allow him time to escape. With urgency, Adam raced around the room turning on every power saw. The noise was deafening.

He slipped through another passageway that led past a few small rooms that the Gibbs used for offices and storage and then quietly out the door.

Adam closed the door behind him as the cold night air engulfed him. The door made a soft click that was barely audible above the drone of the machinery and the heavy thumping on the dock's door.

His eyes scanned the area before him.

There was a wire fence with a large open field beyond. To his right, the river gently bent toward the direction of the road. Adam started toward the fence as he pulled his coat collar up around his ears.

After he carefully made it through the gap in the steel wires, Adam moved as briskly as he could through the snow. His game plan was to try for the mountain pass that was the only access to the outside world.

His legs ached, and each breath burned in his chest as he pushed through snow that was, at times, knee-deep.

A clang echoed across the air toward him. The noise made him turn his gaze back. The farm looked tiny in the distance. A few dots of yellow light blinked through the falling snow.

He deduced that the sound was the main door to the dock finally falling in. The creatures would find beef carcasses to munch on for a while.

Eventually, they would turn their attention to hunting him.

Until then, Adam aimed to make as much ground between them and him as he could.

XXXIV

Miles Freeburg marched from west to east along the southern corridor, peeping into each room as he went, making sure everyone was stocked up with ammunition, food and water. He would fish out water bottles from a canvas bag he had slung over his shoulder if the occupants of the rooms required them and take down orders for food, coffee and ammunition on a notepad.

The veteran firefighter would then relay orders over the walkie-talkie to the occupants of the teachers' lounge who would pack supplies and send either Carl Mason or Deputy Vaughn to deliver them to the rooms.

It was a good system. Everybody felt useful, and it kept their minds occupied.

Tensions and fears had been running at an all-time high since Dawson announced the plan to evacuate women and children. Most of the men were supportive of the plan, but there were a few who believed their lives were just as precious as any kid or woman.

After several heated exchanges and discussions, two men had their noses broken by ex-marines and everyone else continued to do their part.

Freeburg eventually made his way into the last room facing south to see how Deputy Redhawke and the other occupants of the room were holding up.

"I think we've got everything we need at the moment," Redhawke stated. "Thank you, Miles."

"How are things out there?" Freeburg asked as Max Dooley took aim and fired at a group of creatures moving toward the eastern side of the building. Harry Rourke started firing a few rounds into the small group as Dooley reloaded.

"It's been like this all night," Redhawke explained. "They just don't stop."

"Must be the whole town out there," Freeburg suggested.

"And then some," the deputy said. "There are army uniforms out there, civilians, naked ones. Small, big, you name it."

"Kids too?"

"Not so many," Dooley replied as he took aim and fired again. "I think these things might have taken most of them out. Not big enough to fight back."

"The ones out there are the ones who fought back," Redhawke insinuated. "See, we've been thinking Frank Levinson fought back. Maybe he scared one of 'em off, but it got him first."

"Okay," Freeburg nodded, "but where is the one that got him?"

"Hiding," Rourke stated. "It's still in here somewhere."

"Where? We checked everywhere along this hallway. The two soldiers checked down their end. There was nothing."

"Bathroom?" Rourke asked.

"How should I—" Miles Freeburg was laughing. He suddenly stopped and lifted the walkie-talkie he carried in his pocket up to his mouth. "Anyone in western sector copy?"

"Krane here," a static-marred voice responded.

"Freeburg here," he called. "Listen, did you guys check the bathrooms down your end for a breach?"

There was a momentary silence.

"Sharpe, come in," the static voice ordered.

"Sharpe here," hissed a reply.

"Did you or your guys check the bathrooms?"

Another moment of silence ensued.

"What's with the static?" asked Dooley.

"Lemme see." Redhawke put his hand out to Freeburg who placed the walkie-talkie into the deputy's palm.

"That's a negative," the walkie-talkie buzzed. "We thought your guys did that."

"Battery's running low," Redhawke said after scrutinizing the object for a moment. He then lifted the walkie-talkie to his lips, "Someone needs to check in there now."

"On it," replied a fuzzy voice. "Krane out."

Redhawke handed the walkie-talkie back to Freeburg.

"Listening only unless it's an emergency," the deputy instructed. "The battery is too low for regular contact."

Freeburg nodded.

XXXV

"She's been a long time, Sheriff," Barry Webster noted.

"I know," Dawson acknowledged as he gathered the assault rifle he had leaned against the wall and slung it over his shoulder. He then lifted the walkie-talkie to his face. "Sandra, can you meet me near the bathrooms in our sector, please."

"On my way," Upton replied. "Get all the kids in here and send someone to collect all women and children from the eastern sector."

"What age are we regarding as *children?*" asked Lilly Geddes.

"Anyone under twenty-one," Dawson instructed as he left the room.

Upton arrived at the doorway into the bathroom just before the sheriff. He glanced back in the direction he came from and saw Mayor Harold Waring crossing the hallway to the rooms where the children were. Behind him, Barry Webster rounded the corner and headed into the eastern corridor.

"All right," he said in a low voice, returning his attention to the young woman in army fatigues. "You take this one and I'll take that one," he ordered, pointing to the Girls' facilities first, then the Boys'.

"No need," Upton informed him. "She went in here."

Upton raised her M-16 and slowly entered the Girls' bathroom. Dawson positioned his rifle so that the strap was slung over his left shoulder and crossed his body so that the rifle sat under his right arm.

There was a line of twelve cubicles against the left wall, mirrors and washbasins on the right. Three-hand dryers that blew hot air were on the right wall closest to the door. There were also two vending machines. One was for tampons and another for condoms.

Dawson never understood how anyone could allow the installation of these machines in schools. The condom dispensers, that is. It was as if society was inviting kids to find an empty classroom and copulate at school.

Why not have pictures up of genital herpes or photographs of aborted fetuses. Deterring kids from sex would be much more proactive than endorsing it with some branded rubber. They weren't ready for this shit. Hormones exploding or not. Teenagers, particularly in small towns like this, needed educating and reminding of how to zip their pants up and keep them that way.

At least, that's what he thought.

Perhaps he was just old.

Too old to understand.

Cautiously, they moved deeper into the room. All the stalls had open doors. From their point of view, Dawson could see that the first three cubicles were empty.

Upton clicked her fingers and pointed toward the last stall.

The sheriff followed her finger to an object on the ground just outside the last cubicle. It was small and shiny. Even from this distance, the blood was visible.

Dawson spun quietly, his eyes darted high and low for any sign of danger or another individual in the room.

His gaze landed upon the ceiling just above the first cubicle. A hole, just big enough for a small person to fit through, was torn in the wooden panelling.

He walked backward, keeping his eyes transfixed to that spot, all the while staying aware of Upton's position.

Upton paused outside the last stall and moved her eyes from the object on the floor to the scene inside.

"Oh no," she whimpered.

Dawson turned to see the young private backing away with her hand covering her mouth. He glanced down at the object on the floor and saw a set of keys attached to a small plastic dolphin key ring that blared five words back at him.

WELCOME TO MIAMI, BITCH!

He didn't want to turn his head toward the open cubicle, but he found that the muscles in his neck were already engaged in the motion.

His eyes followed small drops of blood that stained the keys, to a tiny trail that led into the stall.

Her feet rested awkwardly at pigeon toe position.

Tears started to well in his eyes as his gaze moved upward.

Her panties were still sitting around her knees and tarnished with large drops of blood.

He sobbed as he scanned what remained of her.

It had ripped her stomach wide open and her neck torn to shreds. Her head was sitting askew, attached by tendrils of flesh.

Dawson quickly turned and bolted for the basins where he exhumed a quantity of vomit. He felt Upton's hand on his back as he turned on the tap and washed his face.

Without looking up, he pointed to the hole in the ceiling. The private turned her head and instantly understood. She lifted her walkie-talkie.

"We've had a breach," she started. "I repeat, we've had a breach. There is at least one hostile inside the complex and hiding in the ceiling. One casualty in the northern sector."

"This is Deputy Vaughn," the radio crackled. "Who is the casualty?"

Dawson lifted his walkie-talkie out of his pocket. "It's Agnes, son."

XXXVI

They heard the wolves circling the cottage, sniffing at the doors and pushing heavily against the shutters. The occasional growl and snort of frustration made Tiffany jump.

She sat on the floor with her back against the wall. Behind her was a door leading to another room. Stan surmised that it was a logger's dwelling and was only empty because the season for cutting trees was three months away. He had found wood, matches and kindling beside a tiny fireplace in the middle of the wall. Instinctively, and out of necessity to get warm, he lit the fireplace before exploring the cottage.

The room contained a small kitchen and a living area. Stan and Tiffany had already dropped the large, heavy fridge onto its side and pushed it against the back door in the kitchen area. They then moved a chest of drawers against the front door and propped the couch against it for extra weight.

Stan placed pretty much anything that had weight against the two entryways before checking the rest of the cottage. He pushed, pulled and threw chairs, tables, cupboards and the like into place to keep the wolves out. Even the television had a prominent place against the front door.

The wolves weren't at all dispirited in their attempts to get in. They continued to circle the cottage.

Testing.

Sniffing.

Searching for any weak spot in the makeshift fortress.

After barricading the doors, Stan went around the cottage to check for any other way in or out. The former occupants had sealed all the windows with storm shutters. The only access was a tiny manhole in the bathroom ceiling.

The access panel was slightly askew, allowing a soft breeze of cool air into the room. Stan stepped onto the side of the bathtub and balanced carefully, placing one hand against the ceiling while reaching for the panel with the other. Using the tips of his fingers, he slid the panel into its correct place, instantly blocking the cold air from entering the cottage.

For the moment, they were secure.

A thud against the front window made Stan jump as he returned to Tiffany. He was too afraid to talk.

Too afraid to ask if she was okay.

Instead, he slid down the wall next to her and held her against him as they bathed in the flickering firelight.

The warmth was no comfort at all.

The sniffing, growling and grunting of the two giant wolves outside kept them on edge.

There was no safety for them.

Not now.

XXXVII

Clinging desperately to the cold rocky surface proved increasingly difficult as he climbed the steep mountainside. He wished he had worn his gloves but had left them in his room so he could fit his finger through the trigger guard on his rifle. This seemed a rather silly decision to have made now that his rifle sat in deep snow near the loading dock on the farm.

His hands had moved beyond the state of cold, to frozen, to numb.

The icy surface of stone, dirt and snow caused him to slip now and then. And now with the onslaught of sleet, gale-force winds and a storm overhead, his momentum had slowed a great deal.

Sheet lightning in the clouds above illuminated the towering menace he scaled, revealing a dark monstrosity of a wet, slippery, sludgy journey ahead. His only saving grace was that he stumbled onto a goat track of sorts, making his footholds easier to find.

He placed his hands carefully on his next hold before lifting his feet into place. His breath escaped in soft rapid wheezes and his heart pounded in his ears. He peered to his right where the river foamed in turbulent rapids before disappearing into a cavern beneath the mountain's surface.

It was far below him now. He could no longer hear the roar of the water as it fell into the blackness below. Instead, the wind filled his ears, and the snow stung his face. Snot had run over his top lip, into his mouth and had now frozen like a grotesque moustache.

He would die out here.

The road was somewhere above him. He needed to get there before his will gave out. He knew that debris had blocked the pass, but he believed that if he could make this climb, the blocked passage would be a breeze.

Judging that he was more than halfway to his goal, Adam risked a look back to the farm. He turned his head to see a vast expanse of darkness. The mountain range spiked like uneven jagged teeth, penetrating through the clouds that seemed to flow like water across the sky.

In the distance, Adam saw tiny yellow lights from the Gibbs' farm. They seemed a long-distance away. An orange glow farther into the valley, must be a fire somewhere near the town. He guessed the folks there weren't having a great night either.

Lightning flashed across the valley.

The fields below him suddenly came to life for a moment.

In the short time that the lightning flared, Adam saw cattle running through the snow, heading in his direction. Behind them was the reason they ran.

Six human-like figures were about halfway between the foot of the mountain and the farmhouse and moving swiftly toward his position.

"Shit," he hissed as he quickly regained composure and turned his attention to climbing again.

Darkness fell upon the valley again, obscuring the view.

Adam moved with intense despair. He accepted that the weather would take his life tonight. He did not, however, want to be eaten alive by these things that hunted him now.

On and on, hand over hand he pressed.

Slowly and gradually he made his ascent toward the top.

He could see the guardrail on the road's edge about a hundred yards above him. It was farther to his left than he thought it would be.

Adam directed his climb toward it as the wind picked up and lightning flashed again and again.

A quick glance back toward the field below revealed that the cattle had moved across the river, but the creatures were reaching the base of the mountain.

He quickened his pace. His heart pounded in his ears and his breath burned as he reached and pulled himself up the steep surface.

Rocks tumbled as he frantically grabbed, kicked and slid toward the road above. He wasn't worried about being stealthy about his movements. Those things knew where he was. They had left the cattle alone and were coming for him.

So, he climbed with all the strength that he could muster.

Lightning flashed, revealing the creatures clambering up the steep embankment with ease.

They were gaining on him quickly.

Adam truly believed they would be upon him before he reached the road.

With a grunt, he pushed harder.

The skin on his bare hands had split and a new pain introduced itself.

"God," he called as he fought his way to the top, trying to ignore the stinging torture.

An excited shrill scream from below echoed up the mountain toward him.

They were closer.

The road was less than fifty yards away.

He wasn't going to make it.

A loud whir screamed above his head and rapidly moved past into the air behind him. It moved too quickly for him to see the source of the sound.

He then saw a new means of escape.

A large concrete drainage pipe stuck out of the mountainside beneath the road less than ten yards away from his location. Adam had no clue where it led to, but in his opinion, it was the best option at the moment.

The whirring from the flying object grew louder as it moved toward him. It was too small to be a helicopter and sounded more like a jet. The creatures below responded to the newcomer with high-pitched screams.

A bright spotlight blinked to life. The flying object was searching the mountainside for him and the hunters.

The light moved back and forth like a searching eye and almost had Adam. Something told him he didn't want to be discovered by this thing. Instead, he put all of his energy into getting to the drainage pipe.

Closer and closer he drew to the pipe.

The light swung past where he just was and moved lower and lower on the surface of the mountain. It found dark stone, snow, dirt, creatures climbing in rapid ascension.

Suddenly, the flying object opened fire.

Rapid machine gunfire erupted. Dirt, stone and snow exploded all around the creatures.

"Fuck," Adam shouted.

He raised his swollen, frozen hand and contacted the drainage pipe with his fingers. A small trickle of water flowed from within.

The water must come from somewhere, he thought.

He started to slide inside the tube.

Sudden shooting pain in his ankle caused him to scream in agony. He looked down to see that one creature had made its way to him. It had sunk its teeth into his flesh.

He kicked with his other foot and connected with the creature's face again and again and again.

"Get off me," he screamed. "Get off me!"

Bright light filled the tube as the flying object trained its attention on the struggle within.

The creature let go of Adam's ankle and turned to confront the source of the light.

Adam turned away and scrambled deeper into the drainage pipe.

The high-pitched scream from the creature reverberated throughout the tube, suddenly cut off by rapid gunfire.

The sound of the machine became more terrifying than that of the creatures. Adam moved quickly, deeper and deeper into the drain.

His hands stung.

His breath burned.

His chest ached.

His ankle throbbed.

The machine kept firing and firing.

Among the sound of the gunfire and whirring engines, Adam heard the distinctive noise of cement and stone cracking and thumping as the exit to the drain caved in.

XXXVIII

Andy clumsily attempted to put his boot on while balancing on one foot. He almost fell several times and had to put his hand against the wall to steady himself.

Tina sat on the floor shaking her head as she laced her boots up.

"Why do boys always do things the hard way?" she asked with a smile.

"I guess we like the challenge," Andy grunted.

"Or you are challenged." Tina chuckled.

The door suddenly burst open to reveal Carl Mason.

"Holy shit," Andy blurted. "What if we were still... You know?"

"You two still in here?" Mason asked. "Okay, get your shit together. You're leaving."

"What?" Andy stomped his foot onto the ground, subsequently slipping it into his boot. "Why?"

"Every woman and person under twenty-one need to move to the sheriff's position."

Andy reached a hand out to Tina and helped her from the floor.

"I don't get it," Andy stated as he and Tina followed Mason out of the room and into the hallway.

"Sheriff has ordered it," the diner owner told them. "You're being evacuated. That's all I know."

With that, Mason walked toward the southern end of the corridor.

Andy stared blankly after the man as he walked away. Something must have happened.

He wanted to know more.

He wanted to follow Mason and ask more questions.

"Come on," Tina tugged at his arm and pulled him toward the northern sector. "He said we gotta go."

Andy grudgingly followed her.

Dawson stood at the door and ushered them into the room. The bag boys and other checkout girls were already inside. There were some children huddled together with six middle-aged women against the wall, sobbing and shaking. Andy could see the fear in their eyes. He guessed that they didn't know what was happening either.

Tina gripped his hand tightly. She was scared too.

Andy peered around the room and saw Principal Geddes and another two ladies standing with Betty Sue Mason. One lady, wearing a nurse's uniform under a parka, looked older than the others, but not as old as his principal. He didn't know them, but they looked familiar.

Perhaps he just saw them earlier in the night.

"Betty Sue," he piped. "Where are Deputy Vaughn and Mister Harris?"

"Greg's out in the hall," she answered. "I don't know where Mister Harris is. Last I saw him he was in the teachers' lounge with Mister Putney."

"Why aren't they here?" Tina queried. "Should we get them? Sheriff?"

"No one else leaves," Dawson instructed. "We had to make some hard decisions. Only some of us get to go."

"Go where?" she asked Dawson. She turned to Andy. "Where are we going?"

"I don't know," he replied.

Andy pushed past the sheriff and ran back toward the teachers' lounge. Both Dawson and Tina called after him, but he ignored them and continued along the passage.

Paul Harris was sitting in an armchair reading a small, leather-bound bible. Resting on the left arm of the chair was a steaming cup while an M-16 assault rifle leaned against the right arm.

Evan Putney, the manager of Stop N' Save, sat at the table nursing his own steaming mug in both hands. His rifle was lying on the table in front of him. He looked up as Andy entered the room and smiled.

"Hey Andy," he said.

"Hey Evan," he responded politely. His eyes, however, were on the old man in the armchair. "Mister Harris, why are you still here?"

"I was about to ask you the same question," Harris answered, closing the bible and placing his full attention onto Andy.

"They've put us all in a room out there," Andy said. "What's going on?"

The old man switched his gaze between Andy and Evan.

"They haven't told them?" Evan asked.

"Told us what?"

Harris returned his focus upon the boy. "Told you that an evacuation is about to happen."

"Under twenty-ones only." Putney sounded spiteful. "I missed out by four years."

"Only some of us get to go," Andy repeated the sheriff's words. "That's not fair. You need to come, Mister Harris. Both of you do. Everyone needs to come with us."

"Some of us need to stay back to draw their attention away from you," Harris explained.

Andy shook his head. He wore an expression of perplexity and the old man could see it.

"Son, I've lived my life, and it was good. I have no complaints. The good Lord above has guided me this far. If this is my time, then I'm prepared."

"I'm not," Putney put in. "I'm twenty-five and have my whole life ahead of me. I've never been laid and I really want to go with you guys. But I know that's not going to happen, so I'll stay here with *Jesus Freak* and hope a bit of his positive attitude rubs off on me."

"So you're going to stay?" Andy asked.

"We're the last line of defence," Harris replied with a smile. "Go back to the others, Andy. I'm staying."

Andy nodded, turned and reluctantly walked back to the room in the southern corridor.

***

The large metal lockers piled in front of the door to the breached room in the southwestern corner of the building had performed well for most of the night. But slowly and gradually, the room was getting crowded. More and more invaders pressed and pushed against the door.

Bit by bit it started to give.

The metal lockers slid slightly.

Just a little.

And a little more.

Deputy Greg Vaughn stood beside Private Upton at the northwest stairwell. It was the first time he had been on this side of the building. They had filled the stairwell with cupboards, students' desks and chairs and a few teachers' tables from what he could see.

"Any sign of the thing that got Agnes?"

"None," Upton replied. "But it had to have gotten by me through the ceiling."

The three doctors walked toward them, flanked by Privates Krane and Sharpe. Vanderberg wore a large backpack and carried two gym bags, all full of first aid supplies. They paused at the stairwell momentarily.

"Ready to go?" Vaughn asked the men.

"I'm not going," Burkley told them.

"What?" Vanderberg quizzed.

"I'm too old to be climbing the outside of a building," he stated. "Get the women and kids out of here. I'll stay and help the men where I can."

"Walter," Vaughn pleaded. "Come on."

"Sorry, son." He turned and headed back toward the laboratory.

Upton led the others down the hallway toward Dawson. Vaughn stayed behind and watched Burkley disappear into the lab before rejoining the others.

Dawson opened the door for the doctors and the three privates.

"Walter's not coming," Vaughn informed his boss.

"What do you mean?"

"He just turned around and went back to the lab," the deputy replied. "He said something about too old to climb buildings."

"Stupid old fart," Dawson snapped. "Okay, let's go inside and work out how we're going to do this."

***

They pressed harder and harder against the door. The doorjamb started snapping and split from top to bottom. The wood splintered near the lock and hinges.

The metal lockers scraped another inch.

Then another.

And another.

XXXIX

Jeff Burrows and Shane Munroe searched the rooms that overlooked the courtyard in the center of the structure. They moved along
the northern corridor from east to west, rounding up all they intended
to evacuate.

Redhawke and Dooley were doing the same in the southern hallway. Both groups moved from room to room, assault rifles at the ready
as they opened each door.

Their intent wasn't just to evacuate people but to hunt the intruder
that had killed Agnes. Mayor Waring had ordered them to find the
thing so it could attack no one else. He feared especially those who focused on other tasks such as keeping the perimeter safe and vacating
the building.

The deputy and the barkeeper had the unfortunate disadvantage
of dealing with noise pollution as they moved through each doorway.
Constant gunfire from the rooms across the corridor drowned out any
possibility to track the intruder with their ears. They could only rely
upon sight to assist them in their search.

The two firefighters, however, were far enough away from the
clamor that they could listen for any strange or inconsistent sound.
Each room they had passed through was empty.

Silent.

Until now.

They both stood outside of a room directly opposite the Girls' Bathroom in the northern corridor. Room 36.

Burrows placed his hand on the door handle and turned it, ready to open the door.

A sudden clatter and shuffle from inside informed them they were not alone.

Munroe poised himself and raised his M-16, prepared to attack. He signalled the other man that he was ready with a nod.

Jeff Burrows pushed the door open hard and moved to the left out of his colleague's way. As he did so, he ducked and raised his own assault rifle, ready to fire.

The door hit the adjacent wall with a thump.

Shane Munroe stepped into the room and swung his rifle from left to right and saw the creature.

It cowered in the far corner across the room, baring its teeth and hissing.

Munroe hesitated. His finger froze to the trigger guard as he looked it over. It was small. Very small.

"Shoot it," Burrows yelled excitedly. Adrenaline pumped through his veins. "Shoot it now."

The creature stood full height. Shane Munroe could see that the thing would stand no taller than his chest height. Its hairless head, pale skin and darkened blood vessels were clear. But the thing that gripped Munroe was the fact that it wore dirty, pink pyjamas with love hearts plastered all over and a large bloodstain from neck to crotch.

Pink pyjamas and love hearts.

This was a little girl.

Is a little girl.

"I can't." Munroe's voice shook as he responded to Burrow's call.

The girl moved her eyes to the ceiling to a hole she had made.

Jeff Burrows followed its gaze and took aim.

She bent her knees and swung her arms back, ready to leap for her escape route.

Burrows quickly took aim and fired.

One-shot.

He hit her in the thigh, causing her to collapse in a heap on the ground.

She cried an ear-piercing shriek of pain. Pushing with her uninjured leg, she backed herself into the corner and bared her teeth at the two men.

Both men stood near the door and stared across the room at the wounded beast.

"What happened to you?" Burrows asked.

"It's a little girl," he replied.

"No, it's not," Jeff informed him. "It might have been once. Not anymore, man."

Munroe nodded. Jeff was right. Anything that these things once were, they now were not.

"Better call it in," he said.

Burrows dug into his coat and retrieved the walkie-talkie.

"We wounded the intruder in the northern corridor," he said as he looked to the number on the door. "Room thirty-six. Repeat, room thirty-six."

"On our way over," Redhawke squawked through the radio.

**

Deputy Redhawke and Max Dooley jogged the rest of the distance of the southern hallway toward the western passage. They turned the corner, passing the metal lockers positioned in front of the breached room and continued northwards.

**

The lockers slid away from the wall slowly.

Bit by bit.

Little by little.

**

Redhawke paused outside of the science labs as Dooley kept going onwards. Inside the laboratory, Burkley sat behind a desk staring at an assault rifle in his lap.

"What are you doing, Walter?"

"Hmm?" The old man seemed to snap out of a deep thought he was having.

"We got one," Redhawke informed the veterinarian. "Could be the one that got Agnes."

Burkley nodded. "That's good, Colin." His voice seemed vague and distant.

"Come on, Walter," Redhawke prompted. "Come with me."

"I'm fine," the old man replied. "Really, I am. I'd rather stay here if you don't mind."

Redhawke lingered a moment. He didn't want to leave but knew there was no way he could talk Burkley into joining him.

He left the old man and ran after Dooley.

All four men stared blankly at the creature recoiling in the corner. It hissed and shrieked continuously as it quickly moved its eyes across each of them.

"It's a little girl," Dooley stated.

Redhawke raised his weapon and fired, hitting the creature in the chest. The other three men gawked blankly at the girl who suddenly slumped lifelessly in the corner.

"It killed Agnes," said the deputy as he slung his rifle over his shoulder.

"Okay," Dawson announced to the small crowd in the room with him. "Barry Webster here will drive the bus out of here. Our job until then is to make sure you all get on it quickly and safely. It also means going outside."

Dawson was met with a chorus of disapproving groans and moans.

"I know, I know," he called over them. "We have a plan. Privates Upton, Sharpe and Krane will drop down first to make sure the area is clear. When they give us the signal to go, Barry will climb down and open the bus.

"The kids go next. Then the rest of you go. That's it," the sheriff finished. He walked through the door and summoned Vaughn to accompany him.

Both men moved into the hallway. Dawson eyed Redhawke and Dooley walking away from them, toward the northwestern stairwell. Jeff Burrows and Shane Munroe still occupied room thirty-six.

"You need to get these people out of here, Greg," Dawson instructed.

"Yeah. No problem, boss." Vaughn smiled.

"I'm not coming with you," the sheriff stated.

"What?" He was dumbstruck. "Of course, you're coming."

"I'm not," Dawson shook his head. "We need to hold them here and give you time to get out."

"No. That's bullshit!"

"Greg. We can't all go." Dawson reached under his jacket and fished out his tin badge. "You're the sheriff now."

"No." Tears formed in Vaughn's eyes. "I can't do this on my own."

"You have to." The sheriff took the deputy's hand and placed the badge delicately in his palm. "Now get those people to safety."

"Where do I take them?"

"I don't know," Dawson replied.

***

Vaughn walked through the gathering, across the room to the window where the three soldiers waited for instruction. He pinned the tin badge to his parka and reached out for Betty Sue's hand. She took him and held him tightly.

"You ready?" he asked the three. They nodded.

He let go of Betty Sue's hand and lifted the window. Quickly, he stood to one side and raised his rifle to offer cover for the soldiers.

Krane went first. His rifle slung over his back, he lowered himself from the window and dropped about two feet onto a carport. The storm above, mixed with the gale-force winds and the snow built up on top of the aluminium surface, absorbed the sound of his landing.

He swung his M-16 back into his grasp and signalled the next person down.

Upton followed him down in the same manner. Krane dropped off the eastern side of the carport and moved to the corner of the building.

Sharpe landed in the same position as the other two and followed Upton off the edge of the carport to the west. Krane and Upton took up position, one on the western side and one on the eastern side of the carport. Sharpe checked around the vehicle underneath. It was a large, yellow school bus with its front parked tightly toward the building.

When he could see all was safe, he turned to Upton who gave him a nod. Krane responded the same. Sharpe moved into the open where Vaughn could see him and waved.

"Okay," he said to Webster. "You're up."

Barry Webster, forty-one and slightly big in the middle, clumsily dangled himself from the window. He let go, but he didn't have the skills of the three soldiers who went before him. Instead of landing on his feet, he fell onto his back.

He quickly gave a thumbs up to Vaughn who was watching the entire fiasco.

Webster crawled to the western edge of the carport and climbed down to ground level. He fished his keys out of his pocket and opened the bus' door. He fitted the keys into the ignition and positioned himself in the driver's seat.

Now he needed to wait.

"Okay." Vaughn smiled. "Betty Sue. You're next. Then the kids."

He lowered her out of the window as far as he could. She felt hands grab her around the waist, making her look down. It was Sharpe. He placed her on the surface carefully.

"Over there and down." He pointed to the edge where Webster had climbed off the carport.

Andy was next. He offered to stand near the carport to help the little kids down. Justin, one of the bag boys, did the same, instructed to stay on the carport to lower kids down to Andy.

Vanderberg's gym bags and three khaki canvas bags came next, passed quickly down the line and placed under the forward seats on the bus by Webster.

They now had a system in place, and it was working.

***

The lockers slid more and more.

The creatures inside the room pushed and pushed.

Slowly and steadily, they were gaining access.

***

The five men by the northwestern stairwell peered back toward the room where the evacuation was taking place. Dawson moved his gaze toward the science labs and decided he needed to have a talk with an old friend.

"This is the last line of defence, gentlemen," he said. "Stay here and keep watch. I'm going to see Walter."

"Want some company, boss?" Redhawke asked.

"No thanks, Colin." Dawson entered the western hallway.

Walter Burkley was still sitting in the chair behind the desk staring blankly at a periodic table pinned to the back wall.

"What are you doing, Walter?"

"Nothing, Tom," Burkley replied. "Just waiting for the inevitable."

"You're not dead yet, you old fart. You could at least do something and come join me at the stairwell."

"Go out with a bang or something?"

"Or, with luck, not go out at all," Dawson sneered.

"There's always hope," Burkley stated. He lifted himself to his feet and strolled over to Dawson. "Well, lead the way."

As the two men stepped into the corridor, a sound made both their heads turn to their left.

The metal lockers rattled and started to rock violently.

"What was that you said about *hope*, Walter?"

Both men turned and ran for the others waiting at the stairwell. Dawson lifted his walkie-talkie, "How are you doing in there, Greg?"

"Almost done," Vaughn crackled through the radio. "Three more people to go, then me."

"You may want to pick up the pace," Dawson suggested. "I think we're about to have company in here."

***

The lockers rocked and rocked until they fell with a deafening clatter.

Figures crawled from the darkroom behind the toppled lockers and into the corridor. They turned their heads this way and that, trying to decide which way to run. The noise confused them as gunfire resounded along both the southern and western hallways.

"Breach," Dawson screamed into the walkie-talkie. "Breach, breach, breach."

The creatures bounded over the fallen metal containers and flooded into the corridors.

Some men came to the doorways and started shooting, taking out as many as they could before being taken themselves. Other men ran back toward the men at the stairwell.

Carl Mason and Harold Waring, both in the southern corridor, opened a crate and found another RPG launcher. Mason looked at the Mayor for advice.

"Better now than never," he said.

Mason placed the device on his shoulder and took aim. He pulled the trigger and…

CLICK!

"What the fuck?"

Harry Rourke lifted the launcher off Mason's shoulder and pressed a catch on the side.

"Safety," he said as he hoisted it onto his own shoulder, took aim and...

BOOM!

The RPG slammed into the stack of fallen lockers and sent shards of metal in all directions. Flames engulfed seven creatures instantly while another twelve ate fire and steel.

Waring and Mason gawked at the disorder and cheered.

From behind the flames, more creatures emerged.

The battle had just begun.

***

Miles Freeburg and Jacob Sorenson were firing at an uncountable number of creatures, which were intent on attacking their section of the building toward the eastern end of the façade. They moved rapidly and clawed over one another as they approached. The two men were having difficulty keeping them back.

The sudden explosion from the RPG stopped them dead in their tracks. Their heads turned in unison toward the fireball at the western end of the building. Unexpectedly, they turned their attention away from Freeburg's and Sorenson's position and bolted for the opposite end of the structure.

"They're all running for the breach," Freeburg called over the radio. "Every single one of them."

***

"Some warning might be helpful in the future," Redhawke yelled after the fireball at the other end of the hallway flared up.

The men took aim as they could see more creatures climbing over the inflamed debris. Dawson fired first, in short deliberate bursts. The others joined in, picking their targets carefully.

Bullets ripped into flesh, taking down creature after creature. But still, they came.

Crawling.

Leaping.

Running.

They kept coming.

XL

The wolves padded around the house slowly, deliberately. Snorting, grunting at intervals, they moved around and around. Occasionally one would growl or thud against the cottage walls.

Each sound made Tiffany jump and emit a tiny sound from her throat. It took Stan a while, but he finally caught onto what they were doing.

Every time Tiffany made a sound, the wolves could work out where inside the cottage their prey was hiding. Stan knew it was only a matter of time before they found their way in.

With no weapons or defensive tools, they were both to become victims to the monsters outside.

Stan thought back to the snowboarding adventure he had with Brad and Andy earlier in the day. In particular, he remembered the carcass of the cow lying on the mountainside.

Something big and strong had ripped that thing apart like melted butter.

He started to wonder if it had been the target of the very creatures that now hunted them.

Tiffany jumped again and snuggled deeper into his chest. How he wished she had gone with her parents today instead of staying behind just to hang out with him. She would be safe outside the valley and he would...

A metallic whirr grew louder and louder, rising above the roar of the wind. It sounded like an aircraft but unlike any that Stan had heard before. He cocked his ear to listen carefully.

"What is it?" Tiffany asked, wiping tears away from her eyes.

"I don't know," he replied as the sound passed high and by the back of the cottage and toward the forest.

The wolves outside began howling as the sound moved around, circling back to pass by the front yard and continue along the direction of the road outside.

The whirring slowly died away and the wolves, padding and growling, seemed to follow it. It was drawing them away.

Stan jumped to his feet.

"We need to risk going out there. Try to find something to fight these things with," he said.

"They're so big." Tiffany lifted herself from the floor and looked around. "There's nothing here that we could use."

"There's got to be." He shook his head, frustrated, thirsty, hungry and feeling useless. He wasn't willing to sign off yet. The need to fight, to survive, was fueling him. With the sound of a man-made machine outside came hope.

"There's nothing," she replied. "You've used everything to barricade the doors."

"Well," he said. "Maybe there's something there that we can use." He started moving objects that he had piled against the front door, looking for anything he could use to hit or strike.

A few smaller items clattered to the floor.

"Stan." Tiffany started to cry again.

He pushed the television to one side with a hefty grunt and dug into the pile.

"Please, Stan."

The television rolled onto the floor with a tremendous crash.

"Stan, stop."

He did.

As suddenly as hope had come, it had gone. He realized they had trapped themselves in here to wait for an end.

Turning, with tears in his eyes, he looked to her for any comfort.

There was none.

Her eyes were looking for the same.

THUMP!

THUMP!

THUMP!

THUMP!

Stan moved across the room quickly and pulled Tiffany into his arms. Both watched as the door shuddered with each hit from outside.

Their interest in the new object failed rapidly and so they had returned.

THUMP!

THUMP!

THUMP!

THUMP! CRACK!

The door split straight up the middle causing the stack of furniture to slide forward.

THUMP!

The door slid open slightly pushing the furniture slightly.

THUMP!

The wolf slid its long snout in through the gap it had created. Its long gray tongue licked the air as frothy drool dangled from its yellow teeth and blackened gums. A guttural growl slowly filled the room as it forced its head into the room.

Bright yellow eyes flicked back and forth until it homed in upon Stan and Tiffany. Keeping its eye trained upon the game, it pushed and pushed until its shoulder squeezed through the door.

Stan knew it wouldn't be long before it would work its way inside.

His brain raced at a million miles per hour trying to come up with a plan.

How the fuck do we get out of this?

He instantly thought of the bathroom and the manhole in the ceiling.

"Come on." He took Tiffany by the hand and dragged her through the bedroom, closing the door behind him and into the bathroom. "Up."

She tilted her head and saw the panel covering the manhole. He grabbed her by the waist and hoisted her toward it. Tiffany pushed the panel to the side and started to climb into the roof space.

A cold breeze gently tossed her hair around as she pulled herself up. It was pitch black inside the roof space and the smell of damp filled her nostrils.

An almighty crash resounded in her ears as she pulled her feet inside. She turned around and lowered her arms to help Stan up.

He reached his hands to hers and grabbed on as he placed a foot onto the lip of the bathtub.

More sounds from the living area made their way to them as the wolves climbed into the cottage, knocking over objects from the furniture pile.

Stan pushed with his legs and jumped toward his girlfriend. He let go of Tiffany with one hand to grab the lip of the manhole.

She hoisted with all her might as he lifted himself upwards.

CRASH!

The bathroom door collapsed inwards easily.

Stan pushed his shoulders through the tight gap. His oversized parka didn't help his situation. Tiffany pulled, grabbing whatever of his she could. He gripped with his fingers and took hold of wooden beams and used every ounce of strength he could.

Something unexpectedly gave way, and he could lift himself to his waist. Tiffany smiled. He was almost inside.

A sudden blood-curdling scream thundered from his throat and he dropped back to his shoulders.

His arms held his head inside the manhole long enough to let him see Tiffany one last time.

"I love you, Tiff," he managed before he disappeared back down into the cottage.

She screamed as she followed him with her eyes.

One wolf had him by his leg and was dragging him across the bathroom floor and into the bedroom. It dug its snout into the soft tissue of Stan's abdomen.

A large spray of blood spread along the floor and up the wall as the monster started feasting on intestines and organs.

Stan screamed and screamed. The sounds filled Tiffany's head so much that she could hear nothing else.

The other wolf slid past the first and stopped at the source of the sound.

It opened its jaws and closed them around Stan's head before squeezing them shut tight.

Tiffany closed her eyes and covered her ears.

It took a moment for her to realize the screams she heard now were her own.

XLI

Blindly, Adam felt his way along the smooth concrete tube as he crawled deeper and deeper into the mountain. His hand occasionally brushed over a small hole on either side of the surface, about the size of his fist. It took a while for him to realize that he was crawling through the stormwater drain that ran underneath the road.

Mostly, the tunnel ran straight without interruption. He did, however, have to navigate a turn or two. These were difficult as they intersected at ninety degrees. The first had turned left and then his journey led him straight on for a good distance. The second turned right before another stretch of straight pipe.

He was now at another intersection that turned right. It was here that Adam realized he was following the route of the passageway in and out of the valley.

The pipe wasn't much higher than Adam when he was crawling on his hands and knees. This made turning a challenge, especially with the wounds he had collected on his journey.

He lowered himself onto his side and bent his body around the corner, pulling with his throbbing hands that vainly grasped at whatever they could. His head pounded and seemed to spin as stars danced about the darkness. The wheeze in his breath had turned into a raspy whistle and the pain in his ankle had moved up his leg and into his groin.

With his left foot against the wall of the pipe behind him and his hands sprawled on both sides of the tube in front, Adam forced himself through the intersection and into the new sector.

His body started to ache incredibly from tip to toe.

Back onto his hands and knees, Adam crawled along another long stretch of straight pipe. The soft trickle of water passing below him brought some sense of calm to his situation as he moved on.

Still, his hands stung with each motion and his elbow joints ached. He started to feel warm, and the stars began to spin and orbit about his head.

His boots scuffed noisily on the concrete, splashing gently in the stream. The stinging sensation in his hands seemed to come and go as the ache in his legs and groin increased and moved into his abdominal region.

Adam suddenly felt parched. His body felt progressively hotter as if he was getting a fever of some sort. He pushed on.

There was no way he would die now.

He had escaped the farm and run across an open field without being caught. He had climbed a mountain in a snowstorm. He had avoided being eaten by who the fuck knows what those things were. And he had dodged bullets from a UFO.

No fucking way was he going to die in a storm drain.

On he crawled.

His hands slid along the curved floor of the tube, feeling for any change in the surface.

His knees scraped over the wet concrete surface as he progressed slowly down the straight section of piping.

His breaths whistled and bubbled with each exhale.

His joints ached.

His lungs burned.

His head spun.

Adam found the next intersection and collapsed in a heap.

Rapid breathing and his own thudding heartbeat deafened him. He could no longer hear the soft trickle of the stream flowing by.

He closed his eyes tightly. His eyelids felt as if they were burning his eyeballs right out of their sockets.

Heat flowed through his body and pain stabbed at every joint like tiny knives. He lowered his head onto the surface, allowing the cool of the concrete to absorb into his skin. A temporary reprieve, but only momentarily.

His intestines felt as if they were being squeezed in a vice, tighter and tighter. A long moan escaped his lips.

The stars spun so fast now that they appeared as streaks of light swirling around and around and around.

He vomited into the stream.

It burned the back of his throat. The burn felt even worse as he breathed in deeply.

He vomited again and again.

He started to shake uncontrollably.

Violently.

The light swirled around and around as he vomited again.

I am going to die here, he thought.

Swirling, swirling like water flowing down the drain.

After all of this, I am going to die.

Swirling, swirling.

Down the drain.

Swirling.

Swirling.

XLII

"Get this bus started," Vaughn ordered as he boarded the vehicle. Upton stood by the open door while Sharpe and Krane lay in the snow near the northeastern corner of the building, watching for any invaders who might slip by the watch of the gunmen at the front of the high school.

Webster turned the key.

The vehicle slowly whirred, but it didn't kick over.

"She's a little cold," the groundskeeper tried to reassure everyone on board. He turned the key again.

This time the vehicle whirred a little faster, but it still didn't start.

"It's okay," he said with a chuckle as he heard a faint sobbing from one woman toward the back of the bus.

He turned the key again and gave it some gas.

The bus whirred and whirred and suddenly roared to life.

Everybody on board cheered and clapped.

"Quiet," Vaughn barked.

Silence erupted inside the vehicle. They could hear only the chugging of the bus.

"How long?" Vaughn asked the groundskeeper.

"A minute or two," Webster replied. "She's been sitting still for quite some time."

Vaughn reached past the driver and tapped on the window, causing Sharpe to glance toward the bus. The deputy held up two fingers. The private nodded; he understood.

Upton looked back into the bus as she watched Vaughn take up position just inside the door.

"Two minutes," he told her.

"I heard," she replied. "That could be a long fucking time."

"I know."

***

Jeff Burrows and Shane Munroe had made a mad dash for the teachers' lounge to stock up on ammunition. It was one of the few places left where the stashed arsenal remained remarkably untouched.

The two men opened every crate and started taking mental notes of what they could find. There wasn't much in the way of bullets, but there were a few cases of grenades and two RPG launchers.

"They've got more grenades down in the front sector," Evan Putney stated.

"How do you know that?" asked Burrows.

"Because Jacob came up here not long ago and took what bullets he could find," Putney replied. "When he saw the grenades, he said they had plenty of those. He also took a rocket launcher. That's what those things are, right?"

"Kind of," Burrows answered. "Does the same job."

"Is everyone out yet?" asked Paul Harris as he shuffled toward them.

"They're all in the bus," Munroe stated.

"Have they gone?" he queried further.

"I'm not sure, Mister Harris. I really have no idea."

"Well then," Harris said, continuing on through the door. "This isn't the last defensive line anymore. I'm heading down to the front with the Mayor and Mister Sorenson."

"Are you sure that's a good idea?" Putney quizzed. "I mean, a man of your age..."

"I can still point a gun and shoot, son," Harris retorted. "I'm not an invalid. Not yet, anyway." With that, he started singing, "Onward, Christian soldiers, marching as to war, with the cross of Jesus going on before. Christ, the royal Master, leads against the foe; forward into battle see his banners go."

***

The creatures massed at the southwestern corner of the building, squabbling and fighting one another to get near the wall. Once there, they continued to claw and shove one another for an advantageous position so they could climb.

Smoke billowed out of the window upon which they all had focused their attention. A flickering orange glow emitted from the darkness within. The combination of smoke and fire burned their throats as they breathed and would turn most other beasts away from advancement.

But the urge propelled them on.

The hunger drew them in.

They climbed up the wall and in through the window.

They crept across the floor and over the rubble within.

They crawled over the fallen debris into the corridor.

They could breathe the scent of fresh flesh and sense the fear of their prey nearby.

***

"I'm out," Dawson called as he searched for another clip.

"Here," Redhawke called as he slid a canvas bag across the floor to the sheriff. Dawson crouched down and opened the bag. There were at least twenty loaded magazines inside. Not nearly enough to last the night.

He reloaded and rejoined the firefight.

Burrows and Munroe returned at that moment carrying very little in the way of supplies.

"All ammo has been utilized," Burrows said.

"What the fuck does that mean?" Burkley called over the blaring noise.

"It means there's none left," Munroe informed the doctor.

"What have you got, boys?" Dawson asked as he continued to aim and shoot in short bursts.

"A shitload of grenades and two RPGs," Munroe answered.

"Okay," Dawson said. "Get ready to use 'em."

***

Webster knocked the bus into reverse. It started making a loud beeping noise.

BEEP! BEEP! BEEP! BEEP!

Vaughn stepped back and allowed the three soldiers to board the bus.

"Anyway to stop that noise?" he asked.

"Not until I put it in *drive*," the groundskeeper answered.

He maneuvered the bus so it faced toward the east.

"Do you know where you're going?" Sharpe called.

"The driveway goes around the side of the building and out the fro—" Webster suddenly stopped explaining. "Oh, I wasn't thinking."

He remembered that the creatures, the very things they were escaping from, were out the front of the high school.

"It's okay, Barry," Vaughn assured him. "Is there another way we can get out of here without getting stuck along the way?"

Webster knocked the bus into *drive* as he gave it a thought.

***

The noise of the reverse indicator echoed across the wind into the sensitive ears of several creatures near the breach. They turned their attention away from the open window and bolted for the back of the school.

***

"I think we can make the service track beside the football field," Webster said. "We can bust through the gate there. It's got a chain and padlock on it, but it won't keep this baby in. From there we can..."

"Oh, fuck me sideways," screamed Timothy, one of the bag boys from Stop N' Save. "A bunch of them just came around the corner."

Vaughn ran to the rear of the bus where the bag boys and two checkout girls had taken position. He wiped some condensation off the glass and saw five figures standing at the far corner looking straight at them.

"Floor it, Barry," Vaughn called.

Webster hit the gas hard. The bus' wheels spun momentarily before finding traction. It lunged forward and fishtailed slightly before descending a steep embankment.

The children started to scream in fear. Vaughn and the soldiers reached up to the overhanging handholds lining the center aisle of the vehicle.

The creatures started running after the speeding bus.

Snow sprayed across the left side of the yellow monstrosity as it hit the bottom of the embankment hard. It didn't slow down, however.

Webster spun the steering wheel to the right and followed the edge of the football field heading directly for a chain-link fence. Beyond the fence was a house made of brick. The vehicle was going so fast that Betty Sue thought they would crash straight into it.

The bus suddenly tilted to the right as Webster turned it to the left. He was now speeding along the eastern side of the field, past the goalposts. Before him, on the other side of the football ground was the gate he had spoken about earlier. He aimed the bus squarely for the middle of it. It was in fact two gates. One was kept in place with a metal pin that slid into the ground and padlocked in place, now covered in snow. The other swung freely, held shut by a padlocked chain that threaded through both itself and the stationary gate.

Vaughn kept his eyes on the runners.

They were leaping down the embankment that the bus had descended moments before. Their path would take them across the edge of the field, a shorter journey than that of the vehicle. At their current pace, they would be on the bus in seconds.

Webster planted his foot down as hard as he could. The bus plowed through the snow and hit the gate hard.

The hinges on both gates snapped. The chain connecting the two gates, however, did not. As a result, the gate now clung to the front of the bus as it spun to the right and headed down one of the back streets in Long Valley.

The five creatures were not far behind. They burst through the narrow space where the gates once stood and turned after the speeding vehicle.

Vaughn could see their pale skin, their yellow teeth and their terrifying lifeless eyes staring straight at him.

***

"We're not going to make it through this, are we?" Redhawke asked. His tone indicated that he already knew the answer.

"Not a chance," Dooley replied.

The other men continued to fire. They knew this to be true, so why argue.

"I got an idea," Redhawke said. "It means having to go down there," he nodded in the direction that the creatures were coming from.

"We'll be torn apart," Burkley stated.

"Just to the nearest science lab," Redhawke replied.

"Okay," Dawson said as he squeezed off a few more rounds. "What's your plan?"

"We go in there, turn on all the gas, throw the grenades down toward the breach, come back here and fire the RPG."

The other men mulled it over as they kept firing.

"Sounds plausible," Munroe put in.

"I'm in," Burrows agreed.

"We can get both labs' gas taps on," Burkley stated.

"What?" Redhawke quipped. "How?"

"There's a preparation room adjoining both labs," the veterinarian informed them. "It has a bunch of chemicals in there. Quite a few have pyrophoric agencies."

"Pyro what?" Dawson enquired.

"It means they go *boom!*" Burrows said.

"Why didn't you just say that, Doc?"

***

Within moments, Dawson relayed the plan to Harold Waring who was engaged in shooting at the same onslaught of creatures from the southern hallway.

"Sad to say, I think it's the only solution, Tom," Waring quantified. "We're running low on ammo and it will only be a matter of time before they have us all. There's just too many of them."

The Mayor looked around at the men within earshot. Jacob Sorenson, Miles Freeburg and Carl Mason were the closest to him.

"If it gives my little girl a fighting chance, we take as many of them as we can," Mason stated. "What do they need us to do?"

Waring looked at each of the townsfolk around him. "Thank you, gentlemen." He lifted the radio to his mouth, "What's our part, Tom?"

"Keep doing what you're doing for the moment," Dawson replied. "When we tell you, throw every grenade and fire any RPGs you have right into those fuckers. After that, anything still breathing deserves to live."

"Okay," Waring responded. "We'll wait for your signal."

"Here we go boys," Dawson said as the men moved in a line into the hallway, firing at the creatures that continued to scramble over the fallen debris near the breach.

The creatures screamed, grunted, spat and hissed in response to the tiny bullets that ripped into their flesh. Some fell, becoming part of the obstacle that the others continued to climb over.

The men in the western corridor worked their way to the first lab easily enough. Redhawke and Burkley ducked inside the door while the remaining men stayed in the hallway, firing at the beasts.

The deputy and the doctor raced through the door to the preparation room, then into the other laboratory. They moved around turning on each gas tap fitted to the benches throughout the room.

"There's no gas coming out," Redhawke called.

"The main tap is under the front bench," Burkley informed the deputy. "The teacher's bench."

Redhawke moved around the bench at the front of the room and peered underneath. He found two taps, one silver and one red. The silver one had a label that said, *MAIN WATER.* The other had no label, tag or symbol.

It was a simple deduction.

At least he hoped so.

He turned the tap on full and placed his hand in front of the gas tap on the bench. Cool air jetted onto his skin.

"Got it," he announced to Burkley.

"Good," the doctor replied. "Let's get the other room gassed up and get out of here."

Both men moved back through the preparation room and repeated the process before rejoining the others in the hallway. The six men then moved backward together, continuing to fire into the oncoming creatures.

Dawson, Burkley and Dooley continued to fire toward the breach as both Burrows and Munroe hoisted the RPG launchers onto their shoulders and took aim.

Redhawke prepared two grenades, pulling the pins but holding the safety clamps in place.

"Ready boss," he announced.

Dawson lifted the walkie-talkie.

***

"You ready, Harold?" the sheriff's voice crackled through the speaker.

Mayor Harold Waring looked at each of the surrounding men. They all nodded. Rourke bore the only RPG they had remaining while Paul Harris and Evan Putney continued to fire their M-16 assault rifles toward the creatures. Sorenson, Mason and Freeburg had all grabbed grenades to throw.

"We're ready," he replied as a strange exhilaration flared in his stomach.

"In three..." Dawson called.

Redhawke poised the throw the grenade in his right hand first.

"Two..."

Rourke targeted just in front of the debris and closer to the southern wall of the hallway.

"One..."

Mason gritted his teeth together, "For you Betty Sue."

"Fire!"

All three RPGs fired simultaneously. Jets of smoke streaked through the air at high velocity. The men holding grenades let fly and threw as many as they could in the time they had.

The creatures continued to climb over the debris of metal, bricks and bodies as the rockets hit.

A large fireball erupted near the breach. Within a moment less than a second, it found the gas that had been expanding silently and invisibly throughout the building. Ignition was instantaneous.

"What a friend we have in Jesus," Paul Harris began.

The flame took hold of the gas and fed on its source, through the pipes and to the main outlet in the building's basement.

***

"Oh, shit!" Andy called.

All heads turned to the rear window of the speeding bus.

The runners were slowly drifting farther away as the bus picked up its pace on the road. But this was not the focal point of the bus riders.

An expanding fireball was engulfing the high school, blowing it apart from beneath.

"Dear God," Lilly Geddes breathed.

"When you get there, turn left on Main," Vaughn directed the groundskeeper. "We're going to the base."

"You don't want to take the Eye?" Webster asked, referring to the only road in and out of the community.

"The Eye is shut," Vaughn informed the driver. "There's no way out of the valley."

XLIII

Tiffany sat with her back against a cross beam close to the manhole. She had replaced the panel, closing out the horrific scene in the bathroom. While she couldn't see what was happening below her, she could definitely hear.

The wet slapping sound as blood-soaked flesh smacked against the floor, the crunch of bones being broken, and the constant growls and grunts of the feasting wolves filled her mind with terrible imagery.

She rocked slightly, back and forth, back and forth, as she hugged her knees into her chest.

"Go away," she spat through slobber and tears to the monsters below. "Go away."

But they didn't go.

They continued to feast noisily upon her boyfriend.

The cold air filled the dark roof space and her exposed face and hands started to turn numb. She rubbed her palms together in vain as she shivered, and her teeth chattered, echoing back at her mockingly as the sound bounced off the tin roof.

You're going to die here, they seemed to say to her. *You're going to freeze to death.*

Why not just face the music?

Why not climb down and join Stan?

Why not get ripped apart?

Let them tear your guts open and tear your insides out.

Why not?

Why not?

She shook the thought away and looked around her for any sign of hope.

Her eyes had adapted to the darkness enough for her to make out the shapes of long crisscrossing beams of wood that held the roof in place. She could see some light at the far end of the roof space.

Cautiously, she lifted herself to her feet and started toward the light. She placed her feet on the beams of wood beneath her, careful to not put any weight on the plaster that was the ceiling. The last thing she wanted right now was to injure herself or, even worse, fall through to the wolves beneath her.

As she drew closer to the light, she realized that it was because of a missing section of cladding on the outside of the cottage. She peered through the gap and could see down the road in the direction from which she and Stan had approached.

The storm had passed and the world outside seemed dead and silent. A thick fog had rolled in, preventing her from seeing more than a few feet past the fence that surrounded the cottage. The only thing to penetrate the fog was light emitting from a few nearby streetlamps.

Her eyes moved to the heavens. Patches of clear sky started to appear in the clouds, allowing the stars to break through.

Something in the street, approaching the cottage, drew her attention.

A figure, like a man, stepped out of the fog and into the yard. He was wearing an army uniform that was blood-soaked down the front, glistening in the starlight. The man stared directly at her with white eyes.

Tiffany's heart skipped a beat.

Does he see me?

Does he know I'm here?

One wolf below her growled angrily. She surmised that they sensed the newcomer's presence.

The soldier moved his face toward the new noise. He started toward the cottage, shuffling his feet through the snow.

A loud clatter erupted from within the cottage. The monsters were moving.

The soldier halted and crouched as he bared his yellow teeth and let out an ear-piercing scream. He stretched his arms out by his sides and leapt.

A wolf suddenly entered Tiffany's view and knocked the man back to the ground.

The soldier clawed at the wolf's face as the beast attempted to clamp its teeth onto the new prey. Eventually, the soldier dug his fingers into either side of the wolf's head just below its ears.

It yelped loudly and tried to pull itself away. The soldier, lying on his back, dug his heels into the ground and tugged, keeping the wolf in place.

Just who was the hunter and who was the prey?

The other wolf now entered the scene and circled behind the soldier who was now getting back onto his feet and dragging the first wolf back toward the fog. The second wolf growled, announcing to the soldier that there was more than he could handle.

Still, the soldier didn't let go. Instead, he screamed loudly.

Suddenly, five other human-like figures burst from the fog and ran at the wolves.

Three of them bowled the second wolf over before it turned to defend itself. The other two ran to the first wolf still in the clutches of the soldier.

As they pounced upon the monster, Tiffany instinctively saw an opportunity to escape.

She carefully made her way back to the manhole and removed the panel that was covering it. Her eyes fell upon the bathroom floor covered with Stan's blood.

Bile rose to her throat, stinging the inside of her neck and back of her mouth. She forced it back down as she placed her hands on either side of the manhole.

Slowly, cautiously, Tiffany lowered herself. She stretched her leg to the bathtub to help take her weight. Eventually, she could place both feet on the floor.

Both feet in Stan's blood.

She knew he was behind her.

At least, what remained of him.

Once she turned to escape, she would see him and wasn't sure how she would respond.

With a deep breath to help calm her nerves she turned.

Her boots lost traction and slipped. She suddenly found herself on her knees. Her hands, with fingers spread, were on the floor holding her body precariously over the blood-soaked tiles.

Over his lifeless body.

He lay half in and half out of the bathroom door. His face was intact and glared lifelessly up to her.

Blood still trickled from the corners of his open mouth, frozen in an everlasting scream.

His arms rested out by his sides, limp and oddly angled. Everything below his chest to his groin was ripped open and removed.

Suddenly the bile returned and there was nothing she could do to hold it back.

Rising to her feet, she warily made her way around him and through the door.

She tiptoed across the bedroom and into the living area. The noise of the battle between the human-like creatures and the wolves was still loud.

Tiffany carefully climbed over the rubble at the front door, remaining silent as she did so. She pressed herself against the cottage's front wall and slid along its length in the opposite direction from the noise of the fighting.

A wolf was shaking one of the man creatures in its jaws. Two other creatures were on its back, biting, clawing and ripping at its flesh.

It dropped the lifeless body of the man onto the snow. It looked in her direction.

She froze in place, feeling her heart skip a beat.

The wolf bared its teeth and growled before rolling onto its back to remove the two attackers.

Tiffany turned and ran around the cottage and into the backyard.

She saw a small tool shed nestled neatly in the fence's corner line and headed directly for it.

The hissing, growling, screaming and howling behind her grew slightly fainter as she slid between the shed and the fence. The gap was just wide enough for her to squeeze into. Eventually, she made her way into the corner behind the toolshed and dropped to her knees.

A small gap in the palings gave her enough of a view to see into the backyard of a neighboring property.

Except for a large house, it looked clear.

She listened to the sound of the battle. The monsters were still there, preoccupied. Her eyes moved to the sky once again, and she saw a tinge of deep purple among the stars.

The sun was rising.

The world was still spinning, and the long night would soon be over.

She saw this as a sign to allow her to hope.

So, she hoped to stay alive.

Her fingers gripped the top of the fence and she pulled her body upwards. Tiffany grunted softly as she pushed her torso over the top of the fence and started lifting her leg over.

It gripped her suddenly around her head with both hands.

White, bloodshot eyes with tiny pinhole pupils locked onto hers.

No!

Long, crooked yellow teeth protruding through blackened gums opened wider and wider as it drew its face closer and closer to hers.

No!

She screamed a loud, chilling scream as it sank its teeth into her cheek and tore a chunk of flesh from her.

Stan!

The scream suddenly stopped as it dug its mouth into her neck and chewed into her trachea.

Mom!

A bubbling, gurgling noise filled her ears as she attempted to call for help.

Dad!

It slammed her to the ground and ripped into her soft flesh around the abdomen with its long white fingers.

God!

She watched the sky as the edges of the clouds turned from a dark mauve to a deep red.

God!

Dawn was here.

No!

Slowly, as she felt her intestines slip from her body, all pain faded.

Hope had gone.

The dark was here.

XLIV

Adam opened his eyes.

There was nothing to see, but he could smell something.

Something alive.

Something fresh.

The water trickled past him in a tiny stream.

He bent his head low to lap at the liquid. When satisfied, he lifted his head and crawled toward its source.

Adam moved with vigor and speed. Navigating the tube was seemingly a second nature.

His first nature was to satisfy the urge.

He sniffed the air that drifted through the piping. Something was ahead. Something that would satisfy his urge.

Adam twisted through the ninety-degree intersection with ease and continued along the next section of the straight passage.

He was no longer troubled with aches or pains. These were things of the past. His body had taken care of them.

His mind was devoid of troubles such as logic, calculations, social responsibilities and education. There was only the urge.

This was the sole driving force that moved him.

It was a hunger that he needed to quench.

The urge pulled him forward and he must comply with its demand.

Adam, the boy who kissed Jenny Swanson behind the drugstore had disappeared.

Instead, a new being crept through the dark passage toward a calling that it barely understood.

Adam, the school dropout who left home to find his own way at the age of fifteen had departed.

Now an emerging organism searched to find fulfilment through an impulse that raged through its body.

Adam, the farmhand who herded cattle and drove tractors, was gone.

The beast had taken control and was intent on fulfilling its one desire.

Adam was dead.

The creature was alive.

It scurried through the drainage pipe, determined to realize its purpose.

To satisfy the urge.

To feed.

XLV

The bus slid sideways into Main Street. The passengers sitting on the barely cushioned seats felt the monstrosity shudder as the tires spun and the back end tilted to the right.

Webster hit the gas again, and the vehicle lurched forward, slipping to the right side of the road before he regained total control of the steering.

"Where did you learn to drive, man?" called Justin from the back.

"I drove a cab in Chicago, motherfucker," Webster called back.

"Children present," Lilly Geddes reminded her groundskeeper.

He had forgotten.

Toppled cars littered the way before him, burning shop fronts and many staring eyes.

"We got company," he called.

"I know," said Vaughn, still watching the five runners tailing the bus.

"He doesn't mean them," Betty Sue cried.

Vaughn turned his head to see three creatures coming at them from different locations. One came from the right, leaping over a flaming sedan lying on its side. Another approached from the left from behind the Sheriff's Office. The last hunkered over a body in the street. It peeped up to reveal sinew strands drenched in blood dangling from its mouth.

"Floor it, Barry," Sandra Upton instructed.

"I already am, baby."

They hit the creature hard. A spray of blood smashed across the windshield. Webster turned the wipers on to clear his view.

The wipers moved the gates that were riding on the front of the bus. Slowly and gradually, the chain metal objects crept upwards until force finally gripped them and sent them flying over the bus.

"Whoa!" Webster let out.

Vaughn and the youths in the bus's rear peered out through the back window. The gates came crashing down on top of the five pursuers, causing them to fall to the ground in a clumsy mess.

It wouldn't stop them for long and there were still two newcomers that were following.

"They're everywhere," a woman sitting halfway along the left side of the bus shrieked. Her public display of fear set a little girl and boy into crying fits.

"Don't look outside," Shirley, Walter Burkley's secretary, told her. "Watch the kids. Keep your eyes on them."

Sharpe tried to open one of the passenger windows. It didn't budge. He peered closely at it and saw rivets holding it in place.

"Do any of these windows open, Barry?"

"No," the groundskeeper replied as he navigated the vehicle between two burning SUVs at top speed.

"Why not?"

"To stop the kids from throwing shit out of them."

"Children, Mister Webster," Geddes restated.

"I know. I know."

The bus passed through the town center and finally hit the open road. Four new creatures had decided to follow the bus. There was no sign of the five that chased them from the high school.

Trees started to replace buildings on either side of the vehicle. Gradually, the four chasers grew smaller and smaller and the bus left them in its wake.

"Do you think they'll keep coming for us?" Nancy asked the deputy.

"They came for me after I got away from them," Andy stated. "And Charlene was a lot faster than this thing."

"Who's Charlene?" Tina asked.

"My car," Andy replied. "Probably scrap metal by now. I left her out-side the school."

They rode in silence for a short time, watching the red sky giving birth to a new day as colors danced on the edges of dissipating clouds.

At least the storm was over.

MONDAY MORNING

I

The school bus smashed through the makeshift boom gate that the army had put in place at the entrance to the base. The vehicle tore along the stretch of road and passed through the burned-out guard post and into the army base grounds.

Webster took the bus along a well-paved road that ceased at a T-intersection, right at the base of a flagpole still donning the stars and stripes. It waved gently in the breeze, displaying a tattered and frayed hem and countless bullet holes.

Several mutilated bodies lay on the grassed area that surrounded the buildings. Some adults covered the children's eyes as they moved past the scenery.

Vaughn felt a sense of despair as the bus turned right and moved along the road a little way before turning left onto a semi-circular stretch of bitumen that trailed to the stairs of a large brick building.

The vehicle halted at the base of the stairs and Webster opened the door. Upton jumped out and ran for the large entry door to the structure. She gripped the handle and gave it a push and pull.

It didn't budge.

She turned back toward the bus and shook her head.

"Door's locked," Krane called from near the door.

"Dammit," Vaughn spat.

"Hello," a man's voice echoed across the grounds of the army base. "Can you hear me?"

The voice seemed to come from everywhere.

Vaughn turned around in the bus, looking out every window for a sign of someone nearby.

Upton instinctively raised her assault rifle to the ready.

"I'm coming over the speaker system, I hope," the voice announced. "We don't have much time. Get everyone to the door."

Vaughn hesitated for a mere fraction of time. He didn't recognize the voice. The speakers made the man sound tinny. Trusting this unseen stranger with their lives was a great risk.

The creatures in the town pursuing them, and any in the immediate vicinity, would have heard the announcer calling out to them.

They had no choice.

They had to move.

"Grab what you can," Vaughn instructed.

"Bags under the seats here," Webster called out.

The door near Upton made a loud *click*.

Upton pushed upon the door and it swung open. She moved inside to a large open area, the foyer of the main office block. A large reception desk sat directly in front of her stationed beneath a giant map of the world with clocks positioned at intervals along the top. Each clock represented a different time zone across the planet. Bullets had made the clocks useless, smashing their glass-encased faces and freezing time on each one.

The women and children moved into the room first, followed by the doctors and the groundskeeper. Vaughn and the remaining two soldiers took the rear, keeping watch across the yard in front of the building. As soon as they were inside, the voice rang through the speakers in the foyer.

"Close the door," it ordered.

Upton complied.

As soon as the door was closed it clicked again, locking shut.

A loud whirring, like a jet turbine, whooshed by the building.

"What was that?" Andy called.

"There," Vaughn said, pointing.

They watched as a small jet-propelled aircraft flew low to the ground back toward the town. It was sleek and black with long, tilted wings.

"It's a drone," Krane informed them. "It's probably surveillance."

"Now what?" Fiona Stevens asked.

"Let's get these people some water," Vanderberg replied as he dug into one of the gym bags he had brought with him. He fished out several clear plastic bottles with labels on them. Spring water. The nurse and soldiers started handing them around to the others.

"Take your time," the voice said. "You are in a safe zone for the moment."

"What do you mean, *for the moment?*" Timothy called out.

"I can see you on the security cameras," the voice stated. "I cannot hear you."

"Well, that's just peachy," Timothy snorted.

"I can lead you through the building to my location," the man announced. "But it is dangerous. So is staying where you are. Surveillance cameras are showing me that a large number of the infected are heading down the road toward the base.

"You could stay there and try your luck," the voice continued, "or you could risk the few that are inside."

Vaughn searched the room for a camera. He found a black dome in the ceiling above the reception desk. Walking toward it, Vaughn waved his hands.

"I can see you, Deputy," the voice reacted.

Vaughn held up five fingers, then ten followed by a shrug with palms up.

How many is a few?

"I understand," the voice told him. "There were eight. They are the original test specimens. I have taken care of two. Two others escaped and I think they may have gotten off the base. I haven't seen them anywhere since this all started. The final four are somewhere between your location and mine."

Vaughn held up one finger, *give me a moment.*

"So," he said to the others. "What do you think?"

"It's only four," Sharpe specified. "We can take them down if need be."

"Agreed." Krane nodded.

"I'd rather take four on than *a large number* that's coming for us now," Upton put in.

"What about the rest of you?" Vaughn asked the others sitting around.

"We can't stay here with the children," said Shirley.

"I'm not so sure," Edry disputed. He had been slinking away in the corner ever since they had entered the foyer. "We locked the door. Who knows what we're dealing with here? What if this guy is a psychopath who wants to watch us... You know?"

"Those things will break that door down the moment they see us in here," Andy snapped. "I'd rather get farther inside this building than be an item on the buffet menu."

"I'm with Andy," Tina told them.

"I'm getting the impression that nobody wants to stay here," Vaughn said. "Any objections to moving on, speak up now."

Edry grunted. He wanted to say something, but he knew that they would shout him down if he did.

"Ammo check first," Upton ordered.

"Canvas bags," Krane informed her. "I packed them before we left."

Sharpe opened one of the backpack sized bags and found various chip packets. He opened another bag and counted twelve loaded magazines for the M-16 assault rifle. He handed four to Vaughn, Upton and Krane each before pocketing four for himself.

"What's in the other bag?" Sharpe asked.

"Chocolate," Krane replied. "I raided the cupboards in the teachers' lounge. They had a great stash in there."

"Andy," Vaughn called as he lifted one of the canvas bags and threw it over to the young man. "Chips. Justin, chocolate." He threw the last bag over to the bag boy.

Vanderberg slung one of the gym bags across his body and over his shoulder. Barry Webster picked up the other gym bag and did the same.

"Everyone ready?" Vaughn asked.

They were all on their feet.

"Sharpe and Krane, take point," Upton ordered. "The sheriff and I will take the rear."

Sheriff.

Vaughn didn't like the sound of that word. It just didn't seem to fit. The badge clung to his chest for all to see, and he was proud to wear it. But he didn't feel that he had earned it.

"To your left of the reception desk you will find a door," the voice informed them. "I have just unlocked it. It will automatically lock again once it shuts behind you."

The group moved past the reception desk and toward a metal door. Sharpe pushed the door open and Krane slid past him and moved inside.

II

The place was a mess.

Ripped panels from the ceiling lay strewn across toppled furniture and the floor. Exposed wires hung loosely here and there. Fluorescent tubes blinked repetitively, sporadically, like demented strobe lights. The scent of bitter smoke from small electrical fires filled the air.

"Go straight on," the voice instructed.

Krane could see a black dome protruding from the ceiling directly in front of him at the far end of a long hallway. Glass panel walls lined their path, smashed and cracked in places, reminiscent of spiderwebs. Blood smeared handprints decorated the panels in areas near the cracks.

Something in the soldier wished he was back in the foyer.

Vaughn was last through the door. He closed the door carefully and heard the lock click in place.

They huddled closely together, keeping the children toward the center of the groups as they cautiously moved along the glass hallway. The blinking lights and stinging smoky smell made them edgy as shadows danced on the broken glass.

They crept toward the end of the corridor, the occasional comforting reminder to a child to remain silent when a whimper started. "Shh."

"Follow the passage to the left," the voice instructed.

Krane complied, keeping his rifle trained and pointed forward as he moved. Sharpe stayed close behind, glancing left and right for any motion.

The glass walls stopped here. Now the room opened up and desks with computers on them and office chairs filled their view. A few had toppled over and were riddled with bullet holes. An aisle, formed by the arrangement of the furniture, gave clear access to another door with a symbol for stairs on it standing about ten yards away.

"Go through the door," ordered the unseen man.

The group moved through the office space gingerly. Everyone anxiously peered around as fear and adrenaline filled their senses.

Sharpe trained his rifle on the door as Krane pushed his hand against it. The door opened with ease. Private Sharpe stepped through the door and into a stairwell that led both up and down.

"Go down," the voice told them.

Into the mouth of Hell, thought Krane as he moved toward the descending stairs.

A sudden ear-shattering scream bellowed through the office space.

Vaughn snapped his head around to the source of the sound. A creature, a large man built like a tank, stood at the passageway they had just passed through.

"Everyone through the door now," Vaughn barked.

The group herded themselves through the doorway and into the stairwell as quickly as they could.

A scream from within the stairwell echoed the first. One of those things was in there with them.

"It came from above," Upton called. "Everyone down the stairs."

Sharpe and Krane trained their rifles in front of them as they hurriedly made the descent with everyone in tow.

Vaughn moved to the side to shut the door. The creature had already made it more than halfway across the room. There was no way that Vaughn would get the door closed in time.

He raised his M-16 and fired.

The beast made it within a yard to the shooter before its face was torn open by a barrage of bullets.

It fell in a crumpled heap near the door.

Upton kept her rifle pointed up. The other creature had not revealed its position. Another scream echoed through the stairwell toward them.

"You can bet they know we're here now," the soldier muttered.

"We better catch up," Vaughn said.

They ran down the stairs after the others. The stairwell swung around to the right where it levelled out onto a small platform before turning right again to continue the descent to the next level down.

It evened out again at the bottom where a door waited for them on the wall to the right. There were no more stairs to descend upon, so there was no choice but to go through.

Krane put his hand on the door handle and looked back at all the others. Sharpe directed his aim onto the door and nodded. Vaughn gave a quick thumbs up.

The private turned the handle and pulled. A great, damp scent of decomposition filled their noses. The soldier swung the door wide open.

A creature was there.

Waiting.

III

"Oh shit," Krane called as the thing reached in and grabbed him around the head with both hands. It heaved him out of the stairwell and into the room beyond.

Frank Sharpe winced as he heard the sickening crunch of bones shattering beneath the beast's grasp. It squeezed the remains of Krane's skull between its fingers as the soldier's body fell lifeless to the floor.

It all happened so quickly.

Sharpe barely squeezed off a burst of rounds before the creature returned its attention to the people in the stairwell.

The bullets hit the abomination hard in the chest. Flesh exploded instantly, sending pink vapor in all directions.

Private Frank Sharpe would not wait to see if one burst would be enough. He squeezed the trigger again, and again, and again until the beast dropped to the floor.

"Move fast," the voice nervously called. "Straight ahead."

The fleeing group briskly progressed into a room lined with computers and terminals with large screens.

Four bodies lay on the floor of the room; Private Dwight Krane and three infected creatures. Beyond this area was a passageway with cinderblock walls and several doors along each side.

"I'm in the last room on the right," the voice said over the speakers. "Be careful. There are at least two more of those things out there somewhere."

Upton moved to point position as the gathering moved into the hallway. Once inside the passage, Vaughn walked backward keeping his rifle aimed at the stairwell door.

Finally, they stood outside the last door on the right. It was a metal monstrosity with an electronic keypad on the adjacent wall.

Sharpe placed his hand on the door and pushed. It didn't budge.

"What the fuck?" he spat.

A scream from the stairwell suddenly set them all on edge again.

The younger children started to cry. The women endeavored to comfort the kids, but the shakiness in their voices thwarted any convincing they were attempting. Shirley slid down the wall and crumpled into a fetal position and bawled uncontrollably. Betty Sue tried to console her by sitting by her and wrapping her arms around the sobbing girl.

They were tired and had seen too much.

Everyone in his or her own way lost it at that moment.

"Open the fucking door," Sharpe called.

Upton thudded the butt of her gun against the metal plating.

Tina buried herself into Andy's chest.

Lilly Geddes and Fiona Stevens huddled together against the far wall.

The beast screamed from just within the stairwell. Vaughn saw it moving in the shadows beyond the doorway they had come through.

The metal door suddenly made a loud click and slid open.

Sharpe gawked at the open passageway, speechless.

"Get the fuck inside," Upton called.

The women and children moved in first, followed by the unarmed men.

Slowly, purposefully, the creature slunk into the room. It set its gaze upon Vaughn and the two soldiers.

"Get in there, Sheriff," ordered Sharpe.

Vaughn hesitated; partly because he forgot he was the sheriff and partly because he felt an obligation to stay and fight.

Upton didn't pause for so long. She immediately grabbed Vaughn by the scruff of the neck and pulled.

The creature advanced quickly and was within the passageway before the soldier had Vaughn in the room. Sharpe fired at the creature as he ran toward it.

"Close the door," he ordered.

"No," Vaughn cried. He was on his back with Upton holding him down from behind.

The door slid shut with a clank.

Locked.

They heard quick bursts of fire through the metal obstruction.

A sudden silence fell.

Upton released Vaughn from her grip. He instantly crawled over to the door and placed a hand on it.

THUD!

He recoiled his hand and stood upright.

THUD!

"It's him," Vaughn stammered. "Let him in."

A shrill scream called from outside the room.

IV

"Private Sharpe is gone, Mister Vaughn," announced a familiar voice. "I am very sorry. I assure you we are safe in here from the infected subjects."

Vaughn moved farther into the room. It was an L-shaped chamber that stretched around the shell of the hallway they had just been in.

A few computers lined the walls on either side. The room then opened up to overlook a large screen that almost stretched the entire wall. The screen was divided into nine smaller screens that blinked to alternating views of the army base from surveillance cameras.

Above the screen was a digital clock counting down;

00:00:04:32.

00:00:04:31.

00:00:04:30.

Beneath the screen, sitting at a large terminal was a familiar face.

Colonel Mike Nelson.

Vaughn had last spoken to this man on the day after the tanker crash outside the base. It seemed an eternity ago.

"Why the fuck are you still here?" Vaughn asked as he slowly approached the uniformed officer. He suppressed his anger as best as he could, but his voice revealed his emotions. "Why aren't you with all of your buddies in your helicopters on the other side of the mountains?"

"Why?" the Colonel replied. "I'll show you why." He swivelled his office chair around to show that he was only part of the man he once was. His right leg was missing from just above the knee. He had bunched and folded his trousers' leg at the wound, tightly tying an electrical cable just above the place it had been severed, acting as a tourniquet. "This is why."

"Dear lord!" Vanderberg exclaimed. He raced to Nelson's side and crouched down. "I need to take a look at that."

"Go ahead, doc," replied Nelson. Vanderberg untied the knot in the trousers' leg and rolled the mass of blood-soaked material out of the way so he could see the amputation.

"This is messy," the doctor stated. "How did you do this?"

"Scissors," the Colonel answered and pointed farther into the room. "Over there."

They followed his finger to a corner in the room where a pair of bloodied scissors lay on the floor next to a severed lower part of a leg still wearing a sock and a boot. Vanderberg saw small scratches in the flesh near the top of the sock, made by four fingernails.

"How are you still alive?" Fiona Stevens asked as she crouched beside the doctor and fished through the gym bag for bandages.

"It needs cleaning," Vanderberg said. "The best we've got is water."

She dug out two unopened bottles.

"I also need those scissors." He pointed.

Geddes retrieved them and handed them to the doctor before wiping the blood off her hands and onto her coat.

Vanderberg started cutting the trousers' leg away to gain access to the wound.

"I guess I should explain," Nelson began.

"I'm listening," Vaughn replied as he put his rifle down on a nearby console and sat in a chair.

"I was upstairs when this all started," the Colonel told them. "When the call came in that the contagion had somehow escaped containment, the first thing we did was a check on *the eight*.

"You met three of them," he continued. "The eight test subjects were accounted for, so we surmised that the contagion infected the first community member after the accident near the guard post out there."

"You're talking about Mister O'Brien," Fiona specified.

"Mister O'Brien." Nelson winced as Vanderberg dabbed a wet piece of gauze against the open wound. "I didn't know his name."

"There's a whole bunch of names to add to that list now, Colonel," Webster grunted.

"Go on," Vaughn ordered. "Tell your story."

"Okay." Nelson nodded. "We got orders to release the test specimens into the community. *Begin the experiment* is what they said."

"So you blew the passage shut and evacuated," Betty Sue sneered.

"Not straight away," he replied. "We found remains of livestock and heard reports of mutilated pets. With those things happening, and publicly reported to the sheriff, they ordered us to cut the valley off from the outside world and contain the contagion."

"Then the experiment began," Vaughn finished for him.

"We released the eight out of their pens," Nelson informed them. "We informed all personnel to stay indoors. But instead of running out into the community, the eight stayed here and entered the surrounding buildings.

"I came down here to help evacuate some people and files of importance. I got all the officers out and was shutting all this down when one of the eight found me in here and attacked.

"It got me, just a scratch on the leg before I could blow its brains out with my Glock. The other attacked at that moment, but I got him too. I crawled in here and radioed for help. They told me I could be infected and, they all left."

Nelson looked down at the stump that Vanderberg wrapped in bandages.

"Why cut your leg off?" Andy asked.

"I didn't want to become one of those things," Nelson replied. "I watched on these screens as those things attacked all over the base. Most of the remaining soldiers fought, but the specimens were quick. We ended up with a lot of dead personnel. The injured, who went somewhere to hide, turned quickly. They attacked others, infecting more and more as they went."

He turned his attention toward Upton. "How did you get out?"

"We ran while you were still loading the choppers," she informed him. "Something didn't sit right, so we loaded a truck and got the hell out of here."

"Good idea," Nelson slurred. "Was it your idea or the doctor's there?"

"What?" she asked, shooting Edry a quick glance.

"It was the doctor's idea to cut and run, wasn't it?"

Edry felt the eyes of everyone in the room upon him.

"You didn't think I'd remember you," Nelson sneered. "Did you, Doctor Edry?"

"I don't understand why you're singling me out," Edry replied.

"Because you're a coward," Nelson affirmed. "Did you know, Mister Vaughn, that the *good* doctor is the brains behind this beast?"

"He told us he conducted blood tests," Vaughn replied. "That's all."

"Oh, he did," Nelson agreed. "But he also is the creator of the goop that spilled out of that truck on Friday night. He didn't tell you that now, did he?"

"No, he did not."

"He chose the subjects personally," the Colonel continued. "Men with no families and no social ties. Men who would not be missed. He also chose the location for the experiment. A small secluded community with the advantage of an established army base to run production from."

"Is that so?" Vaughn turned to face Doctor Edry.

"Sure is." Nelson smiled. "But you can't lay the whole blame on him. The military purchased the product and agreed to set up shop here. Just a shame that poor Doctor Neville Edry won't get to spend the fortune he made from selling his wonderful biological weapon that he created."

"Fuck you, Nelson." Edry had turned beetroot red with anger. "Fuck you all. They didn't take me either. They left me here too. They said I worked too close in proximity to the infected. They feared that I might have become infected. But I'm not. I helped you get out of here before it all happened," he said, turning to Upton.

"We should put him out there with his invention," Webster suggested.

"No need," Nelson informed him. "See that timer there. That's how long we've got left."

Their eyes fell upon a digital clock above the giant display. It was counting down: 00:00:02:16

"What is that?" Andy asked.

"Count down to the end, son," Nelson explained. "One of those drones that have been flying around all night observing the infected and rating their performance will deliver a payload shortly."

"Payload?" Tina asked.

"A bomb," Upton answered.

V

"A big bomb," Nelson replied. "*The* bomb. Part of the experiment was to contain it after it was complete. What better way to accomplish that than to incinerate everything that might be infected? Merry Christmas."

"Is there any way out?" Vaughn asked.

"What?" Nelson asked, wide-eyed as he craned his neck to see the clock. "In one minute? Are you crazy? We're talking thermal, nuclear explosion. This whole valley is about to be vaporized."

Upton slid against the wall and down to the floor placing her head in her hands. It was over.

Betty Sue started to hyperventilate. Vaughn quickly got up from his seat and held her in his arms.

"Sorry Doc," Nelson said to Vanderberg. "I probably wasted your time letting you patch me up. Seems a waste now."

"It's what we do," he said, and smiled, shooting Fiona Stevens a look of gratitude. She put an arm around his shoulders and gave a squeeze.

The women dropped to the floor and hugged the children tightly. Shirley crawled over and joined them.

"I don't want to be alone," she slobbered.

Nancy and Timothy held hands and watched the large screen. The images continued to change as the clock counted down. Different angles from security cameras showed more creatures assembling outside the complex. They rapidly filed in through the gates, sprinted across the grounds into the building like a torrent wave of bodies.

00:00:01:10

341

Justin and Rose huddled together in the corner.

Andy gently kissed Tina on the forehead. With him holding her tightly in his arms, they started to sway like a slow dance.

Webster parked himself next to Lilly Geddes on the floor beside a computer terminal near the door.

"Well, boss," he said. "I just want you to know I loved working for you."

"Thanks, Barry." She smiled, tears welling in her eyes. "And you were a lazy bastard who barely kept the gutters clean. But you were the best groundskeeper I have ever known."

The large monitor showed a crowd of infected people swarming over the parked bus.

THUD!

The test subject had returned its attention to the metal door, hitting with all of its strength.

THUD!

00:00:00:45

THUD!

Greg Vaughn brushed a strand of hair out of Betty Sue's face.

"I love you, Betty Sue Mason," he whispered.

"I love you, Deputy Greg Vaughn," she returned.

"That's *Sheriff* Greg Vaughn," he smiled.

"Sheriff Greg Vaughn," she whispered before touching his lips with her own.

00:00:00:03

THUD!

CRANG!

The door buckled and the top rail keeping it in place broke, causing the metal access to fall slightly open.

00:00:00:02

The creature reached through the gap with outstretched claws, frustratingly grasping air inches away from Vaughn and Betty Sue.

00:00:00:01

They held their embrace, wrapped in each other's arms, as the beast let out a terrifying, shrill scream.

00:00:00:00

VI

A blinding light filled the entire valley, casting shadows of the surrounding mountains across the terrain in all directions.

It dissipated as smoke, dust, rock and vapor lifted, gathered and absorbed into its heat.

The giant winds from the explosion suddenly turned direction as the air quickly rushed to fill the void that the fireball had created.

Gradually, the mushroom cloud raised itself into the sky, leaving a hulking crater in its wake.

EPILOGUE

The small circle of light ahead of him grew larger and larger. The scent of fresh prey was overwhelming.

He quickened his pace as he crawled through the cement piping. Cool air flowed across his body as the circle of light drew him nearer and nearer.

His hands grasped the edges of the tube as he pulled himself into the open. The morning sunlight was bright, and the colors were mesmerizing.

Snow clung to everything, but the green of the trees was unmistakable. The scent of the pine forest filled his nostrils as he breathed in the fresh air for the first time.

In that breath, he smelled prey.

The urge took control again.

His purpose.

His reason.

It was to fulfil the urge.

He scanned the landscape with his eyes.

His gaze landed upon a line of vehicles some distance away. There were people nearby.

That was his purpose.

That was his reason.

***

Roadblocks on the turnpike prevented traffic from accessing the road that eventually wound its way into Long Valley. Instead of logging vehicles and civilian traffic, a row of nine Humvees and a group of men stood on the road near the turnoff.

All men were facing toward the mountains that surrounded the township. Some wore dark suits and ties. Others had khaki uniforms with stars on their shoulders.

"Damn fine execution," said one of the uniformed men to the others. "Any chance of exposure reaching surrounding regions?"

"None whatsoever, sir," said a young man in a dark suit. "The natural enclosure of the valley's mountain range will contain any fallout."

"Good," clucked the uniformed man. "Good."

"What about contamination from the bio-weapon?" another uniformed man asked.

"We'll send in three more drones to explore the valley after the cloud has dissipated," the suit replied. "We should be able to ascertain whether there were survivors or any escapees by then. In the meantime, we've positioned patrols around the outside of the valley and drones have been surveying continuously since the experiment began."

"Nothing to worry about," the first uniformed officer offered.

"Absolutely not," the suit responded.

"Well gentlemen," the second uniformed officer said. "I think we can retire for the day. Let's rendezvous back at the officers' club at, say, fourteen hundred."

All men nodded and smiled before heading toward their allotted Humvee.

A sound resonated around them, causing them to stop dead in their tracks.

All men turned, some cocking their heads to hear more clearly in their old age.

Wisps of snow streamed across the ground like loose ribbons caught in the breeze.

The trees swayed and creaked gently each time a gust of cold air blew down from the mountains.

The wind swam through the pine leaves, sounding like a rapid stream flowing violently.

A shrill scream echoed from the snow-covered slopes before them. The first uniformed officer peered toward the source of the sound. "What was that?"

THE END

About The Author

Robert E Kreig was born in Newcastle, Australia and grew up in its outer suburbs. He has always had a love for books, particularly well-told stories involving action, adventure and fear.

Some of Robert's favourite authors as a young reader included J. R. R. Tolkien, Stephen King, Orson Scott Card, Ray Bradbury and Frank Herbert. As he grew into adulthood, the list continued to lengthen, adding more great writers such as George R. R. Martin, Matthew Reilly, Nathan M. Farrugia, Dan Brown, James Patterson, Michael Connelly and Lee Child just to name a few.

Inspired by movies like Star Wars, King Kong, Jaws, Jason and the Argonauts and other great adventure pieces, Robert listened to the voices in his head and entertained the strange visions dancing through his mind to assist him with writing his fantasy series The Woodmyst Chronicles.

Robert has penned ten books for the series which follows the lives of many characters, particularly focussing upon a family who must face many trials before the epic conclusion. Clashing swords, strange creatures, flying dragons and sorcery inhabit the world surrounding Woodmyst.

OTHER BOOKS BY THIS AUTHOR

I Am Calm Voice

No one in the remote town of Edwards Hill could have known that she was capable of such carnage.

Least of all her parents, the first to die.

Driven by the gentle words of the Calm Voice, she inflicts a barrage of carnage and death, leaving a trail of blood in her wake.

Her goal is to bring death to all who have hurt her.

All she needs to do is listen to the Calm Voice.

All she needs to do is just focus...

Just focus...

Focus...

I Am Calm Voice by Robert E. Kreig is a dark psychological novel surrounding the actions of one girl on a fateful morning in April 2017. Kristin Matthews is fed up with her life, her oppressive parents, and her bullying schoolmates. She is compelled by a soothing voice thrumming in her head to seek revenge on those who have wronged her. At the top of her list is a trio of girls who have taunted her to breaking point. After careful planning, she embarks on a deadly rampage through Edwards Hill State High School, bent on destroying all her pain one final time. What follows is a haunting description of the day's events, culminating in an ending no one will expect.

THE WOODMYST CHRONICLES

From a faraway land...

...comes a new adventure.

The Woodmyst Chronicles is the story of a small community that face the hardest of trials in a world filled with darkness, violence and magic.

Books In This Series...

THE WALLS OF WOODMYST

THE SONS OF WOODMYST

THE HEIR OF WOODMYST

THE WARLORDS OF WOODMYST

THE HUNTRESS OF WOODMYST

THE SHADOW OF WOODMYST

THE BRIDES OF WOODMYST

THE GODS OF WOODMYST

THE WEAPONS OF WOODMYST

A FAREWELL TO WOODMYST

9 780645 235401